# PRAIRIE
# EDGE

# PRAIRIE EDGE

## A NOVEL

## CONOR KERR

UNIVERSITY OF MINNESOTA PRESS
MINNEAPOLIS
LONDON

First University of Minnesota Press edition, 2024

Published by arrangement with Strange Light/Penguin Random House Canada



Published by the University of Minnesota Press
111 Third Avenue South, Suite 290
Minneapolis, MN 55401-2520
http://www.upress.umn.edu

Book design by Kate Sinclair

ISBN 978-1-5179-1723-4 (hc)
ISBN 978-1-5179-1725-8 (pb)

LC record available at https://lccn.loc.gov/2024006959

Printed in the United States of America on acid-free paper



31 30 29 28 27 26 25 24 10 9 8 7 6 5 4 3 2 1

For Marguerite

# PROLOGUE LATE 1870S

We had no relief from the mosquitoes. Vast itching clouds of them rolled across the prairies, urged on by the sun's rays pounding the earth. After those torrential spring rains, the relentless heat had brought them out. We could always hear them coming. From miles away, screeching across the land, until they tornadoed into the wood-spoke wheels of the Red River carts, the constant barking of the dogs. The tension in the hunting party rose around us like ripples of heat off the ground. My mother gripped the reins so tight her brown hands turned white. The horses picked up their trot without us asking. They wanted out too.

An Elder named Violet, who rode in her family's old wooden cart a couple wagons over, motioned for the hunt captain to come over. I tried to listen in to what they were saying. But it was impossible. I doubted that either of them could hear each other over the itch and the squeak below their seats, the creaking and groaning of the carts, the braying of the draft horses hitched up to them, the barking dogs that seemed to be everywhere, the mosquitoes' roar above it all. A few families played out rhythm songs on the fiddles, spoons, and drums, to carry us in beat across the rolling grasses of the prairie. A welcome distraction. The Elder and the hunting captain communicated with hand gestures and read each other's lips, a skill we had all learned from living within the constant noise. I knew she was telling him to rein it in. We needed to get off the trails and down into a river valley, or ravine bottom, or slough of some sort, to hide out from the swarms.

Violet and the captain came to an agreement, and the captain rode off to the front of the hunting party. I watched as his men circled up around him. They conversed for a bit, and then the men dispersed on their horses to the family cart groupings they had been assigned back when the captains of the hunt had been chosen, before we set out. They let us know what was happening. A young guy, barely older than me, maybe sixteen or seventeen with a wispy three-hair moustache and old hand-me-down full-brim hat, rode up beside us.

"After the next ridge, we're going to turn off towards the creek, circle up in the mud and get some brush piles burning," he told my mother. He seemed so serious, but at the same time such a boy. He still had those big chubby cheeks that a little kid would have. I wondered if he would grow into them or if he'd always have the classic Métis round face.

"Won't be too late?" my mother asked. I saw him shrug and our eyes caught. I stiffened up in my seat, trying to look older than I felt.

"It is what it is," he replied. He rode off towards the next cart. I wanted him to look at me again.

"Stop it," my mother said. She took a hand off the reins and swatted my thigh. "Don't think I don't know what you're up to."

The horses picked up the pace until we caught up with the others and joined in with them. They wanted to keep running but she lifted up on the reins, slowing them down to keep our cart in check with everyone else. "Damn mosquitoes are so loud. Can't even hear your father."

I looked behind us and there he was: still sprawled out in the back, snoring under the loudness of it all. His body splayed out, legs, arms, chest, head everywhere. He slept in his underwear and wore his hat and sweated beads that ran out from under the brim until they evaporated in the dry prairie air. I turned back around to watch the boy gliding from family to family.

"We should have turned off as soon as we heard them. We're already too late. Old lady over there is losing her hearing. Should have had her daughter warn her. You're going to warn me when I'm an old lady, right?" She rambled on after that because she didn't want my answer. She didn't want me to talk, or look, or do anything except sit right next to her.

I didn't know if I wanted the boy or if I wanted his freedom. To ride with the hunt captains up front and patrol the camps at night. Untethered to this bench, beside my mother, forced to listen to her and my father yell whenever he woke up.

My father used to be one of the main men working for the hunt captains. But he got into the whiskey one night and stole a set of beautiful moosehide gloves that were gifted to a family from our nehiyawak relatives who lived down in the Beaver Hills. I don't know what he was thinking. It's not like something like that would go unnoticed. Was it something within the beads that drew him in . . . When was he expecting to wear them . . . We were constantly surrounded by all the other Métis families who knew exactly whose gloves those were. The next day, when the search began, he was found passed out not far from the family's tent. He was wearing the gloves. The community publicly shamed him for it. He went into the circle and judgement was passed down from the Elders and the family he'd stolen from, and he was forever labelled a thief, which is about as low as one can get within our world. He hasn't recovered any pride since. That's just not something you do.

I don't think the community ever really forgave him. My mother definitely didn't. She always noticed the looks from the other women whenever she cut up the bison; she didn't even want to come on the hunt. She thought we should all stay back at our river lot and just work on farming, and then we could trade with the hunting party when they returned. But rumours had gone around that this hunt was the last one. We'd been hearing that for a while now, but something felt like this time it would be real. The nehiyawak and niitsitapi had signed a Treaty, and the traders whispered about how the bison weren't coming back when they crossed the Medicine Line this time. The Elders had worried during every one of the fifteen winters I'd been on this planet about this happening. Now we were at that point.

I remember when you couldn't see the end of the herd. When I was little, it stretched as far into the horizon as you could possibly see and the next person could possibly see. Herds that my kohkum used to tell me carved the river valleys and ravines with their movements. They were so numerous that when they stopped to drink at a lake, they would drain it dry and it would stay dry until it filled once more with snow and rain.

And then, right around when I got my first moontime, I could point to where the herd ended on the prairie. And then the next year on the hunt the herd only stretched halfway to the horizon. Elders talked about America's war against the bison. They finished killing each other out east and switched their focus to the bison and the Sioux. The Sioux fought hard. But the bison just moved as they had always done, and it took them right into the paths of America's guns. When my father got too drunk, he would rant to us about the cowardly Americans. How the Americans couldn't fight the Sioux straight up like the Métis and our Cree kin had at the Grand Coteau. How instead they had to kill the bison to try to starve our kin out of the prairies, and in turn how they would starve us. My mom would tell him not to be dramatic and that we could just farm.

"You think the government and the Mounties are just going to let us farm?" he'd say. "You really think they'll let us settle down and farm the land that we want to?"

"Why not? It's not like there's any shortage of land around here," my mother replied.

"Give your head a shake. You remember what happened in Red River when they wanted that land."

"They won't do that here."

"Yes, they will. They'll take it all and leave us the scraps."

"No one in their right mind wants to live in this god-forsaken country."

"I do," I joined in. They both gave me a look that carried lightning and told me to shut up.

Later my dad came and sat down beside my bed. He looked beat-up, weathered, old, like we had just gone through a long winter, but here we were in the middle of the spring; his nose pockmarked red and cheeks swollen and flushed from a permanent state of drinking. He didn't carry himself like he used to. The shame and the drink had withered him into the last leaf on the tree. The one that shouldn't remain.

"I want to live here too, my girl. I promise that I'll do whatever I can to make sure we never have to leave."

Part of me believed that it was just another story. How could the bison really be gone? They had probably just been wintering farther down south, and since now the Treaties were signed, maybe they'd come on back up. It might have just been niitsitapi rumours to discourage us from setting out. I couldn't fathom what my life would be without the herds running as far as the eye could see. It was all I had ever known. All my family had ever known. I loved the adventure. All the communities together, in our carts, heading south on the bison trails, wheels squeaking. It beat the rest of the year when we sat around tending to gardens and trapping the rivers and streams. Sitting around the river lot got boring. Sure, we'd go down into the ravine or out to Lac Ste. Anne to visit family, but it wasn't the same as the thrill of constantly travelling, on the move behind the herd. Being part of something bigger than just our survival.

Following behind the hunters and finding the tokens left on or next to the bodies of the bison. A glove here, a sash there, a locket, a wallet, anything to let us know that this was the bison we needed to start getting ready for the journey back home. The way we helped each other find them, how the women yelled out to direct each other. The feeling of the warmth of life as we split open the rib cage and ran our knives down the belly to clean out the innards. The smell of digested grass from the stomach that bounced out on the ground; the blood that flowed from the bison back into the land. Working together to process a whole animal, loading it into the cart and moving on to the next one. Every part was ceremony. Every part made me love the bison more than anything.

The carts circled up in the mud flats off of the river. I ran out with all the other kids, young women, men, anyone physically able to help, and piled up the found sagebrush around the ring we had created. The mosquitoes caught up to us as we piled the brush. The thunder cloud descended and the sky all around us was dark with bugs. I swatted my arm and my hand turned black with dots of my own fresh blood from the dozens of them that I had killed. I looked over at the girl beside me, whose face was completely covered. I could feel them doing the same thing to me. In the middle of the circle, the horses and dogs howled and bayed; the riders struggled to keep their mounts under control, causing a panicked stampede through the camp. I lost track of where I was. People were running and screaming and trying to find respite in the water away from the bugs. The hunters tried to maintain their composure and not follow the crowd into the river, but even a few of them turned tail. I went to make my way to the water but got disoriented and fell to my knees.

"Get that brush lit now!" the captain hollered.

The piles went up and the thick dense smoke hung in the air. People came running back from the river into the circle of carts. The smoke had created a layer of protection from the bugs. We had to calm the panicked horses and get them covered in mud to prevent them from going wild from the bites and bolting. All the people that had been piling brush now switched to gathering mud in big slop pails and running it back to the horses and slathering them with it. The horses' eyes held the same wild look as a moose's when it's being hunted, and I was careful not to get on the wrong end of one. One kick and it would be over. And these horses were all kicking and bucking away.

When the horses were safe and under control and more sagebrush had been piled up to keep the fires going for a while, we gathered. It would be a bit before the bugs left and we could get going. The instruments were out, and fiddles could be heard switching from the keeping-time rhythm songs to the dancing reels. My father had crawled out from the back of the cart and took his sprawl on the ground beside the cart, sipping at his glass whiskey jar again. My mother had wandered over to where a bunch of other women sat around pouring each other cups of muskeg tea from the cast iron pot that dangled from a tripod over the fire. I did my best to imitate my father's sprawl beside him and together we watched the dark billowing smoke suffocate the itching clouds. The odd bug still got through, but it was bearable now.

"What are we going to do if the bison are really gone?" I asked him.

"We'll figure it out," he replied.

"What if we never see one again?"

"They'll come back. They always do. It might not be this year. It might not be in my lifetime. It might not be in your lifetime. But they'll come back. These prairies were meant for the bison and we were meant to follow them, to work with them, to respect them. The bison are the land just as much as we are."

"The Elders said—" I started.

"The Elders say a lot of things," my father interrupted. "They're just as scared as we are. If there are no bison then who are we as a people? Who do we become? Do we just cease to exist? I don't think so. You see the strength in how we survive. We're not going anywhere and neither are the bison, even if it's just in our dreams. And if we can keep memory then we can keep story, and your kids' kids will know who we are and who the bison are." He leaned back against the cart wheel. His nicotine-stained yellow beard and moustache glistened with sweat. He pulled out a pouch of tobacco and his rolling papers and fashioned himself a cigarette. He put it up to his lips and lit it and blew a cloud into the air.

"But don't listen to me. I'm just an old drunk. Listen to the Elders," he said.

I closed my eyes and thought of a big bison bull skull. Not like the ones from the hunts, but the ones from long, long ago that turned up in the sides of the cliff faces after floods went through. The skulls with the horns that stretched on forever.

---

We followed the herd until the Medicine Line stopped us. Years ago, we would have just kept going. But the war between the Sioux and the Americans had made the territory south of the line too dangerous. And who knew what might happen if we ran into the Blackfoot, or what the Mounties would do when we crossed back over.

The carts lined up on the top of a ridge, and off in the distance the last thousands of a herd that once was as numerous as the mosquitoes kicked up the prairie soil, crossed over, and eventually disappeared.

I looked beside me. Violet, the Elder, stood there staring off into the now-empty prairie as the dust settled.

"That's it," she said. "It's over."

# ONE

# EZZY

Around two in the morning, Grey dropped me off at an outskirt suburb of Edmonton. The kind where there were no numbers to tell you where you were on the grid, just the name of a landscape feature like Rolling Meadows, followed by a Blvd., Way, Point, Lane. I assumed that rich people loved not having numbers in their addresses. Why else would you live out here? Grey took off down the block in her beat-up Honda CR-V. I watched the tail lights until they disappeared around a suburb bend. Rich people also loved curves in the road.

The neighbourhood that I grew up in was on the central grid. Straight-line avenues and streets as far as the eye could see. You couldn't steal a vehicle in the neighbourhood. Everyone knew who you were there, or people would be out and about. If you were into stealing vehicles, you would catch a lift or take a bus out to a random sleepy suburb just like the one Grey had dropped me off in and jack a truck out there. Then the cops couldn't pattern you either. I used to be quite good at it.

When I saw the older Ford F-150 parked on the street, I felt that old familiar rush kick up. The one I used to live with constantly when I was on the edge of either being locked up or becoming rich. That instant shot of adrenaline. As badly as I didn't want to go back to jail, letting Grey down would be worse. If she dreamt bison, I'd make that happen. What else did I have going on? Being a bison rustler made me feel like I was living in an old-time western movie. The kind that hired Italians to play the Indians.

I jimmied open the door of the F-150 with a coat hanger I'd brought with me. I used a flathead screwdriver to snap the wire case open. I couldn't make out the individual wires in the darkness, and had forgotten to bring a headlamp or something that would allow me to see. Back when we did this regularly, we used those headlamps you could get at Safeway or convenience stores. The cheap ones. Then everyone started using the phone flashlights. I had neither with me now. I'd have to try to turn on the cab light. No problem in the city, but out here in suburb territory, any light would draw attention. Banking on the darkness of a neighbourhood without streetlights and asleep under 2,500-square-foot roofs for some sense of anonymity. I hoped it was enough to get this done.

I pulled out the bundle of wires that held the power for the battery, ignition, and starter, stripped back the insulation on the red battery wire and brown ignition wire, and wove them together. The dashboard came alive. I had to move fast now. I took the last dangling yellow wire, stripped it of insulation and touched it to the connected battery wire, just enough to get a spark going. The engine kicked up and I revved the truck like a kid would a standard when he was learning how to shift. I cranked the wheel to the left to break the steering lock and I was gone. It was a skill that a person would never forget. Like riding a bike or throwing an ace up your sleeve. Once you learned it, you always had it.

You had to love the older vehicles. No alarm systems, and the wires just hanging there ready to roll. It really didn't take much. I wasn't sure what would happen with the newer, more computerized vehicles. I had never tried to steal one of them before. But something told me that they didn't make them this easy. My buddies used to tell stories of the old ones where you could just jam that flathead screwdriver in the ignition and it would always turn. Then they put in the anti-theft thing, but the wires would still work. Then the companies got smart and started locking it all down with the new computers that ran the whole thing. I was sure someone had come up with some way to steal those too, but that was a little too much for me. I had enough trouble turning on a computer at the library, let alone hacking into some car. I'd leave that to the kids. Still, I never felt bad about taking these older vehicles. The insurance payout was probably worth more than the unit itself.

Grey figured that we would get the bison from the same field that little khaki nerd boy had told us about before telling us to move along. From the main gate you could be in and out of there in five minutes, tops. The bison were usually milling about on the viewing road that arched through the field in a semicircle, especially at night when they'd want to lick the salt off the road. It was the same spot the park had set up with the corrals to load and unload the bison. They also put water and leftover feed there during the winter to keep the bison close. It kept national park tourists happy if they could see the big beasts without leaving their vehicles.

I pulled into the loop and saw Grey parked there in a big Dodge dually pickup truck with a livestock trailer hitched up to it. I flashed my lights at her and she fired up the truck, and I drove to where my headlights would help guide her. Grey backed the livestock trailer up to the corral with the precision of someone who had done this a hundred times in a life. I was about to step out to help her align the livestock trailer with the loading ramp, but could see that this was something she didn't need any assistance with. She rammed the loading ramp with the gate, hopped out of the truck but kept it running, walked around to the back to open the trailer's doors, and hitched the chains around the fence sides to keep them propped open. When she was done, she walked over to me. Beads of sweat were running down my face, freezing in the cold air before they hit my mouth. My hands had been gripping the steering wheel so tightly that they started aching with a dull pain. Grey got into the passenger seat and I immediately felt better. I took my hands off the wheel and stretched them out.

"What are you doing?" she asked. "We gotta get going."

I pulled into the field and drove over to the first group of bison—a bunch of cows and calves.

"Push 'em," Grey said. I nudged the bumper of the stolen F-150 into the butt of a cow. It didn't like that. It started trotting forward, snorting and spitting and making little buff barks as it went. The rest of the herd followed suit.

Every dark form hunkering over in the bush was a blacked-out prairie semi-truck ready to come charging out of the shadows and hammer into the driver's-side door. Nothing about this screamed safety. I bet one of the big guys could tip this truck right over. I thought about getting crushed in by a bison. A cousin of mine had been crushed on an oil field construction site back in the day when a tank fell off the crane that was lifting it up. Splat. There couldn't have been anything left. That was a closed-casket funeral. If a bison smashed into you, I thought, would it be that different?

That first load took longer than expected. I couldn't get the hang of pushing them in. The herd kept moving just out of the path of the F-150. They didn't want to get loaded up. If a bison doesn't want to do something, it's not going to do it. I kept trying to get them up against the fence line we were using as a barrier on one side, but they always turned off at the last minute and returned to the rest of the herd. I'd circle back around in the truck and then try again.

"Just hit them," Grey yelled. "You're not going to hurt them. They'll get the point."

"I'm fucking trying," I yelled back. My hands white-knuckling and trembling on the wheel. I couldn't quite get used to the idea of how to keep an animal calm while nudging it with a massive truck. Grey got fed up with my lack of ability as a rustler.

"Move," she said, and I shuffled over to the passenger seat while she climbed overtop of me into the driver's. She started using the bumper of the truck to manoeuvre the herd against the corral fencing. On her first try she got them into place. She pushed the bumper of the truck up on the butt of the cow that was hanging back in guard mode and, with a sense of assurance, started driving the truck forward. The cow moved with the truck. I kept expecting it to panic, but it just kept docilely moving ahead.

With the bison pinned between the fence and the truck, Grey was able to push them into the livestock trailer. They were more chill than I'd imagined. I'd expected a war zone or something, with ropes and wrestling, bison and cowboy carcasses littering the earth. I didn't know why. My dreams tended not to be realistic.

When they were all in, Grey hopped out of the truck and ran around to the back and locked up the doors, then got behind the wheel of the dually and started the drive back into Edmonton. I followed in the stolen F-150.

Our next run went smoother, and the next. Grey had lost all hope for my bison-rustling skills and just took the lead right from the get-go. I opened the livestock trailer gates and hung out on the other side of the fence while Grey pushed them in with the truck. When they were all inside and Grey had parked right at the loading ramp to discourage any from trying to back out, I hopped over the fence and closed the gates. A job I could handle. Though even this one shook me—I could feel the heat, musk, and size of the bison looming within the trailer. These weren't even the bulls, either. Just a bunch of cows and calves. But even the smallest calf probably weighed as much as the F-150, or at least it did in my mind. Still, I couldn't believe how easily they just trotted in, but Grey reminded me that they were national park bison and were probably used to tourists gawking at them and national park employees moving them from field to field, examining them, and the general presence of unwanted human interaction.

None of the park staff were around tonight, though. Grey had heard that they only had about two full-time staff after the summer busy season.

"How has no one come by?"

"You really think someone's pulling a fall night shift out here?" Grey said. "The employees are on government time. They've been home since two p.m., I'm sure."

"If we had to go chase them through the field, someone might notice," I said.

"Who? And even if they did, they'd just think we were a contractor. No one gives a shit about the bison. They just exist out here. They're the ultimate prairie animal. They don't need our shitty human help to survive."

"Then why not just snip some fences or something?" I asked.

"You want these things running all over the highway? Up in the north, there are still wild bison all over the highways in the winter, licking up the salt. If you think hitting a moose is deadly, imagine hitting one of these. You'd be done instantly. Just erased."

"It's amazing that we were ever able to hunt something like this."

"Never underestimate the Métis," Grey said. "This is just us establishing a new herd. The parks did the same thing in Banff. We're just doing it in the middle of the city."

"Got it," I said. If this was all part of Grey's plan, then it meant something. I didn't know much about protest movements, but Grey did, and I had no problem falling in line behind her. She radiated confidence in her decisions, and it was hard to imagine that she could do something wrong. I hadn't seen that happen yet.

Dank waves poured out of the air vents on the double-axle cattle trailer. The smell of two moose mating in the skankiest of muskegs. I'd gotten used to plugging my nose and breathing out my mouth, just like I did whenever I went into a public toilet, but the odd whiff would still break through. If it hit the wrong way, it made me want to vomit. But something about the bison being so close to us made me feel connected to some sort of higher purpose. We were actually doing it. No more bullshit. I was confident that this was the right thing to do.

Inside the trailer, ten big blocky heads followed me as I walked back to the gate. Even without the smell, you could feel their presence permeating the air. I knew they would like to stampede right over my body. Trample it. Return it to the land. I couldn't blame them. Even though here we were, about to give them their freedom. Bison don't like getting enclosed. Especially within a fence. Especially not in a tight old rusted-out cattle trailer.

"Alright," Grey said, her face illuminated by the red glow coming off the trailer's tail lights. It had taken us about an hour to drive into the city from when we got the last bison into the truck. Grey made a point of driving exactly five clicks under the speed limit.

If anyone saw us, they'd just think we were a couple ranch hands moving cattle along. "I'm going to undo the latch. Then let's hightail it back into the truck. I don't want one of these bison thinking we're crash-test dummies on their way out." She looked more the part than I did. Black cowboy hat, black bandana, black hoodie, black jeans, and black cowboy boots. She'd grown up on a ranch on the Pembina Creek Métis Settlement. Horses and cows were second nature to her. Maybe not bison specifically, but bison were the prairie itself.

I was a city boy. There was no connection to nature in the beat-up concrete avenues and alleys of forgotten neighbourhoods that commuting people passed over. I grew up not far from the park where Grey and I had parked the trailer. Eighteen blocks north at best. While Grey had been learning how to round up and load livestock into a trailer, I'd learned how to sneak through the city in the darkness. Both necessary for the plan.

"Last run," I said.

"Thank god," Grey replied. She reached down and picked up a hammer.

She undid the latch and cracked the gate so the bison would get the idea. We started walking back to the truck, and she clanged the hammer onto the metal trailer siding a couple times. The noise thundered throughout the trailer, and the bison came streaming out. They looked around confused, then noticed the rest of their herd over by the park pavilion and trotted off to join them. Thirty in total. Three trips, around ten each time. Thank god the nights were long this time of year. We had been going at it for what felt like days at this point. The rising sun began to turn the cloud line over the river valley purple and pink. The bison's hulking forms got more pronounced with every minute of more light, as they stomped and snorted around the picnic tables, gazebos, garbage cans, and locked-up bathrooms. The steam from their hot breath rising through the frost and into the sunrise. Somewhere in the near distance, coyotes howled their morning census songs to greet the new arrivals to their river valley landscape.

"How long until someone notices?" I asked Grey.

"I'd give it an hour or two until some early morning dog walker or jogger calls it in. But who knows, could have already happened."

We were back at Grey's uncle's mobile home. I'd ditched the stolen truck in a McDonald's parking lot on our way out of the city and grabbed us a couple coffees and Egg McMuffins. I devoured mine and guzzled back the coffee as soon as I was physically able to stand the heat. Grey waited until we got back to the kitchen table. She picked away at the edges of the sausage patty that hung out of the sandwich.

"What if they just round them back up?" I asked. "Then what was the point of all of that?"

"I dunno. To prove that the River Valley doesn't belong to us?" she replied. "I don't think it'll be that easy for them. It's going to be very confusing."

I was still starving. Grey's barely touched sandwich stared back at me. "You gonna eat that?" I asked. She pushed the sandwich across the table to me. I ate it in two bites. "Being a buffalo cowboy is hard work."

"Do you ever wonder what it would have been like a hundred and fifty years ago?" Grey asked.

"No Egg McMuffins."

"We would have been in the carts going down into the Dakotas to hunt. You wouldn't have had to go through all that foster care and group homes. I wouldn't have had to constantly fight for the right to exist as a Métis woman without colonial oppression. We wouldn't even need any of that. Just us and the prairie and the buffalo."

"I'll steal bison every night and let them out wherever you want me to. I'll let them out on the legislature grounds and watch them trample the marble buildings into dust."

"We'd need a lot of buffalo for that."

"We'll find them," I said. "Who knows? Maybe people will start freeing bison everywhere."

"Somehow I doubt it'll get that intense," Grey replied. "But you never know."

I crashed hard after those breakfast sandwiches settled into my gut. Late that afternoon, I woke up on the couch. I stretched and peeked over the back of it at the bed. It was empty. I stepped outside, and the truck and the trailer were gone. I reached into the cooler and pulled out a Lucky Lager. Maybe she'd just gone back up to the settlement to drop the trailer off at her parents'. I cracked the tab and took a big swig. In the distant sky, thousands of cranes migrating south for the winter whooped and called their way above the city skyline. I watched as they caught the thermals coming off the bison breath and soared in tornados upwards into the infinite sky without lifting their wings.

A few days earlier, Grey and I had been sitting across from each other at the kitchen table in the acreage we were renting off her uncle. "Acreage" is how her uncle had described it. I'd pictured a log cabin surrounded by soaring trees with a view over a little pond and little deers and little moose frolicking through the little fields, and little songbirds calling out from the little surrounding trees. I'd pictured two rocking chairs on the porch overlooking everything, where you could drink a couple Luckys and watch nature.

Clueless. A musty old one-room trailer with black mould growing along the upper walls in a swamp surrounded by rusting-out vehicles and abandoned farm equipment would have been more accurate. Grey told me that her uncle didn't like people calling it a trailer, thought that was low-class. When he bought it, it had been advertised as a mobile home on the acreage, and he was sticking to it. Out of respect or mockery, I couldn't tell which, Grey referred to it as the "mobile home." But we didn't have many options or the money to get something better. I wasn't even sure if Grey was actually paying him rent or not.

"I hate it," Grey said.

"Hate what?" I dealt us each six cards. Grey looked at her hand. She frowned, then pulled two of the cards out and placed them in my crib.

"Just thinking about how this used to look. How it used to feel," she said. She took a sip of her tea. "All I want is to see a herd of a million bison storming across the prairie."

"Could you imagine?" I asked. "How wild something like that would be."

"Think about them all running. I wonder how the earth would feel, how it would sound when they travelled through . . ."

"How much do you think it would cost to buy Saskatchewan?" Grey stared at me. "Like, could the Amazon guy buy Saskatchewan?"

"I dunno, probably."

"All we have to do is convince him to buy Saskatchewan for us, and then we can get the buffalo herd going." I put down a ten of spades. "Ten."

Grey shook her head, took another sip, and laid down a five of hearts. "Fifteen for two."

"Just think about it. A million buffalo running back to Saskatoon. Pretty sure that's what The Tragically Hip were singing about." I laid down a six to make it twenty-one.

"The Guess Who," Grey said. She put down a ten and pegged out two for the thirty-one.

"Huh?"

"It wasn't The Tragically Hip. It was The Guess Who."

"Whatever, same old shit, anyways."

"I'm serious."

"Serious about what?" I asked.

"I want to bring the buffalo back," Grey replied. Then she skunked me.

Grey slept in the bed across the trailer from where I'd sprawl out on the couch, listening to her soft snores, trying to time my breathing with hers. A leftover habit from foster care and the group homes and having to share a room with someone. I always hoped it would help me fall into the rhythm of sleep. Something that never came easy to me. At night, Grey would tell me the stories that she had heard from the old ones in Pembina Creek growing up. They'd told her of the last days of the Métis bison hunts on the prairies. Before borders, barbed wire, and Mounties took away freedom of movement for us and the bison both, and left the land barren and empty for agriculture. A new game for prairie survival that we weren't allowed to participate in. She told me stories of great bison that were double the size of what you see now. About how the plains ecosystem relied on these animals to guide it. They were a natural form of keeping the land healthy. All the other animals—from the grizzlies to the coyotes, magpies, and wolves—their worlds all revolved around the bison.

"You ever think about why magpies are such a nuisance?" Grey asked me once.

"Can't say I have."

"Why they're so angry?"

"Nope."

"It's because they're sad that the bison went away. Their entire existence for millennia was built around being a part of the bison. Following them around, cleaning their fur, scavenging from the dung, they had this beautiful way of being with each other. And now that one's gone, the other is restless and takes it out on us."

"I dunno if watching magpies tearing through bison shit is beautiful," I said.

"You gotta get your head out of your ass sometime and just think."

Grey talked about bison a lot. One of the reasons she'd wanted to move into this trailer was the proximity to the herds at the national park. Grey would drive up there for sunrise to watch them. Most nights we'd play game after game of crib, and she would tell me about the different bulls and the newborn calves' orange fur. How those calves stuck out like angels on the prairie. How the older bulls tended to spend time by themselves off in the woods, and the younger ones grouped up together. One time she told me how the older boys were confident, could just do their own thing, but the younger ones had to try to build up their macho energy by hanging out together, humping each other and wrestling away. Not any different than the young bros strolling up and down Whyte at night. She'd often chat with the Parks Canada staff that worked out there about the bison, and when she returned to the trailer, she'd tell me all the facts about the herd, about government bison reclamation, about big programs that planned to reintroduce the bison into other national parks and areas across Canada.

Most of the time, she went alone and was long gone before I'd woken up, but I did accompany her out to the park one day. We pulled out onto the highway and Grey put the speedometer up to one nineteen, exactly nine over the speed limit. Enough to get there just a bit faster, not enough to warrant getting pulled over by the cops on the way. We drank our coffees and sat in silence as we listened to an Ian Tyson playlist on Spotify. As soon as we hit the park gate, Grey turned the music off and rolled both windows down. I gave her a look.

"Better to hear everything," she said. I reached over and turned the heat up. It wasn't exactly summer weather out here. An early fall morning had left frost on all the white poplars, aspens, and willow trees that ran up and down the main road into the bison areas. The sun hadn't risen high enough yet to burn it off. We puttered along until we came across two big bulls standing along the side of the road. Grey pulled off a few hundred yards away. Enough room to give them space. Though it didn't look like they cared one way or the other.

"These are the young ones," she said. "The old boys would never hang out together like this."

I nodded like I knew what she was talking about. A guy doesn't realize how big a bison is until you're next to one. They carry themselves with the swagger of an animal that knows that nothing can touch them. We definitely couldn't.

I caught a glimpse of a vehicle pulling up behind us in the rear-view mirror. It had the lights and the green stripe signalling that it was a national park truck.

A man got out. He wore the outdated khaki pants and green uniform that had been a staple of federal park workers since the days when they'd come into our schools to give presentations on the bison herds and the moose and elk that also called the park home. I don't remember much from those presentations, but I felt like they mentioned at some point that the herd was descended from some Texas ranch where a guy had squirrelled away a bunch of bison before they were completely killed off.

"Hey there," the parks man said as he walked up to the truck. Grey nodded at him and kept her eyes trained on the bison. I didn't acknowledge him. Never acknowledge authority. Only bad things can happen when they're involved.

"Pretty beautiful, eh," he continued. Grey nodded again. "They'll be getting shipped out soon here. The park's at carrying capacity again. Can you believe that? Bison just keep on keeping on." He forced a laugh.

"What's hard to believe about that?" Grey asked.

"About what?" he stammered.

"That they survive perfectly on the landscape? That just makes sense. It's not something hard to believe."

He seemed confused. The interaction wasn't going the way he'd thought it would. I held back a grin and kept my eyes fixed ahead on the bison. They still could not give a shit that we were here having this conversation.

"So you're going to have to move along," he said.

"Why? We're not bothering anyone."

"It's unsafe to be parked on the side of the road. If you continue on to the next loop, you'll be able to pull over. There may be a herd in there."

"Herd's deeper out right now. You should know that," Grey said.

"You're going to have to move along," his tone had shifted to an authoritarian one. I could see him itching to execute his ultimate bro move and pull a weapon on us.

"Can you imagine thinking that it's a miracle that bison survive on the prairie? What kind of useless university degree did he have to get to not know that," Grey said as she watched the parks guy walk back to his truck in the rear-view mirror. Her brown eyes were a darker shade than normal. I felt like you could see the embers of anger burning in them. She lowered her ball cap over her forehead and relaxed her grip on the wheel, colour returning to her pale fingers. She turned the radio back on and Buffy Sainte-Marie sang "Darling Don't Cry" to us. "Come on, let's get out of here. That fuckwad ruined the vibe."

Grey did a six-point turn on the road. Somewhere above us an owl hooted away. Beside me Grey shivered and rolled the windows up. We continued back down the road we had come in on, and back to our trailer existence.

"I've been thinking about what you were talking about," Grey said, later that night.

"About what? I say a lot of dumb shit," I replied.

"About buying Saskatchewan."

"I think that was the sixth Lucky Lager talking, Grey," I said. "Speaking of . . ." I walked over to the old blue Coleman cooler I kept outside the door of the trailer. A few months back, I had scribbled out all the Coleman branding with a Sharpie and then scribbled "Yeti" all over it. That made me laugh every time I reached into it for a Lucky. I came back into the trailer and sat down at the kitchen table with Grey. She kept shuffling the cards over and over.

"I don't know if we need Saskatchewan," she said. "I think we have what we need right here." I raised my eyes towards her and motioned for her to pass me the deck of cards. She ignored me. "What do they always say? That Edmonton has the biggest park in the world or something like that? With the River Valley and all."

"Yeah," I replied.

"That's a lot of land for bison."

"Yup."

"We could bring the bison to it . . . They're not going to make it there on their own. But when they got there, wouldn't that be something."

"I dunno. Can you get arrested for something like this?" I asked.

"You can get arrested for just existing when you're a Métis man. You know that better than anyone. So what difference does it really make in the long run? It's either do something monumental or just fade into an inevitable jail cell," Grey replied.

Still, even if it was inevitable, I had zero interest in seeing the inside of Fort Sask Correctional again. Ever. One of the reasons I liked being stuck in a swampy, mouldy trailer with Grey on the edge of the city: no trouble to get into.

"Wouldn't it be worth it to see a bison herd, a thousand strong, running through the River Valley? Going from park to park? Becoming a part of the land?" Grey stared at me. "Wouldn't it be worth jail time over something like this? Better than smashing car windows and snagging loonies."

I took my black toque off and ran my hand over my freshly shaved head, and then put it back on. I cracked another Lucky Lager. "That's not why I went to jail."

"Basically the same thing," she said.

"You don't even have a plan."

"We'll borrow my dad's truck and trailer. Then we'll just drive into the park and load them up."

"It's probably not that simple. I mean, how do you load bison into a trailer?"

"Round them up."

"With what? We don't have horses. And even if we did have a horse, I don't know how to ride one."

"You know how to drive a truck though, right?" Grey asked.

"I don't have a truck, either."

"When has that ever stopped you before?"

Three days I waited in that trailer. Playing solitaire and staring into the distant swamp. The Lucky ran out after the first day. The coffee on the second. That's what got me moving. If I'd had the supplies, I could have chilled there for weeks waiting for Grey to come back. But on the morning of that third day, out of my liquid mental reinforcements, I decided that it was best to keep moving. Grey had a habit of finding me when she needed me. She moved on her own time, and I didn't want to be a burden to her. I left a note saying that I was headed into the city and would probably crash at Auntie May's, and I started walking. It would take me most of the day, but what other option did I have? If someone decided to pick me up, great, but I wasn't going to resort to trying to beg a ride from someone. I couldn't bring myself to hold that thumb up on the highway. That wasn't my style.

I'd known Grey seven years. Two of those years I'd wasted in jail. And, at the beginning, I wouldn't say I really *knew* her—I *wanted* to, more than anything, but she mostly kept to herself. She had just finished a degree in Native Studies from the University of Alberta. I had no idea what that really meant, still don't, but it sounded like something that would get you a social worker job later. Or maybe a job with the government or band office. I had been hanging around with a couple guys from the neighbourhood. We figured that our best bet to meet women was to attend the protests going on all throughout that year. We would bike or take the train downtown and join in on whatever event was happening. These guys couldn't really give a shit about the causes; they were just fired up about the beautiful women who came to the protests. The idea was that white university women would love the authenticity of a bunch of native guys supporting the protests. It never worked out that way, of course. We were all too shy to actually talk to anyone. After a few weeks of going to the protests, my friends faded out, the dream of dating white university women dead, but I kept showing up. I liked listening to the different speakers talk about climate change and Indigenous rights. Something in the messaging spoke to me. It made me feel like maybe all of this shit we had to live with was placed there by a system and not because we just didn't know any better. I liked the idea that we were descended from warriors and people who fought for their rights. That our ancestors didn't just roll over and let colonizers onto the land. The kind of pitiful narrative that I had been taught when I was a kid. This contradicted that shit.

The afternoon I met Grey, the speaker talked about the Papaschase Cree and renaming the Oliver neighbourhood because of the shit that Frank Oliver did back in the day to natives. I was trying to remember what my grandfather had told me about the Papaschase Cree. We were descended from them. That I knew. But I couldn't remember exactly how. As the protest filled out, a group of people ended up standing right beside me. Grey was with them.

"What an asshole, eh?" one of the women in the group said to me. I just nodded. What was it my grandfather had told me? Something about how the south side of the river should have been our reserve lands, but it never materialized, which made sense now when the speaker talked about land rights of the Papaschase Cree. He'd said we'd had the run of the prairie until Treaty was signed and the army, disguised as a police force, moved in and forced us into these tiny-ass areas. I didn't get how a paper could force anyone to do anything, but I did understand how a cop could. They carried war hammers on their belts.

After the speaker wrapped up, I side-eye glanced at the group beside me. They were my age, somewhere around twenty years old, natives and a couple white people who could have been native but just white-passing. That was always a tricky one to figure out. The group milled about and didn't seem in any hurry to leave. I stood around too, not saying anything, hoping that someone would talk to me again.

"What'd you think?" another woman from the group asked me.

"I think that guy was a dick," I said. "How has no one realized this until now?"

"Grey Ginther nitsikasowin, Pembina Creek ohci niya," Grey said, introducing herself.

"Ezzy. Sorry, I don't know much Cree," I replied.

"You'd say apsis nehiyawewin then," another person in their group chimed in.

"Okay," I replied. "Hiy hiy, I know that one."

"We're going to go and sit by the river," Grey said. "Do you want to join us?"

I tagged along for the rest of the spring and summer. They all went to university together, and most of their conversations were about the different graduate schools they were going to in the fall. Everyone was excited to leave Edmonton and move to Montreal, Vancouver, Toronto, and New York, places so foreign to my limited inner-city skull that I couldn't comprehend how far away or how vast they were. Except Grey—she wasn't going to grad school. Her friends liked to bug her about that. She'd tell them it wasn't the time. "I just hated four years of an undergrad. Grad school sounds like more of that same bullshit" was another favourite of hers when the conversation veered that way. Which it always did. I liked hearing about the other cities, though, even if I would never go—and the idea of leaving, about their futures and what another degree would bring. Most of the friends seemed to want to work as academics, professors, writers, or activists and such. They never straight up said that, but I could tell from the way they idolized their former professors at the University of Alberta.

No one ever asked me what I wanted to do. I brought legitimacy to their group with my upbringing and not much else. Since I hadn't gone to school, even high school, I didn't register in any of the oh-so-important conversations about the future. I was okay with that. I didn't want to do much of anything. Just getting by was enough for me. One time, my friend and I were in the grocery store, wandering down the beef jerky aisle, and he stopped and stared at all the different packs, and then he turned to me and said, "I'll know I've really made it in life when I can afford to come in here and buy as much jerky as I want." I thought about that a lot.

That summer ended, and Grey's friends took off for their intended destinations. Even though I was never really a part of the conversations, I missed hearing their ease about life and where it was going. When the biggest problem was grades on papers, you had it made in my books. They gave me a glimpse into a world that I would never be a part of. I thought about their adventures in new cities constantly. I don't think they thought about me twice. I had vague notions of someday going and visiting them, but we were never good enough friends for that. No one would want some punk-ass guy like me showing up to their new city with their new friends. And there was no way in hell I could ever afford a plane ticket anyway. It seemed like a lot of them had constant grants coming in that afforded them the luxury of travel. I didn't know how someone got one of these grants, but if they were throwing money at people, sign me the hell up.

Grey and I continued to hang out. Of all the people, she seemed to have a bit more of an understanding of the world I came from. She never ignored my voice in the group, was really the person who had welcomed it in the first place—the only one who would actually ask me what I thought about the latest racist policy rolling out or whatever pipeline was going through whatever traditional territory. Though one time I did make the mistake of mentioning that I thought a job was a job and people worked in the oilfields or forestry because it paid the bills and they had families to support and probably didn't think too much of it outside of that. Her friends did not like that, and even Grey frowned at me. It's that type of attitude that continues to enforce resource extraction dynamics within the colonial state known as Canada, they replied in unison. A group decision that if you were some poor schlub like me, trying to make a living to support family, that was bullshit. I wanted to tell them that not everyone can laze around on a grant and criticize people. But I didn't. I didn't think that would have landed any better than my first comment. I didn't speak up after that.

I liked to think, though, that Grey viewed my opinions and thoughts as valid. After everyone left for their new worlds, we walked down all the trails in the River Valley, through summer green into fall yellows, browns, reds, and finally into the October snows and freezing winds. When I say we walked down all the trails, I mean that. We were both out of work, though Grey had a job lined up at a non-profit as soon as their grant landed. We didn't have money for pubs, cafes, or movies. I didn't think I could physically sit through an entire movie without twitching out hard. My attention span tended to force me into constant movement or drinking to keep entertained. I could get behind walking, though. There were so many different birds to check out and people who were also doing the walking thing.

Grey's new job was going to focus on climate change activism. She talked a lot about the lack of response and movement that non-profits made towards actual sustainable goals, but that everything started to mount up towards an inevitable revolution. Maybe. Grey would also tell me about the things that she'd learned at university. She talked about the Papaschase and the illegal land surrenders, about Treaties and their nuances, about cultural appropriation and reclaiming identity.

"One of the things that always pissed me off was this urban idealization of the country," Grey said. "My friends would always talk about how if we just went back to the land or went back to the rez or the settlement, things would be so much better than they are here."

"I dunno," I replied. "I like the idea of being out in a cabin on a lake somewhere."

"That's because you've never spent a night outside of the city. Everyone thinks it's going to be an Instagram ad but forgets the work that goes into rural life."

"Sounds nice though, being around animals and shit."

"I really don't think people understand the work. Much less the solitude and loneliness," Grey said. We stopped walking and looked out at the High Level Bridge that spanned the river. "It's just really fucking hard, okay," she continued. "I don't ever want to go back to Pembina Creek. I don't know if I want to stay here, but I know that I don't want to go back there."

I thought she was going to start crying. But she just walked down to the river, picked up a stone, and skipped it five times until it hit the bridge pillar. Twenty feet above the spot where the rock hit the post, someone had spray-painted FUCK COLONIALISM in red. I marvelled at the graffiti. They would have had to climb down on a rope from the bridge's rafters some hundred or more feet above them. Made the little tags thrown around the neighbourhoods seem wimpy.

"The funny part is people always talk about this idea of being Métis," Grey said. She threw another stone. This time it plunked right into the river with a big splash. "But it's not like my family had in-depth conversations about being Métis or anything like that. It's just who we are. Sometimes I feel that people want this idealized compact version of a Métis person."

"All I know is that's what was written on the social worker's records, Métis, and I guess my grandfather told a few stories here and there when I got to see him."

"No one in Pembina Creek was driving around congratulating each other about being Métis. I often feel when people get their . . . card . . . that they feel this sense of entitlement without any of the histories that come with it."

"I thought you were all for people reclaiming their lost identities?" I asked. I picked up my own stone. Instead of skipping it, I hucked it towards the graffiti. It missed horribly.

"I am. Don't get me wrong. But I don't feel any kinship, at least not yet, to someone who comes flying in but hasn't really been there. Does that make sense?" Grey said.

"I dunno. People are always going to be weird about that stuff." I didn't understand why someone would want to be native if they really weren't. I didn't think anyone would really want to switch places with me. That would kill the romance of being native fast.

When winter really hit, Grey and I switched to crib. My grandfather had basically been a semi-professional crib player. He went to all the tournaments at the friendship centre and played matches with his friends around the shelters. Anything that he could to try to make a little extra cash. When one of the social workers set up family visits with him, it was often the game that we'd play. My grandfather was ruthless, though. Even as a little kid, if you missed counting points, he'd count them for you and then add them to his own hand. "Muggins," he'd say, and then peg out two for the weird fifteen-count that my eight-year-old head had missed. "Nothing in this world will ever come easy to you. You gotta take, or it'll take it first." That first crib game between Grey and me, she had no idea what was coming. I skunked her. In the second game, I almost double-skunked her. She had played the odd time before on her family camping trips or with a friend from university—enough to know the rules and get by, but not enough to get ruthless.

"Fuck," she said. "This game is horseshit." I had just played a twenty-four-point hand. Sixes, fives, and fours, beautiful combos. "I'm not playing this stupid game anymore."

"We could play go fish?"

"Asshole. Fifteen-two, a run is five, and a pair makes seven. Suck it."

That was the same cold, cold night we almost made out. We were both wearing double hoodies, toques, and had knockoff Pendleton blankets wrapped around us. We even had a space heater going in her apartment. Still, we weren't warm enough. Grey never really drank, but on that night she brought out a bottle of dusty whiskey and poured us each a shot into our Red Rose teas.

"Fucking heater doesn't do anything so we'll have to warm up somehow," she said. We drank our whiskey teas and leaned back into our spots on the couch. The crib board and deck of cards separated us. I looked at her eyes. Something I realized I never really did. She was staring back at me. Time slowed down for a moment, cheesy-movie style. I realized I had no idea how to approach this. I didn't know if I had ever been basically sober when I'd hooked up with anyone. Then I got too in my head thinking about the different ways this scenario could play out and if I even really wanted it to, and did Grey really want it to, and I was just imagining the tension in the room. The buzz was fleeting. Neither of us acted on the moment, and it passed.

Not long after that, Grey invited me over to her apartment to show me something. I really wanted to try to kiss her again. I thought that was why she was calling me over—we were going to hook up. I got incredibly nervous. Everything in me screamed go and have a couple shots, that'll numb you out, you'll feel normal. Maybe then I wouldn't act like some twitch bag. It took me everything not to have a drink. If Grey found out I had been drinking before coming over to see her, we definitely wouldn't be hooking up that night. She wasn't that big on booze. I asked her about it once and she told me that, back when she was in high school, she drank too much at a bush party and ended up waking up alone in the back seat of some shitbag's truck with her pants off. The truck was parked in the middle of town and there was no one around. She couldn't find her pants or the cell phone that would have been in her pocket and ended up running all the way back to her parents' place half-naked, broken, beat-up, and she swore off booze. If some asshole came at her again, she wanted

to have herself all together so she could give him hell right back.

I had never imagined that I would be friends with someone like Grey. Now she wanted to move that forward. Right on. My hands were trembling when I punched in the code to her apartment building. The buzzer never worked, and the elevator was sketchy sometimes. She just gave me the numbers to access the building rather than having to go down twelve flights of stairs to let me in. Should I make the first move when I got inside? My friends always talked about how you should just go up and kiss someone, don't even hesitate. But my friends also didn't kiss too many people. And I couldn't imagine it working like that. My stomach lurched with the jarring of the elevator as it plodded up. I got to Grey's apartment door. I knocked and then opened it, ready to embrace this new phase in our relationship.

"Ezzy! I got some good news," Grey said. She walked over to greet me at the door. Was she going to try to kiss me first? Then she went for a hug. I turned my head to see if she would lean into my lips, but she just put her face into my shoulder. She pulled away from the hug with a shit-eating grin on her face.

"I figured out how we're cousins!" That was not the news I was expecting. I followed her over to the kitchen table. She had a copy of her family tree laid out. Beside it was a copy of mine.

"Where'd you get this?" I asked. I had never seen it before.

"Métis genealogical office."

"Are they allowed to give this out?"

Grey shrugged her shoulders. "Don't know," she said. "Here, check this out." She pointed back three generations to a lady named Lizette Desjarlais. "Now, from what I can see, Lizette had a whole crew of kids down here when she was young. Then she moved up north and had another crew of kids. Twelve total. Can you imagine?" I stared at the family tree. Lizette would have been my grandfather's mother. I didn't know anything about her. "Or it could have been the other way. A bunch of kids up north and then came to the city. But I think based on this and who the other kids married that it was the city then north," Grey continued. I spotted my grandfather's name under Lizette's. Then it branched off to my mother and Auntie May. Then there was my name directly under my mother's. I looked back past Lizette. The document stretched into the early 1800s.

"A lot more Cree names back then," I said.

"Oh yeah. Pre-Canada and assimilation out here, though, have to remember that." Grey pointed to a spot on her family tree. "So here's where Lizette shows up on my tree. She'd be my grandmother's aunt."

"You sure it's the same person?"

"Oh yeah, absolutely," Grey said.

"So, that would make us . . . ?"

"Pfffft cousins?" Grey laughed, and went to bring us tea.

"This name sounds familiar," I said, pointing to a John Quinn Gladu on my tree.

"That was the chief of the Papaschase First Nation when they signed Treaty 6. You probably heard us mentioning him at one of the protests. His name comes up quite a bit around here."

"So if he's my relation . . ." I paused.

"Yeah?" Grey asked.

"Then I'm Edmonton as fuck."

---

Three days in the trailer was long enough. I wandered down the dusty, washboard gravel driveway to where it met up with the secondary highway. I stood there for maybe ten minutes debating if I wanted to start the walk or not before a grizzled, fat old redneck picked me up. He could have been anywhere from thirty to sixty years old, but had the scars of a hard-lived life. The three teeth he had left hung on precariously under his nicotine-stained moustache. The pockmarks on his face screamed meth head. The orange on the logo of his Oilers hat had turned brown from dirt, and a salty sweat line was permanently etched on the brim and reached halfway up the front of the cap. He drove a blue Chevy single-bench pickup, and the stench of tobacco and stale beer hit me when I opened the door. I pushed through the fast-food bags and smelly-ass empty cans and made myself a spot on the passenger seat.

"Smoke?" he asked.

"I'm good, thanks," I replied.

"Nah, I was asking if you had one."

"Sorry, all out."

"Well, better keep going then." He pulled back onto the secondary highway and brought the truck up to 80 km/h. "Was really hoping you were going to have one, you know."

"Sorry, man," I said.

"I can drop you off at that gas station on the edge of the city. I don't like driving in any farther than that. People are crazy in there."

"That's perfect," I replied.

"Only good thing about the city is smokes and whores," he said. Then he started laughing at his own joke. He laughed so hard he started coughing and hacking uncontrollably. I thought his chest was going to burst open. Each retch came from somewhere deep in his lungs and I expected little pieces of them to start splattering on the dash. He somehow managed to keep the truck moving straight during this fit while other vehicles zoomed by us. He finally settled down long enough to ask what I was doing in the city.

"Looking for a lady," I said.

"Ahhhh, that's the spirit, my boy. You're a good one, aren't you?"

I nodded. He started telling me stories of sex workers that he used to visit.

"Would love to go and join you, but my goddamn willy don't wanna work no more," he said. He started laughing weird again. Eventually, the man chilled out, right about when we pulled into the gas station. He parked. I opened the passenger door and meant to hop out.

"Wait. You gotta give me some cash," he said.

"Fuck that," I replied. "You picked me up. I didn't ask for a ride."

"This look like a goddamn bus service to you? Twenty bucks."

"Do I look like I have twenty bucks?" I asked. I got out of the truck. He stepped out on his side.

"I don't give a flying fuck what you look like. Pay me twenty fucking bucks right now," he yelled.

I started walking away and could hear him running up behind me. When his wheezing got close enough, I turned around and punched him right in the gut as hard as I could. He doubled over. His Oilers hat went flying off onto the sidewalk. The wind knocked out of him. He hit the ground and started groaning.

"Fuck, I can't breathe," he said. "Help me."

"You can talk, you can breathe, you old fuck." I booted him in the rib cage, then stomped on his ankle and the hat on the ground beside him. I thought about taking his truck and driving the rest of the way into the city with it, but cops love greasy old rednecks. I mean, they're glorified rednecks themselves, just with uniforms and badges. If he called, they would leave whoever they were busy racially profiling and come running at his beck and call. I don't know much, but I know that. I strolled away, keeping a slow pace even though my mind was telling me to get the fuck out of there. But one thing I'd learned at a young age is you didn't want to run or bolt from a scene—that made you look suspicious as all hell.

I figured I could find Grey at the park, making sure the bison were doing alright. She would want to see in person what was happening and what kind of reaction they'd be getting from the public. Same thing that brings arsonists back to the sites of their fires—a person needs to see their creation in action. I knew she'd feel responsible for dropping them in the middle of the city and take it straight to the gut if something went wrong. At least until they got established, and people started leaving them alone. I hoped they were doing well, too. It would be a shame to move them just to have someone move them right back.

I hopped on a bus heading downtown. Fares were expensive, but I learned long ago that if you just threw some random change into the payment bubble thing, ninety-nine per cent of the drivers wouldn't give you shit. The one per cent that did would be getting in fights constantly. It was a popular move, and why the hell would you care if you were a driver? You were still getting paid and still driving your route. What was one more person? This guy rolled with that and didn't question the pennies and dime that I put in. Just motioned with his lips towards the back of the bus. I took a seat and stared out the window, half expecting the redneck to come running up, though I was pretty certain he wouldn't be moving too fast after my last boot-smash down on his ankle. Some of those guys had big meth energy going and wouldn't be stopped by a little pain. He didn't show, though, and the bus took off through the suburb city, through the industrial wasteland of oil refineries and manufacturing yards, and into the downtown core.

I got off outside the library. For a minute, I thought about saying fuck it and walking the blocks north, back up towards the neighbourhood. It would be so much easier to just fall back into old routines and not continue on with being a bison cowboy. Get back in a rut of trying to scrape by but having a good time doing it. I could find an old friend to crash with for a bit. We could get some Luckys. Tell made-up tales from our younger days about glorious shit we almost did. I'd love to think we had hockey stories or good-time stories, but ours revolved more around the times we almost got rich and the times we almost got arrested. They tended to go hand in hand. But I was getting too old for that. There was never leniency for kids from our neighbourhood. And stealing cars and bikes and clothes from the mall and catalytic convertors didn't land the same when you were in your twenties, especially since I didn't have a habit to support. I got it if you were in that place, but I was probably more destined for grunt labour, four-month construction gigs on all the new downtown skyscrapers. And I wasn't going to risk another prison stint for some petty-ass change. Not that I had any petty-ass change to my name.

Northside dreaming as I walked into the library.

I got on one of the computers and booted up local news headlines from the past few days. *Bison in the River Valley . . . The Dawson Park Herd . . . Jogger Runs into Bison on Early Morning Run . . .* I started back from the first day we had dropped the bison off and moved forward to see the general progression. The first articles were all pretty similar, questioning how the bison had got there, where they came from, if they were harmful, giving warnings to avoid them. But the second batch was different, talking about how the city planned to remove the bison, and their statements to the public to avoid the area altogether. In the pictures in the articles, you could see tons of people standing in the park watching and taking photos of the bison with the downtown skyline as their backdrop. I tried and failed to spot Grey, but I knew she wouldn't be in the crowds anyways. Then the third round of articles mentioned protestors moving in so that the city would leave the bison where they are and got into the weeds of their demands. They called on the city to view it all as a form of reconciliation, thinking in particular about Land Back and a return to Indigenous governance systems and economies, and then ended with calls to create a ceremonial space for Indigenous peoples in the River Valley. We have churches, we have mosques, we have synagogues, we have temples—the statements went—but we have no place for Indigenous peoples to practise ceremony.

I had read enough. I figured that I had better head down there and see if Grey was kicking around. Northside dreaming could wait.

There were a lot of people in Dawson Park. The streets of the bordering River Valley neighbourhood and the parking lot were lined with cars. People stood around in big groups. I walked through them to get closer to where the bison were. Everyone had a nervous excitement about them, that buzzing, pulsing energy. This was turning out differently than I'd expected. I had assumed there would be a military presence, an 1885-style Canadian army moving in to squash the bison rebellion, enacting those old starvation policies and shooting them all on sight. Conversations with Grey and her way of thinking had definitely been wearing off on me.

I managed to push my way through the crowds to the edge of the park field, and climbed up the riverbank so I could get a good lookout over the area. Grey might be somewhere around here, and I hoped that I could spot her if I had some elevation. It was apparent from up there that the crowd was mainly white middle-class people. But in the back, a group of young native guys were standing around. I tried to see if I could recognize any of them, but it was too far, and they hid their eyes behind dark sunglasses. From my high-up vantage point, I could see the North Saskatchewan River running low and clear, its shallow surface reflecting the leaves' yellows and browns and the downtown buildings that towered above. Some of the bison waded in the water, trudging through what had been an old garbage dump turned into a park, where you could still see the remnants of old toilets and rusted-out car frames in the bank of the river. The rest were up on the park grass, against the riverbank's tree line. I tried to count to see if they were all there, but kept losing myself when they shifted positions. A line of police and peace officers were preventing the crowd from moving any closer to the buffalo herd.

Then the crowd changed. New people showed up. They were young, probably university-age, and carried banners, signs, and megaphones to announce their arrival.

"HEY, HEY, LET THE BISON STAY," the lady leading the procession called out. The people following behind her echoed her words back. "HEY, HEY, LET THE BISON STAY." The crowd that was already there parted to allow these new arrivals to walk through to the front. I scanned for Grey again. Nothing. I started reading some of the signs. BUFFALO FOR MAYOR. BISON STRONG. LAND BACK. The group began another chant.

"HEY, HO, BUFFALO, TELL THESE COPS THEY HAVE TO GO."

One of the cops was trying to tell the protestors not to use the megaphone around the bison. If you looked at the bison, though, it was apparent that they didn't care what was going on around them. They just wanted to munch grass and lounge around. I had to remind myself that these were national park bison. They were used to tourists, to people and noises. If we'd brought some bison from up north where they still ran wild, or one of the farms where they weren't as used to getting gawked at, they might not be as chill. But then again, who knew. Well, Grey probably would. She had that big bison energy down. Myself, I didn't know shit. Never had. Never would.

---

I felt like most of my life so far had been waiting. When I was a kid, I waited for someone to adopt me. When I turned twelve and realized that was never going to happen, I waited until I aged out of foster families. After that, group homes. Then I went out on my own, and I waited for something, anything, to happen to give me direction or purpose. Floating through life was fine, but I felt like there must be something missing. What motivated people to try to do something different than the generations before them? I couldn't grasp it. All I knew was survival mode. If there was food, eat it as quick as possible before someone took it from you. If there were drugs or booze, do them all before someone else could. If there was money, spend it now, or else it'd just be whittled away. Survive. Survive. Survive. No purpose, no direction, nothing—just waiting for that moment to happen.

When I went to jail, I waited to get out. Grey and I didn't communicate then, not once, but I didn't think much of it. I was used to people disappearing from my life. It happened all the time. Grey being gone didn't faze me. She was a friend and then she wasn't. No different than anyone else I had ever known. Still, it was hard to wake up excited to greet the day. One guy I knew in prison used to yell out "waniska bitches" every morning. He was a tough guy, connected, funny. He did alright.

When I got out, they sent me to a halfway house meant to transition ex-cons back into secure housing. Apparently, I had the potential to not reoffend. High praise, Judge. It must have been one of the Gladue rights guys who everyone back in remand hoped to be put before. Most judges were old hard-asses who still believed in prisons as the be-all and end-all of justice. But every once in a while, you got someone like I did, and when they made those decisions, the system put a few more resources into you than they would with the gang boys or the hardcore cons. Most people just got kicked right back out onto the concrete.

It turned out that a social worker who had been working with me and the other guys to try to find us jobs was one of Grey's friends. She was just out of university and still had that "I'm going to change the world through my practice" mindset. Goes away pretty fast after a few years of working in the system. I'd seen it happen all my life. A bright, shiny, new social worker assigned to you who's going to finally make everything right in your life. A year later they're burnt-out; a year after that on leave. Five years into it, they're haggard or they just quit. We had a good group of guys in the house, though. Most of us kept to ourselves during the day. At night we'd get together to smoke cigarettes and play poker. No booze or other substances allowed. None of us had any money to bet with, but we still enjoyed the act of it. We all played along nicely with the social worker and dutifully went along with her instructions. They were mainly about how to get a job and "reintegrate into normal society." Grey would have called it becoming a tool of the western capitalist overlords who had overrun our world. Had a better ring to it than "normal society."

The social worker brought us to different classes, all taught by people with zero emotion. Must have drawn the short end of the stick and been forced by whatever organization they volunteered or worked for to come in and try to smash lessons about resumé writing, workplace interactions, and time and money management into our thick skulls. The lessons were a way to pass the time, though, which is why we sat through them. But all of us knew that no one was going to be hiring a bunch of ex-con Métis and Cree guys. You could get a job at the bowling alley if you wanted, and that was about it. Maybe scaffolding or concrete if you were really lucky. So we each waited until our turn to leave the house came up. Forever waiting. Then, one morning, while I was sitting on the front stoop drinking coffee and staring down the never-ending avenue, Grey pulled up in her old Honda CR-V.

"Hello," I said. "Long time."

"I heard you were here," she said. She walked up to the bottom of the steps and stood there. I didn't get up. I didn't know if a hug was appropriate or not.

"You want a coffee?" I asked. I raised the cup I was sipping up to my lips and then towards her. Apparently, I hadn't quite figured out how to act normal yet.

"Why don't we go for a drive, and I'll buy you one?" she replied.

"That sounds good. Let me grab my jacket."

Grey bought me a coffee from the McDonald's drive-thru, extra-large black. She got herself a tea. Then we drove down to the river. We didn't say much. I wasn't sure how to talk to someone who wasn't a social worker, cop, or from the prison. It had been a long time since I'd had a conversation with anyone who wasn't involved in the system. Grey never felt the need to fill silences with unnecessary words. She just let stillness fill the SUV.

That was fine. I needed to get my thoughts together. We sat there sipping on our drinks and watching the water flow by us. In this city, there was no avoiding the river. Even if you actively tried to, like most of the settlers did for the longest time. The old high-rise apartment buildings they built in the sixties and seventies didn't put any balconies or windows facing the River Valley. They situated them so that you could ignore the landscape and instead look towards the brutalist structures rising from a concrete downtown. But even then the river made its presence known, moving through the city like a vein carrying the lifeblood of a people with it.

"You look good," I said. Grey shrugged. I tried to catch her eye, but she kept her gaze deadlocked straight. Fuck-off vibes.

"It's been a hard few years," she replied. "And I see prison made you fat."

"You know what they say. Fat or fit. I ended up on the fat side," I said, patting my new gut. I hoped that she would laugh at the joke, but nothing. Silence surrounded us again. This time it didn't feel fine. It felt like one of the fat prison guards sitting on my chest.

"So what have you been up to?" I asked.

"It's okay not to talk sometimes, eh?" Grey said.

We finished our drinks. I took the sticker off the McDonald's coffee cup and put it on the little cardboard counter board it came with. Seven stickers to get a free coffee. Grey passed me hers. Neither of us had said anything else yet. I was starting to wonder what the point of this was. Why had she come to see me if she didn't want to talk? Let the dead be dead.

"So, can you take me back to the house?" I asked.

"Ezzy?"

"What?"

"I miss you," she said. I looked over at her. She was still staring straight out the car window. Her long black hair in two braids coming down from the ball cap that had *iskwew* spelled out in syllabics on it. She wore subtle metallic purple and orange beaded earrings with abalone shell fragments. The shell fragments caught the sun and reflected it into my eye. I looked away and looked back, and I saw that she was crying. No sound, just tears coming down in overwhelming silence. I didn't know what to say.

"Why'd you come find me?" I asked her.

"I don't know. I heard that you were there. And then I remembered playing crib and how easy it all seemed then. I guess I thought that if I saw you, it might get easier."

"Nothing's easy," I said. Grey threw her hands up in the air.

"I don't know. This. All of this, I hate it." Fresh tears started rolling.

"I don't think anything will ever be easy for us, you know," I said. "We're not the kind of people that easy comes naturally to . . ."

"I legit thought that we were going to change the world," Grey said. "I was so fucking stupid. We can't change the world. We're living in the apocalypse, and there's nothing we can do about it."

"Apocalypse?" I asked.

"This is our version of hell. The apocalypse happened when they all arrived." She gestured towards the university campus and the high-rises on the other side of the river from where we were parked. "I don't know what to do anymore. We live on this beautiful land, but it's just fucking dying around us, from all of this."

"You talk to any Elders?" I asked.

"Still? Just Mary. Quite regularly. She just tells me to slow down, though. That things will come. But I just want to tell her that I can't. We can't slow down anymore. This is all moving too fast to fix."

"You don't need to fix everything."

"Fuck you. If I don't, then who will? You?" Grey said. "You'd just sit around all day playing cards and drinking coffee."

"It's part of my process . . . I'm an artist."

"You're bullshit," she said. Then she laughed.

---

Grey and I had started fading out before I got arrested. I was getting bored of the protests that occupied all of her time. Walking around the legislature holding signs was never going to change anything. At least that's the way I saw it. Grey and her friends would spend every waking hour organizing, making signs, planning events, posting on social media, reading, researching about issues. They were dedicated. I'd give them that. But it was also way too fucking boring for my ADHD-riddled brain. The people who joined in with Grey always followed a similar pattern. Later-year undergraduate students from one of the universities, usually women from the suburb communities around Edmonton, the kind where every house looks the exact same. They had some extra time to burn before they took off to their graduate school of choice. The ones who stuck around a while were the people who were native or Black, the ones who grew up on the northside like me or out in the rural reserves, without any real formal education and no prospects to move forward with. But even they would eventually move on, too. It was a high-turnover kind of trade. A lot of emotions and drama. Maybe they just got sick of the ongoing discussions behind the scenes that told of a different future that we would never be a part of.

Other activists started asking Grey to come and help organize protests in different cities. She had built up a bit of a social media following. Instagram videos of her speaking passionately were spreading, the crowds fired up while she called on different levels of government to give the land back, recognize and start doing something about the climate disaster, dissolve the Indian Act, fix the systemic racism that put thousands of Indigenous people in prison or the child welfare system. Whatever the topic, she could nail it. The Land Back one was what she really wanted to focus on, though she would tell me that it was all connected at the end of the day. Non-profits would fly her out to their conferences, professors would bring her in to university lecture halls, she was on the road more than she was back home. She never said it explicitly, but I could tell that she was excited that she was getting the same opportunities that her graduate student friends were, without the nightmare of going through the doldrums of one of the programs herself.

For me, my fascination with listening to the others talk about other cities and places and universities and a future with hope wore off. Just like before, when I had tried to be a part of a larger conversation and realized it was about a world that didn't

concern me. Even though they liked to talk about this idea of community, the community that really came through was their own, which was fine, but it wasn't mine. I disappeared back up into the avenues north of downtown. An area that most of the people who participated in the protests that Grey organized would never venture into. At least until gentrification hit.

With Grey being gone for weeks on end, I decided that my time following her around was coming to a close. If I could have gone on some of the trips with her, that might have been different. I sometimes wondered what it would be like to be the centre of attention, up there in front of everyone. What message would I bring? But then my hands would start shaking and a blackness would flow out of the pit of my chest, rising until it took over my head and blocked out all thought—even just imagining it. If it was actually happening? Bad news.

Grey and I would go months without seeing each other. She was doing an extended tour out east with a couple of international trips. It was the longest we had been apart since the day two years back at that Frank Oliver protest when I met her. She didn't message me, and I didn't message her. But she was never one to just reach out to make chitchat over text. I couldn't imagine it. *Hey what's up? Not much you? Not much. So who do you like?* I hadn't messaged anyone like that since the junior high MSN Messenger days. Back when my friends and I would scramble over to the library as fast as we could to log on after school. Throw up some emo band lyrics and hearts around a crush's name. Good times.

I had been crashing in my auntie's basement. A 1960s wood-panelled wannabe sex dungeon with mirrors in the weirdest places and blue-purple shag carpet. The carpet had stains that I didn't want to think about. My Auntie May had gotten clean in her early thirties. While doing that, she'd gone back to school and earned a nursing degree. And now, she worked with native kids who struggled with addiction. May put everything into the job. When she got home, usually late at night, she'd sit on the house's front steps for hours smoking cigarettes and drinking decaf double-doubles from Tim Hortons. Auntie always let me stay in her basement if I needed to.

One day I heard that there was a climate change protest happening down at the legislature. I assumed that Grey would be there, and I hadn't seen her since she'd taken off on that tour. I figured, what the shit? I might as well go down and see. Maybe catch up with what she'd been doing and join back in again.

Not many people showed up. The enthusiasm for climate change protests had worn off. Now it was just the die-hards, the people who attended every rally ever, and Grey's crew. The masses had stopped coming when they realized that reversing climate change and returning land to native people would severely challenge their white stranglehold on the world. I got that line from Grey.

It wasn't hard to spot her. She was on the legislature steps. A spot that she was very familiar with. She was speaking calmly into a microphone that someone had brought for her. Outlining the impacts coming in the next decade if we didn't start reversing the current trends. Grey never yelled. A lot of people speaking and running protests would be screaming their heads off, but she was always calm and collected. Something was different this time, though—something was off. I didn't think anyone else had noticed it, but after listening to her speak hundreds if not thousands of times over the past few years, I could tell instantly. I thought she might be sick or something. But then I realized it wasn't actually Grey at all that was bothering me. It was beside her. Someone new. A tall, lanky guy standing there. I could only ever remember Grey being a singular presence when she spoke. But you could tell this guy thought he deserved his own audience. He used his physical presence to overshadow Grey, even though he was behind her and a little off to the side. A seemingly supportive position. I didn't like it.

After the rally ended, I waited for the handful of people in the audience to disperse. Grey was always one of the last to leave. She made a point of having a conversation with everyone who wanted to chat. It was a habit that would drive me crazy back in the day when all I wanted was to get the hell out of there and go down to the river. I didn't need to sit around and listen to some nut job running their mouth about flat earth theories. Those were always the people who took up the most time. Never any normal chill-asses. In the conversation they were having with the rally participants now, I noticed that the tall, lanky dude talked more than Grey did. I walked up beside them.

"Grey, how's it going?"

"Ezzy, I saw you in the back there."

"Yeah . . . a lot less people than there used to be, eh?" Grey shrugged her shoulders.

"People will come and go, but the message remains the same," the tall guy butted in. He was wearing a black collared ribbon shirt and a beaded medallion the size of a hubcap. The medallion had a bear paw in the middle of it. The bear paw was made from red and white beads, and the outer edges were yellow and orange. Someone had put a lot of work into it.

"Tyler, this is Ezzy. Ezzy, Tyler."

"Ezzy? Like Esmeralda?" Tyler asked. He had a smirk on his face.

"Isidore," I replied. Then I immediately regretted sharing my actual name with him. Why had I done that?

"Come on, Grey, let's get going. I'm starving," Tyler said. "See you around, Ezzy."

He started walking towards the LRT stop. Grey turned to me, shrugged, and then followed after him. I watched as they faded across the legislature grounds and eventually disappeared down into the train tunnels. Whatever. I had to go to my new job anyways.

A couple guys I knew from my group-home days fancied themselves entrepreneurs and had a new racket going to start making some cash. They were stealing catalytic converters from vehicles around the city and selling them to scrapyards. Most of the places would pay two hundred bucks for one, and they never asked questions about where it came from. It was one of the easiest rackets that I had ever heard of. It didn't have the violence of drugs or the danger of straight-up stealing vehicles or robbing places. It was just simple. We'd pull up to a vehicle, one of us would hop out with the saw and slide underneath it. Two big cuts, one on the back, one on the front, rip it out and boom, gone. Once you got enough practice, you could cut one out in a minute tops. The best part was that the vehicle was still there, and people wouldn't even notice anything was up until it started making noise. They'd have to bring it to a mechanic. By that time, we'd have already unloaded the catalytic converter on a scrapyard, along with the dozen or so other ones we could get in a night. On an average night, we were clearing six hundred bucks each. That was more money than I'd ever had in my entire life.

The two guys that got me into it were former bike thieves. They'd spent years stealing bikes and selling them to wholesale people who specialized in stripping them down or reselling them. That didn't pay anything, though. Not compared to this. We were making drug-dealer cash without the risk.

After a few weeks, we had enough to rent a house with a garage not far from where Auntie May lived in the central core. After crashing with other people for years, it felt good to have my own spot. I even bought a bed. Do you know how bougie it feels to sleep in a bed instead of just on a mattress on the floor or someone's couch? I had it made. There was lots of cash for booze, too. I kept bottles stashed all around my room. Fancy stuff. Good glass bottles. Captain Morgan, Crown Royal, Jägermeister. Not the cheap plastic bottles of vodka and whiskey, Russian Prince crap, that I usually drank.

The three of us fell into a good rhythm. We'd wake up sometime in the afternoon. Watch full seasons of some stupid show or play video games on the big-screen TV we bought together. We'd order some food. Usually, it was half-priced pizza from Domino's. I had a university discount code that Grey had told me about. Though there was a good Vietnamese place not far away that I'd order us bowls of pho and vermicelli from.

Sometime around eleven at night, we'd head out. We'd grab one of the last trains down to the southside and get off at either the university or one of the suburb neighbourhoods, and start looking for a van or a truck. Something nondescript that wouldn't draw attention to itself. When we found a good one, we'd take it quickly, then find a new licence plate, just in case. I didn't think anyone would be waking up to call in a stolen vehicle until the morning. We'd drive around until we found a similar-looking van or truck, then swap the plates and leave the stolen vehicle's on the parked one. Then we were off. We'd cruise around neighbourhoods way out in different areas of the city, looking for the right vehicles. The best ones to hit up were trucks or SUVs. When I saw a big Dodge or Ford, my adrenaline would start kicking in. They were already high enough off the ground that you had room to work. That and the catalytic converters that came from them were worth a bit more. Most nights, we went until three or four in the morning. We'd hit up one of the twenty-four-hour fast-food spots for something to eat and go drop off what we had in the garage at the house we were renting. We'd ditch the vehicle at one of the mall parking lots and take early morning transit back home.

The rule was whoever woke up first had to bring the converters to the scrapyard. I drank more than the other two guys, so it was rare for me to be the first up. I would make up for it by paying for the food later on. My one friend had his granny's old minivan that she had given him, which was our main transport wagon. We had all the seats taken out of it so we could fill the back with our haul from the night before. The scrapyard dealer didn't care about what we brought in. He had his own cash racket going, and the more we brought him, the more he made. No questions asked.

It all went smoothly until it didn't. I probably was drinking too much. That's when it started to get sloppy. After a couple months, our one friend bailed. He said he was going to clean up and didn't want to be involved anymore. We figured there would just be that much more for the two of us who were left. Problem was the guy who took off was the voice of reason. He made sure we didn't drink beforehand and that we kept to the system we'd created. We got lazy without him. I'd start sipping as soon as I woke up and would be good and buzzed by the time we left to grab a vehicle. The friend who was still doing it with me would be into his cups too. We stopped switching licence plates. That seemed unnecessary. We also stopped parking the stolen vehicle over at a mall. Taking transit or an Uber back to the house seemed like a chore after a night of work, so we started ditching the vehicle just a couple blocks over from the house. Neither of us was too aware of what was going on around us. It was strictly steal the converters, sell them, and move on.

I never did figure out who called us in. It might have been one of the neighbours, who usually would have kept quiet but didn't like that stolen vehicles were getting parked on their street. That often happened with drug houses. Any extra attention on the block and the dealers would start getting mad. Maybe the cops figured out what we were doing. I wouldn't want to give them that much credit, though. Either way, one night, when we had a Dodge Caravan loaded up with converters, the cops were waiting outside the house when we got back.

They charged us with everything they could find. Theft over five, trespassing, vandalism, the classic resisting arrest they always throw in when dealing with native dudes. Most of it stuck, but we got reduced sentences because the crimes weren't violent in nature and because of our histories in the child welfare system, thanks to that bleeding heart judge. Still, two years. Long time to be locked up.

---

I waited out the rest of the bison protest, hoping that Grey would emerge from somewhere as the crowd thinned out. She gave direction to my wandering, but she wasn't around. The best I could come up with was that she had driven back up to Pembina Creek to get rid of the Dodge dually and the livestock trailer at her parents' place. The autumn darkness was settling in and the temperature dropped with the sun. I'd had enough, and decided that a bowl of smoking-hot hamburger soup or stew at Auntie May's sounded like the perfect thing to warm me up. There was a good chance that she'd have a fresh batch going. If not, she'd heat some up out of one of the many old ice-cream containers full of it in the freezer.

I started up the old wooden stairs out of the River Valley. When I was younger, kids would come and hide out here when they were escaping whatever they needed to escape. No one ever really talked about the details, just a bunch of kids happy to be with each other and away from whatever hell was happening back at the group homes, apartments, foster homes. Here or the cracked cement under the Hotel Macdonald were the good spots, mainly because the access points between the concrete slabs were a pretty tight squeeze, so adults never came in. But once you got inside, it was a perfectly sheltered space for a bunch of kids to hang out in. Not many of the ones I knew from then were still around.

When I got to the top of the River Valley, I walked along the sidewalk until I reached a viewpoint. You could see the dark forms of the bison down below. I watched them until they melted into the darkness.

"You staying sober?" May asked. We were sitting at her kitchen table. She had taken out an old 4L ice cream pail from the freezer that was full of hamburger soup, and heated up a few scoops in a pot.

"Trying. No hard stuff, you know."

"Beer isn't sober," she said as she ladled me out a giant bowl. May always took leftovers home from the events she attended for work. She'd use them to feed the youth she worked with, or family members like me who needed some help.

"Yah, yah, yah. I know," I said.

"You can't stay here if you're drinking. You know that."

"It's all good," I said. "I don't have cash for that kinda shit, anyways."

"I started doing more over at the friendship centre when I cleaned up," May said. "Lots of volunteer opportunities there. You could head out with one of the Elders to chop wood for the ceremonies. They always need wood." Every time I swung by her house, she always tried to get me involved with the friendship centre. She loved the community that hung out there, but I always felt judged when I went with her. Like they knew something about me that I didn't. Most people had done jail at some point—just part of our existence—so it couldn't be that. We'd walk in, May would start greeting the locals who hung around on the daily, I'd say hi to a few people that I knew, and then I'd stand by one of the noticeboards staring at outdated posters for round dances, powwows, healing centres, writing circles. No one ever bothered to take them down; they'd just stick another one up, right on top.

Even just minding my own business, I'd feel people staring at me. Why the obsession with what everyone else was doing? It felt like there was no way to do good in there. I'd never be able to live up to the weird unnamed expectations of a community member. I asked May about it once and she said they were just worried, checking to see if I was doing alright. But it definitely didn't feel like that.

"I'm good right now," I told her. "I'm just doing my own thing, you know." I lifted my soup bowl to my lips and gulped down what was left. "This is so fucking good."

"Hey, no swearing, chah."

Trying to fall asleep that night without the beer fog sucked. I tossed a lot and thought about Grey. I worried about her. In my experience, if someone disappeared, you didn't see them again. Even the women who would kick the shit out of anyone who side-eyed them never came back. That's how it went. I wanted to dream about her. The two of us sitting around a kitchen table playing crib and not thinking about anything except the hands of cards in front of us. Outside our trailer, a herd of bison, the bright orange calves tumbling around in their royal rumble flanked by bulls and cows. But you can't control your dreams. I fell asleep at some point, and it was just emptiness.

I wasn't sure how long I'd been asleep when I woke up. The basement at May's didn't have any windows to let you know what the sun was doing. It was always just dark down there. When I walked upstairs, Grey was sitting at the kitchen table drinking tea, while May was at the stove frying up eggs.

"What, you sleeping like a high school kid again?" May said as she laughed away at the eggs. "Think a grown boy would wake up before nine." I ignored her.

"Grey! Hey." I poured myself a cup of coffee from the old drip machine on the counter. "What's going on?" I wanted to hug her, but I didn't.

"I must have just missed you at the trailer," Grey said. "You hungover? Why'd you sleep so late?"

"It's dark down there. Relax, everyone," I said. May flipped two eggs onto a plate with a piece of white toast and brought it over to me. She inhaled deeply as she passed me the plate.

"Nah, no booze on this one," she said.

"What, you think I'm just gonna be crushing Luckys downstairs by myself?" I asked. May shrugged her shoulders. "It's *dark*! Geez."

May put some eggs on another plate and put it on the table for Grey.

"Thanks, Auntie," Grey said. "This looks delicious." May sat down with her own plate and cup of coffee.

"You got any ketchup?" I asked. They both shot me a look.

"Get your own ketchup," Grey said.

"You working today?" I asked Auntie May.

"Always." She gulped her coffee. "Have to go try and find a couple kids who didn't show up back at the group home last night."

"I hope they turn up," Grey said.

"Me too. I'm sure they will," May said. "These two usually just end up at the mall. If you're not back when I get home, well, it was great seeing you, Grey. And you: stay off the booze." She pointed at me with her lips, then put her leather jacket on and left, her plate barely touched.

"Where you been?" I asked. I didn't want to make her feel guilty or like she owed me an explanation. I've never understood people who feel like they need to control every situation; I've never felt like I've been able to control much of anything. I did want to be there with Grey, to help her, to be beside her, but I knew I had no right to try to fence her in. It's like with bison—sooner or later they're just going to get pissed off, stampede, and leave you with a noseful of prairie dust.

"Up at my parents'. Got everything back there and laid low for a couple days," Grey said.

"Did they ask any questions?"

"Nah, why would they? I used to always go and grab the trailer to help move friends or different things around when I was back in the city. They didn't think twice about it." I briefly thought about asking why she hadn't told me where she was going. But that wasn't any business of mine.

"You see the news?" I asked.

"I went and checked in on the bison the first day," Grey replied. "It's funny that there are so many people protesting to let the bison stay."

"I went down there yesterday to see if you were around. It was packed. Lots of people."

"Did the bison seem to care?"

"Not really, but I dunno. They seemed pretty content, I guess," I said. "No counter-protestors either. That was cool."

"They're coming. When people can't take their dogs off-leash through there anymore, or a bison charges someone, or they can't do a marathon or a yoga class, or some shit, people will start getting mad."

"True." I stood up and started doing the dishes.

"So . . ."

"Yeah?"

"I was thinking . . ."

"About what?" I replied.

"That we go back."

"Like, back out to your uncle's trailer? Sure."

Grey stood up and started drying the dishes and putting them away. "To another park in the city," she said. "We'd have to go soon, though. I still don't think they have any idea where the bison came from or how they got there. Eventually, someone is going to check the tags and figure it out. I'm actually amazed no one has yet."

It didn't seem as intimidating an idea as it had the first time. "Would we get the bison from Elk Island again?" I asked. Already

I was minimizing the difficulty of trying to get them into the trailer. That kind of fun where it's scary as all hell then, but afterwards it doesn't seem so bad.

"No," Grey said. "I have a better idea this time."

"Do we need to?" I asked.

"You don't have to do anything," Grey said. "But if we're going to create a sustained presence, we're going to need to keep it going. They'll get this first herd sorted out soon enough and it will fade. But if we get a second herd into the city . . . Who knows, maybe they'll even start making their way back in on their own."

Later, we drove an hour southeast of the city, following Grey's directions down a range road until we came across a bison farm. You could see a herd of a hundred or so buffalo eating the prairie grasses and lazing around the field through the full-on nine-foot-tall prison-style chain link fencing. Only difference being there was no barbed wire angled inwards at the top. No one in their right mind would climb in with the bison.

The longer I watched them, the more I realized just how stupid I'd been to start thinking that it wouldn't be so hard. That these animals weren't all that big or bad. I started to get nervous. What if one of those massive units decided it didn't like me? It could crush my chest with a little kick. Or stampede right over me, trampling my bones into prairie dust. Or headbutt me and send me flying all the way back to the city. I wondered if I had just been naive about the first time we'd gone. I'd had so much false confidence. That was probably why it had gone so well. I hadn't realized what could actually go wrong, I'd just gone along with it all because I trusted Grey. If she said I wasn't going to get hurt, I wouldn't get hurt.

But had she actually said that?

"The farmyard is a couple quarter sections away," Grey said.

"Sure." I pretended I knew what a quarter section was.

"And they're working the harvest right now, so no one's around."

"How long have you been watching this yard?" I asked.

"Day or two. Basically since I dropped the truck and trailer back off at my parents' farm."

Grey switched the radio station from Windspeaker to CBC to catch the hourly news update:

*"Today on CBC am, we're going to talk about the ongoing bison dilemma. Then we have a calligrapher coming on the program to talk about what they've been doing. That'll be followed by weather and traffic. Now, let's get into what's been on everyone's minds. It's been determined that the bison in the River Valley have come from the Elk Island National Park herd. City officials are saying to exercise caution when using the River Valley trails as there may be more bison on the loose. Representatives from Parks Canada are currently determining the best course of action to remove the bison from the River Valley. But some people want the bison to stay. CBC reporter Cory Pepper spoke with local activist and community leader Tyler Cardinal about why the bison matter and what this means for Indigenous peoples."*

Fucking guy. Grey turned the radio off. I could feel her withdrawing, folding in on herself.

"What now?" I asked.

Grey broke out of her trance-like state. I felt helpless beside her. The reality of a second run made my body tense up. That fight-or-flight shit they always liked to talk about in all those group therapy sessions over the years. The prissy-ass counsellor would give advice like it was just an easy choice to bring your mind back to normal and make a decision like you had an 80K-a-year job and a paid-for house. But when it came to my brain freezing the fuck up, it felt like I had no control over anything. I'd never had any control, so it wasn't a new feeling, but I wanted Grey to give me something, even if I wasn't sure what I wanted.

Physical pain had never scared me. And according to all the social workers and counsellors, my entire life had been mentally traumatizing. None of them ever had a problem telling me that. But no real right way of fixing it. White people love telling you what your problem is and then letting you wallow in that shit while they go about their daily business of making money.

"I think we're going to get the bison in the middle of the day," Grey said. "We'll just pretend that we're working for the farm or whatever and do it right in the open. No one will even question it."

She made it seem so simple. Like, yeah shit, of course it was obvious that this was what we were going to be doing. "Yeah, good call," I said. "And if we were going to do it at night, they would spot our headlights too, so we'd be busted fast." I was trying to add something to the plan. To be a part of it. To help out.

"You can turn vehicle lights off," Grey said.

We took off back to the trailer. For a moment I thought that maybe we shouldn't stop driving. We could keep going until we ran out of highway and then start something new there. People up and left all the time, whether by choice or force. We could get ahead of it, go live somewhere different. Wherever the hell that would be.

We turned onto the driveway that led back to the trailer. Something was off. The smell of a burning building came right in through the vents on the CR-V. An unmistakable smell. I was used to it from meth house explosions back in the city. A house doesn't burn like a campfire or a forest fire. There's too much plastic, and garbage, and other shit. There's nothing beautiful about it. That fucking smell penetrates everything.

The trailer had become a pile of black hell. Embers still burned with little puffs of smoke from where it had once stood. Charred wood beams stuck up towards the sky and the melted plastic from the siding curled and bubbled within the ashes. No one had attempted to put it out. It had just burned in on itself until there was nothing left.

We kicked around in the smouldering ashes. I grabbed a long stick from the forest and poked around. I wasn't sure what I was looking for. Grey and I didn't have possessions. Just a couple changes of clothes and the crib board. At one point, the trailer had housed Grey's uncle's family. He'd raised a bunch of kids out here by himself after his wife passed away in a car crash. All those dreams and hopes for the future, all those tears, drinks, laughs, fights, and loves long gone with them as they got older and moved on. I'd never met them. Grey never spoke of them. But sometimes I liked to think of what the family might have been like. In my mind they used to try to fish in the slough even if they knew nothing was in there. Maybe in the early mornings they would drink their coffee and a moose would wander by. Late at night they'd sit around a fire under the stars and tell good ghost stories and old histories of the family. I saw myself right in there with them.

Running through the woods in late-night kick-the-can games, booting that beer can as far into the sky as I could when I got to it. Surrounded by my friends and family. Everyone laughing.

But Grey's uncle had left a few years ago, and you couldn't sell a place like that. No one would buy it. Grey wasn't even sure if he had properly owned it to begin with, or if he'd just been squatting on the land. "Land Back" is how Grey would have referred to it in her protest years. Her uncle had just been reclaiming what should have rightfully been his. Something that had probably seemed like such a permanent fixture to all of Grey's cousins. And now, poof, gone. Just like that.

"I didn't turn on any burners when I came by," Grey said. "Maybe just electrical? I don't know. These things happen." She seemed pretty nonchalant about the whole thing. I didn't know why I'd been expecting an outpouring of grief, but she just maintained her normal collected self. It was just another problem to analyze and think through. Probably one that didn't really register that high on her list of priorities.

"Nah, a trailer doesn't just light up if no one's there," I said. "I wonder why none of the neighbours called it in."

"What neighbours? And even if there was anyone around, they probably would have just thought someone was clearing brush," Grey replied. "Would you have called something in?"

"No."

"Exactly."

"I'd probably go check it out, though," I said. "When I was a kid, and a house went up, every person in the neighbourhood would be all up in it. It would turn into a block party real fast."

"That's morbid, people love misery."

"Do you think someone torched this place?" I asked.

"Not sure. Could have just been kids fucking around. I should probably call my uncle and let him know."

We kept poking around, but there was nothing to salvage. The trailer had become another ruin on the side of a backroad swamp. It started getting dark. The shadows from the tall trees were making the area feel small and crowded. Ominous even.

"What should we do now?" I asked.

"Probably go to your auntie's. You think she'd mind?"

"Not at all. Let's go. I want to get out of here. This place is giving me the fucking creeps."

"Yeah. I don't want to be here if someone comes by. Maybe I'll just let the cops or whatever call my uncle. Then I won't have to deal with this shit."

"Sounds good to me."

"Hey, wait. Look at this," Grey said. She had been walking back towards the vehicle. "You can see where someone was limping around in the mud here. It looks like they were dragging their leg."

"Fucking kids," I replied.

"I just don't get why they would do it?"

"Wonder if it was your uncle. Thinking about insurance or something? And he just waited until you were gone," I said.

"You think my uncle had insurance? Or ever thought about this place through the whiskey? Give your head a shake."

We got in the CR-V and took off down the driveway, out to the secondary highway. The road only led to the trailer. There were no other houses back in that swamp. Grey had told me once that it was probably an old oil field survey road. That was why the county had quit maintaining it. They didn't actually own it. But then, did they really own anything?

One night, a while back now, when Grey and I were sitting around at the trailer, she'd told me stories of the Papaschase people and the places they'd fled to after the reserve was stolen from them. She told me that, after the North-West Mounted Police torched their houses and agricultural equipment, killed all the animals, and prevented the Papaschase from going back onto their land, they'd had to go somewhere. Most of them fled up to Slave Lake or the bush north of St. Paul. Some went down to Maskwacis, and others went out to Enoch. But there were a few families who stayed around Edmonton, and a few families who came out to this area east of the city, the muskeg of Beaver Hills, to eke out an existence not far from the lands they had known.

The families had lived in old wooden shacks. They were probably similar to the trailer that Grey and I had been staying in. You couldn't farm in the muskeg, so they got by hunting, foraging, and doing seasonal work. It wasn't much different to what most people were doing back on the reserves to survive. I couldn't imagine growing up in the muskeg. It seemed so outside the city world that I knew. When I'd first started staying with Grey out at the trailer, the lack of city noise had really got to me. It wasn't quiet or anything like that. It was just a different type of noise. I was used to the never-ending sirens, people laughing and fighting as they went by, cars ripping up and down the roads, the muffled loudspeakers from the football stadium broadcasting the games, the songs from the outdoor concerts I never got to attend. That was the background soundtrack to my life. I didn't want to fuck with the screeching of bush bunnies when coyotes ran them down, or the nightly howls. I remember asking Grey about that. Why did the coyotes always start howling right at dawn and dusk? She told me that they were doing a roll call, basically. They just wanted to see who was around, where they were, and if everyone was up and ready to go out hunting. One night I was drinking a Lucky on the deck, and I thought I heard a wolf howl. But Grey told me that when a wolf howled, there would be no mistaking it. In the summer months, it was the never-ending hum of bugs coming off the slough. Just this incessant din: buzz, buzz, buzz. It got in your ears no matter what you did. Hard to get it out. I hate bugs. Give me concrete and sirens any day.

We pulled up outside Auntie May's house. She was sitting on the porch having a cigarette and drinking tea. Grey was about to get out of the car.

"Wait," I said.

"What?" Grey asked.

"Let's not tell auntie. She'll get fired up."

"No shit," Grey said.

"Just tell her that you have some work to do in the city," I said. "You sure we're going to go get those buffalo tomorrow?"

"What else do we have to do?" Grey sighed and leaned back in her seat, and I thought for a minute her toughness was going to melt back into the cushions. "You know, I'm going to miss that place."

"What about it? The mould and the mice?"

"It kind of felt like home."

"You two hungry?" May yelled from the porch. She stubbed out her cigarette and started heading inside, not bothering to wait for us to respond. "I'll heat you up some moose stew."

"You sure you don't want me to come with you?" I had offered before to help get the big Dodge dually and the livestock trailer, but Grey didn't want me to come up to Pembina Creek with her. She had never invited me up in all the time we'd been hanging out, and I thought a lot about why that was.

"Nope," Grey said. "My parents will start thinking that they're going to be getting grandbabies if you come with me. They'll just get in our way."

"What babies?" I asked.

"No babies."

I followed her inside and we all sat down in the living room on the big pink chairs that took up way too much space in Auntie May's tiny house.

"Did someone say babies?" Auntie May called from the kitchen. "I would love some big chub babies around." She came crashing into the living room at full speed and sat as physically close as a person could get to Grey on the couch.

Grey gave me a look.

"See what happens when you mention babies around these ones?" Grey pointed her lips at Auntie May.

"But they would be soooo cute," Auntie May said. "Did you see the video on Facebook of that little chubster jigging up at the Kikino rodeo?"

"No, I don't have Facebook," Grey replied.

"Neither does this one." Auntie May pointed at me.

"That shit's for old ladies," I said.

"Watch your mouth. You're not going to be able to talk like that when the baby comes. Here, Grey, come look. I'll show you that video." Auntie May pulled out her phone. I went over to check it out too. A little brown kid in black jeans with a tucked-in ribbon shirt wearing a sash was bouncing around to the fiddle. His cheeks seemed to take up the entire screen. Auntie May started squealing while she watched it.

"Oh, he's just so cute," she kept muttering. Grey just stared at the screen, her face blank.

When the video ended, Auntie May went into her bedroom to make some calls to check in on the youth she was working with. Grey pulled out her phone and started doom-scrolling through the news.

"So apparently the protestors aren't letting any trucks into Dawson Park," she said. I looked up from the beadwork book that I had been pretending to read. "Last night the city tried to send in a couple livestock trucks and animal control people to round up the bison. But the protestors met them there and blocked the entrance to the park."

"Wild."

"It's going to take all the attention away from the other parks and potential areas."

"Won't they just clear it out?"

"Eventually, but they can't do it right away. All the politicians will have to figure out how to spin it so that they can look like they support the protestors as well as the bison. You know that classic systems shit where they pretend they're going to change something but they really won't. Law and order in the west above all else."

"Have they made any demands for action?" I remembered that from when I'd hung around with Grey years ago. She'd always said that a protest didn't really matter if there weren't concrete demands for action that came with it.

"Not yet. But they will. Tyler's a lot of things, but he's not dumb," Grey said.

"You think he's involved?"

"You heard him on the radio. Of course he's involved. Anything that has even the slightest chance of attracting attention, he'll suck the blood out of it like a tick."

"Okay there, bush girl. A tick, really?"

"Guy's a fucking parasite."

Grey was going to head to Pembina Creek that afternoon to borrow the truck and trailer. She'd spend the night with her parents, then meet me in the morning. My job was to go borrow another truck, probably real early, and drive out to meet her. I didn't want to go get one, drive it back to May's, and then go back to sleep for a few hours. I figured I could just get it all done in one shot.

Grey left, and I went to bed right after supper. I tossed and turned. Another night struggling to fall asleep sober. When I was alone at night in my own head without a fog, my brain would fall back into these patterns of playing out memories of my grandfather's visits from my childhood. I didn't know how accurate they were, but as I stared at the dark ceiling, I thought I could picture his face, the wrinkles and crow's feet from too many laughs and the spots from too many drinks staring back at me. He had been my one and only connection to family when I was a kid. This was before Auntie May got clean. My parents were long gone. And the only thing that I'd wanted in the world was to live with my grandfather. I couldn't understand why this man, who would come visit me, and take me to the parks, playgrounds, hockey rinks, and round dances, couldn't take me back home. But it was a long time since he'd passed on, and an even longer time since I'd realized that was never going to happen.

I didn't sleep. I had hoped for a few hours' rest, but it never came. I brought an old alarm clock from upstairs down with me so I'd know when it was late enough to leave, and when it hit three in the morning, I got up and put on my jeans, a black hoodie, and a dark blue toque. I flipped the hood up over the toque and quietly left the house.

The city blocks carried dark shadows with pockets of streetlight. I started walking north. Once I crossed the Yellowhead and got to the official northside, I could steal something. I'd rather go out to a suburb to grab a truck, but the buses out there didn't start running for another couple of hours, and there was no way I could ask Auntie May for a ride. I passed a McDonald's just on the other side of the freeway. Three people were sitting on the picnic tables out front drinking cheap wine. An old man with long braids and a wispy moustache winked at me as I walked by them.

I went another couple blocks and found an old Jeep Cherokee. Another easy vehicle to snatch. Coat hanger through the window, connect the wires, the fuel tank reading three-quarters full, see ya. I drove out to the main street and headed towards the freeway.

When I passed the McDonald's again, I looked over and the people were gone. In their place, three magpies pecked at the crumbs of French fries and the burger dust.

We had agreed to meet at an old, abandoned county campground not far from the bison farm. Grey wasn't there yet when I pulled up. I stepped out of the vehicle to go take a leak. The cracked pavement was covered in discarded cigarette butts, condoms, and Slurpee cups. I lined up at the bushes on the edge and let loose. The place gave me the creeps. It was the kind of place where people ditched bodies when they drove them out of the city. I got back in the vehicle, reclined the seat, and took a nap.

When I woke up, Grey was rubbing slough mud all over the truck and livestock trailer's licence plate. I rolled the window down and was about to crack a joke, but the look on her face told me she wasn't in the mood. She didn't say a word, just nodded at me and then got back behind the wheel and took off. I started the Jeep up and followed behind her as she drove the exact speed limit on the single-lane highway. When we turned onto the range road, the livestock trailer started kicking up gravel. The Jeep Cherokee's windshield took a couple chips and I slowed down, giving Grey more space and keeping the glass from getting completely chewed. If my vehicle got stolen and then found again, I would hope it wasn't fucking trashed. But then again, I'd never owned a vehicle.

We passed the farmyard. No vehicles seen. Grey mentioned the kids were off at school, and the wife worked in Camrose. She figured with the way the farmer and his hired hands were working the crop rotation, they should be almost three kilometres away in another field, in the combines until late that night—maybe even all night if the harvest was slow. Not coming home anytime soon, either way. Well, at least until three in the afternoon; that gave us almost seven hours to get in and out of there. We pulled into the pasture, and I got out of the Jeep and stood in view of the passenger-side mirror. I pretended to guide Grey with hand signals as she perfectly backed the trailer up to the corral. Anything to help. In the distance, the herd showed no interest in what we were doing. They kept right on munching away on the prairie grasses.

"Okay, I'm going to head out in the Jeep and move them towards this pen," Grey said. "When they get inside, I want you to run behind and close the gate. It needs to be done fast, or else they'll panic and start trying to back right out."

"No problem." I looked into the distance. These bison didn't seem that big compared to the ones from the other day.

Grey got in the Jeep, and I watched as she bounced across the pasture in an arcing semicircle towards the herd. Every little noise would take my attention back towards the gravel road. I imagined the dust clouds parting ways to reveal hordes of angry farmers in their pickup trucks driving towards us, carrying pitchforks and burning torches as they came down the road, honky-tonk music blaring, and then Grey driving off, leaving me to fend for myself. I'd been in those situations before.

I lost sight of the Jeep for a minute as Grey went over a slope and down towards a slough. Then the Jeep popped up again behind the bison herd. There were twenty-five or so in the main group. Grey started driving towards them. They didn't budge. I heard the horn beep in the distance, and a couple of the cows and their calves started trotting towards the corral. Two big bulls stood their ground. The younger bulls moved with the cows and calves. Grey drove around the older bulls and focused on the moving buffalo. I double-checked to make sure I knew where the gate latches were and how they would swing. The herd was moving closer. One of the bigger bulls started following the Jeep. There was no more thinking about angry farmers. This was getting real very fast.

The buffalo picked up steam trying to get away from the Jeep. I could feel the ground trembling underneath me. They were getting close enough that I could see their deep black eyes staring through me at a supposed freedom far away from this harassing thing that had suddenly dropped into their world. They got closer and closer. Then the herd veered towards the right of the corral. Grey accelerated up their flank and pushed them back in the proper direction. I could see their spittle and snot flying everywhere. I climbed on top of the corral fence. When they went inside, I'd swing out on the gate and close the latches as fast as I could, as long as they didn't trample right over the fencing and take me out with it. Visions of Mufasa from *The Lion King* being crushed by a herd of wildebeest flew through my mind. Then they were here.

Half the herd broke off around the left side of the corral. The other half went right in through the door. When they were in, I swung out on the gate. It clanked closed, and I slammed the latches across and down to lock them in. The bison inside the corral ran around it in circles a couple times, and then they stopped. They formed a ring with the calves in the middle protected by the cows and then the few young bulls who had come with them. Twelve total had made it inside the corral. The other half of the herd kept right on going. Their prairie pasture dust kicked up all around us. I could feel the heat coming off the bison inside the corral as they stared at me. They didn't want to be there any more than I wanted to be on the other side looking in.

Grey parked the Jeep. She hopped out and ran up to the cab of the truck, grabbed a large blue tarp and brought it out.

"Here, take this." She passed me the folded-up tarp, then jumped up and undid the next series of gates that would lead into the open livestock trailer. "Okay, we're going to each take an end, then walk through the pen towards the buffalo, pushing them into the chute."

"We're going into the pen? No fucking way."

"You got a better idea?"

"We didn't have to do this last time," I said, but Grey jumped up onto the corral fence, then used her arms to push herself up and swung her leg over with a practised motion that could only have come from a childhood spent on a farm. I followed with way less grace and tumbled over into the corral.

Grey grabbed one end of the tarp and walked calmly to the other side. We were about fifteen feet apart. I held the top edge up as high as I could, and Grey did the same with the other end. We walked slowly towards the herd. The bison stomped and pawed backwards, then bluff-charged towards us. We got closer to them. I could smell that dank musk all around us. A couple of the cows turned and ran into the chute that led into the trailer. Their calves followed them. Finally, the bulls turned around and ran in. Grey dropped her side of the tarp. She ran as fast as she could towards the last corral gate, leapt up, and slammed it shut. The bison were inside. They rustled around and brayed and snorted. I started shaking. I couldn't move my legs. My teeth were chattering. Grey turned to me with a big grin on her face.

"See?" she said. "Nothing to it." I leaned over and puked everywhere.

Grey started laughing. I felt drunk, even though I hadn't drank in days. The exhaustion from not sleeping combined with the adrenaline had done me in. I stumbled towards the gate of the corral. All I wanted to do was get back into the Jeep and close my eyes.

"Ezzy, *wait*!" Grey called out from the other side of the corral. Her voice was drowned out in my spinning head. I climbed onto the fencing and swung my leg over it so that I was straddling the fence. "*Ezzy!*" Grey screamed again. Then it hit me, and it all went black.

I woke up with Grey's hands under my armpits, trying to lift me into the cab of the truck. My head was on fire, screaming. I tried to stand up and my right leg buckled under me. More pain screeched through my body. I looked down. My lower right leg was mangled. I could see fragments of bone popping through the skin and my foot looked absolutely crushed. I wanted to vomit.

"We need to get out of here *now*," Grey said. Her voice shook. I could hear bison stomping and snorting in the trailer behind us. I stood up on my left leg, with one hand on Grey's shoulder, and grabbed the handle above the open door. I pulled and Grey pushed me into the cab. I leaned forward and puked on the ground. I wanted to go to sleep. Grey slapped me across the face.

"You can't sleep now! *Stay awake*," she said. "You smacked your head real good when you fell off the fencing." I tried to lean back to ease the pain. Nothing worked. Grey ran around to the driver's side. She jumped in the cab and put the truck into gear. We started rolling forward. Each bump of the prairie pasture sent shivers of pain hammering through my body. All I wanted to do was go to sleep. I closed my eyes. Grey punched me in the shoulder. "*Ezzy no*," she said. She rolled down my window and cranked up the radio. We turned off the range road and back onto the secondary highway. It was less bumpy, and as we picked up speed, the cold fall wind whipping by felt good on my face.

"What about the Jeep?" I asked.

"Fuck the Jeep," Grey said. "We need to get you to a hospital."

"What about the bison?" I asked. My head was clearing up.

"Oh shit—I forgot to close the pasture gate." Grey slammed the steering wheel. "Fuck."

There was a pack of Canadian Classic cigarettes sitting on the dash. I reached forward and took one out and lit it with the lighter that was resting inside the pack.

"What are you doing? You don't smoke," Grey asked.

"I need something," I said. The smoke tasted good. Like the smokes I used to steal from foster parents or group home workers when I was a kid. I could feel my blood rising with the nicotine. The pain in my leg seemed to subside a bit. But then we'd hit a bump, and I'd get another surge through my body. I winced. If I looked down, I'd puke everywhere. Grey gave me a sidelong glance, not really taking her eyes off the road. She didn't have any emotion on her face.

"What are we going to do?" I asked.

"I don't know. I might need to just drop you off somewhere." Grey passed me her phone. "Can you google where the nearest hospital is?"

"Won't people ask questions?"

"Just say you got your leg crushed by a truck or something. It's not like you got shot or stabbed. People get crushed all the time."

"Yeah, but not when they're stealing bison," I replied. Things were starting to come together a bit. My head didn't feel quite as foggy.

"They don't need to know that."

"It says here that the Sherwood Park Hospital is probably our best bet. It's right off the Yellowhead Highway, too," I said.

"Okay, perfect. I don't think I could drive this rig through downtown Edmonton. People might get suspicious if they saw a trailer full of bison going through the city right now."

I lit another cigarette.

"What happened?" I asked.

"One of those big bulls that was following us charged when it saw you hopping over the fence. You're lucky it only got your leg and that you fell back into the corral and not out into the pasture."

"Fuck me," I said.

"How the hell didn't you see it?" Grey's eyes lit up for a moment before going back to her usual reserved self.

"I don't know."

"Fucking city boy," she said. Then she started laughing. "You smacked your head so good when you fell. I thought you were done."

"I feel like I'm done."

"You'll be fine."

The hospital was in the far reaches of an outlet mall in Sherwood Park, just off the main highway. It shared a massive concrete parking lot with the mall and a Walmart. Grey parked the truck at the far end of the lot, as close to the road as possible so she could easily drive off without having to back up the truck and trailer. I watched as she sprinted to the hospital, grabbed a wheelchair that had been left outside the main emergency room doors, and ran it back.

"Let's get you into this, and then I'm gonna get the hell out of here," she said. She came around to the passenger side and helped lower me into the chair. "You can wheel yourself in?" she asked, more of a statement than a question.

"I'm good."

"I'll come get you later," she said. "Try to get them to keep you here for that long, at least."

I faux-saluted her and started wheeling myself towards the emergency room doors. She took off as fast as a truck and trailer filled with bison could go, not bothering to stick around to see if I made it inside or not.

# TWO

# GREY

I figured the yard at my uncle's was large enough to turn the truck and trailer around in, a good spot to lay low until after the sun went down. It got dark early this time of year, but I'd have to wait until at least midnight. Even if Ezzy was done in, I still had the trailer and a job to do. As I drove down the road, I wondered if anyone had contacted my uncle about the fire yet, but when I got there, it still looked like Ezzy and I had been the last ones in the yard. People didn't just come down this road. You needed a reason to be out here.

I parked the truck and stepped out of the cab. The remnants of the fire long burnt out. I walked through the ash and kicked it around. I wasn't sure what I was looking for, but I felt like there was something left. This was the last spot that had made me feel close to something real. It had brought me back into connection with something that had been missing, helped me process and think about all the shit from the past few years. Shit I would probably never deal with properly. I thought about Ezzy and how stupid he was sometimes. He would be fine. But his right leg was fucked. When that bull smashed into him, the crunch of the hard skull pounding flesh and bone up against the metal fence had almost sent me crashing down too. And I didn't think I'd ever fainted in my entire life. He would be fine, I was sure of that. He was tough, and it was just a leg wound. I was more worried about his skull after he fell. That had been the second thud. Lucky that corral dirt wasn't concrete. The idiot could have just paid attention. I still wasn't sure how he hadn't noticed a two-ton snorting, stomping, buffing bull outside the corral's fence. But he hadn't, and now I had to unload these units by myself.

I didn't have much to do except watch the sun until it dropped below the treeline. I sat in the cab and pulled my phone out and began scrolling through news feeds. I had deleted my social media apps years before. I used to have access to Instagram through one of the Land Back organizations' logins, but after I broke it off with my ex, he made sure that they changed all the passwords. I could probably guess what he had changed them to—something like *Imafuckingsnake69*.

The articles talked about the blockades that Tyler's group had set up to prevent the city and national park from removing the bison. He always made sure that he was front and centre in any media pictures. The guy had an uncanny sense for being able to track and hunt down any opportunity to get attention. If there was an interview, he made sure that he was at the microphone. If there were photo ops, he was always positioned with a perfect grimace that told the world just how angry he was. But the thing was, he wasn't angry at all. He was just an opportunist who'd figured out that protests and activism were cool things to be involved with. I put my phone down. Typical fake shit. Old story. Behind me, one of the buffalo let out a big, belchy fart. More real than anything on social media trying to sell me a dream.

I wanted to throw my phone into the slough, but I just went back to kicking through the trailer's remains. I didn't find anything. That thing I was looking for didn't exist. The trailer had been sparse to begin with, Ezzy didn't have anything to his name, and I kept minimal possessions. I had a bit of a sentimental attachment to that crib board. We had always tracked who skunked who on the back of it. That was really what I wanted. Something to hold on to from our time out here. The hours of small talk and small math and avoiding a future. But it was just a toy, and a toy could be replaced.

If I could have texted Ezzy, I would have. But he hadn't had a real cell phone in years. He was thousands of dollars in debt to every cell phone company—both on his own and from letting friends of his use his information to sign up for cable or internet or phone plans when they couldn't get their credit score through. They wouldn't connect him unless he paid those off. Every once in a while, he'd get a burner with a pay-as-you-go plan, but those only lasted so long before he ran out of minutes or texts. He never called anyone anyways, except his parole officer when he was under probation.

Inside the trailer, the bison were resting. I peeked through the vents and thought about wrapping myself up in a bison rug, laying down by a fire somewhere under a winter sky and just sleeping. The bison looked warm. But they always did. Even in the depths of a blizzard, even when the snow got too deep for cows to survive, a bison would just keep on chomping away.

A comfortable natural silence settled around the trailer. I appreciated the different level of quiet in this clearing. Natural settings hit different. I needed to cut out the extra noise that a city created. It never did me any good, and it sure as shit wasn't about to start to now.

The rumble of an engine broke through the trees. It got louder and the panic came. I could feel myself going snake-mind and thinking about tearing off through the bush. For a brief second, I thought it might be Ezzy, but it was only a couple hours ago that I'd dropped him off. He would never hitch a ride back out here from the hospital, and wasn't in any shape to steal a vehicle. No way he wasn't all drugged up in some back room. I looked at the truck and the trailer. No use attempting to hide those plus a dozen bison. I looked in on the bison again. They didn't give a shit about the engine rumble. The rumble wasn't their problem. If it was the cops or fire department, how would I explain my way out of this? I didn't have anything that said I lived at the trailer, and even if I did, no cop or firefighter would take the word of a Métis lady out in the bush by herself. Throw in the trailer full of stolen bison, and I wasn't getting out of there without handcuffs on.

I climbed up into the cab of the truck and looked behind me into the back seat. My dad sometimes left his rifle there underneath a blanket in case he came across a moose when driving around. I moved the blanket. Nothing. He must have taken it out when I borrowed the truck. I looked through the truck windshield back down the road, expecting a cop car to come ripping into the yard at any moment. Then an old blue single-cab pickup truck emerged from where the road bent around the slough.

*Who the fuck is this?* Must be lost or something. It was getting close to hunting season; maybe it was someone tracking a deer. But in the months we'd stayed in the trailer, I had never seen or heard another vehicle come down this road. There was no reason to drive out this far.

As the truck approached, I saw the outline of a fat man behind the steering wheel. He parked right in front of the semi, blocking the road. We locked eyes. He looked confused, then pulled his Edmonton Oilers hat down over his eyes and stepped out of the truck. I was about to roll down the window. Then I saw the gun.

The hunting rifle pointed at me through the windshield. The man had an unlit cigarette tucked into the corner of his lip, the filter hidden by a patchy beard that exposed the pockmarks and spots staining his face. He walked with a limp around to the driver's side of the truck, keeping the rifle pointed at me the entire time. I froze. I wanted to put the truck into gear and smash through his pickup. He tapped the driver's-side window glass with the barrel of the rifle.

"Get out of the fucking truck," he yelled. I pretended I couldn't hear him. He raised the rifle and fired straight up into the air. The blast hammered through me. My hands began shaking uncontrollably. The shaking woke me up from my fear-freeze. He cycled out the cartridge, and another one slid into place. He tapped the window with the barrel again.

"Next one's coming your way if you don't get out of the fucking truck right now." His tobacco-blackened spit splattered on the glass. I raised my hands in the air. I strained against the fear of movement and reached for the door handle. He smashed the barrel into the glass again. "*Move*," he shouted. I opened the door and stepped out of the cab.

He pressed the rifle against my stomach. I could feel the cold death of the barrel through my hoodie. Everything in my body convulsed and then tensed up, bad, bad, bad, bad.

"Where the hell is he?" the guy asked. He spat on my face. The smell of his beer and chemical breath penetrated my nose. Then he turned the rifle around and drove the butt of it into my stomach, hard. Knocked the wind out of me. I gasped and dropped to my knees.

"Who?" I said, as I sucked for air.

"The guy who lives here. I owe him something," he said. He spat on the top of my head. I struggled back to my feet. He jammed the barrel underneath my rib cage.

"What are you talking about? What do you want?" Tears started welling up in my eyes. I tried to choke them back. I didn't want to encourage him.

"*Ahhh fuck, where is he?*" The man was sweating profusely. It poured down his face. His eyes twitched back and forth. "If you don't fucking tell me right now, I'm going to shoot you, fuck you, and then shoot you again, you fucking stupid bitch." Behind me, the bison stomped and snorted.

"No one lives here," I said, surprising myself with how calm my voice sounded. It surprised him too. I saw the hesitation on his face. He lowered the rifle and then raised it back up after he realized what he was doing. He gave me a good jab, right under my breast. He lifted the barrel up so that my boob went with it. He moved the barrel back so that it fell down. He chuckled to himself and did it again, sniffling uncontrollably. Each time he sucked back snot, it echoed throughout the clearing where the now burnt-out trailer used to stand. "Just leave," I said. "I won't tell anyone."

"Who the fuck would you tell anyways, stupid bitch?" He regained his composure. I could feel the barrel digging deeper into my chest. "It's just you and me." He leaned in close. I could feel his cold sweat dampening my skin and then the stickiness of his tongue as he licked, starting at my jawline and slowly moving his way up to my ear.

"I wouldn't be so sure," I said. I could feel his saliva dripping down my cheek.

"Is he fucking hiding? *Come out here, you fuck!*" He turned around and surveyed the bush. The light was starting to fade over the clearing, and the shadows were getting stronger. He paused when he saw the trailer. For the first time, it seemed like he recognized that something was inside of it. I watched as he shook his head and kept searching the bush. "*I'm going to fuck this stupid bitch right now unless you come out*," he screamed. "*Fuck her good*." All the increased twitching pronounced his agitation. "*You hear me?*" Sweat kept pouring off of him, and he frantically pointed his gun at all the waving shadows from the trees blowing in the wind in the dimming light. Inside the livestock trailer, a bison bellowed. "Fuck you have in there, girl?" he asked. He walked over to the trailer and looked inside. When he saw the bison through the vents, he turned back towards where he'd left me. He sneered and giggled and put the barrel of the gun through the hole in the grating. He put his head on the scope.

"No, please . . ." I cried, then there was the BOOM of the hunting rifle going off, sending the trailer rocking as the bison bucked and smashed back and forth. One of the buffalo let out a howl. Then there was another shot and the howling stopped. The man cycled the round out and a copper bullet casing flew into the air. The bullet casing arched up, floating in what seemed like slow motion as it caught a glint of sunlight. When the bullet landed, I charged him.

He was focused on the bison inside the trailer and didn't see me coming until it was too late. I drove my shoulder into him, and he spun into the dirt. The gun fell next to the trailer. He hit the ground and started scrambling. I leaned down and picked the gun up, shouldered it, and put him in the open sights. He stood up, his hands stretched out in front of him like he was calling it in.

"Relax," he said. "It was just a joke."

I used to go out hunting with my dad when I was a kid. He always told me to shoot for the lungs. It'll drop an animal, he'd say, and they'll have a clean, quick death. It's how we honour them and the meat we get from them. The last thing we want to do is make an animal suffer. Suffering ruins the meat. Think of that poor animal and what it would have to go through. Nobody wants that.

I aimed at his dick and pulled the trigger. A bang, an explosion of red mist and skin, and he fell to the ground. He screamed out. I chambered the next bullet. It was the last one. I walked to where he lay on the ground. A gaping hole oozed blood and body out of where the crotch of his jeans was. I put the barrel on his stomach.

He gasped out, "Don't." When he tried to climb to his feet, I pulled the trigger and his flesh splattered everywhere. He clawed at his stomach, trying to stop the bleeding in a frenzy. Then, with a last suck of breath, his eyes clouded over and he stopped moving.

I sprinted over to the trailer. Inside, a bison, one of the young bulls, lay in a blood pool, breathing heavy. The other bison had calmed down and circled it. The young bull stared at me without any expression in its eyes. This had been their fate for so long. Destruction by men for no reason other than the wrong place and time. The young bison tried to stand up, and when it did I saw its blood had matted the fur on its underside. The hind legs buckled underneath it, and it fell back down. I started crying.

I checked the rifle again, just to make sure there were no bullets left. Nothing. The last thing I wanted was for this prairie god to suffer. I walked over to the redneck's truck. Somewhere on the edge of the clearing, the owls hooted to one another. The light faded so quick in the fall.

There was an open box of rifle cartridges on his truck's front seat, next to a stained glass pipe flecked with burn marks. I pulled two out of the white plastic packs and chambered them into the rifle, then walked back to the livestock trailer. The bison looked up at me as I shouldered the rifle and aimed it underneath the shoulder blade, where the bullet would hit both lungs. I pulled the trigger, and the *whoomph* of the bullet hitting its mark echoed through the clearing. The buffalo stopped moving. The others started bucking back and forth. I worried that one of the calves would get trampled or that one of them would hurt itself trying to escape. "Easy, easy, easy," I said, drawing out each word in my best calm voice. But I could feel everything shaking. I thought about firing the last bullet into the guy's skull. Then I looked over at his lifeless corpse, a bloodied stain on the land.

I went to move his truck out of the way. He had left it running the whole time. In the box of the truck, I noticed two red jerry cans. It all clicked. This was the guy who had torched the trailer, and "the guy who lives here" was Ezzy. What the fuck had Ezzy done?

I grabbed one of the cans and shook it. Empty. I grabbed the second one and some gas sloshed around inside. Everything that was fucking wrong with the world. I drove the truck and parked it beside the dead body. Part of me wanted to go through his wallet or the truck or something, to figure out his name. To learn something about him. But that would humanize someone who didn't want me to exist, didn't want the bison to exist. We didn't deserve that. That bison hadn't deserved to die. The smell of blood and shit clouded the air around the man. I felt my guts rolling. I leaned over to puke, but nothing came. I retched a couple more times, then my stomach and nose adjusted to the smell. I grabbed the man's corpse and dragged it into the cab of his truck. The same move I'd had to do with Ezzy earlier in the day. A lifetime ago. For the first time since the truck pulled up, I thought of Ezzy over at the hospital, pumped full of painkillers and oblivious. I threw the rifle into the cab with the body. Then I doused the truck with the gas left in the jerry can and lit it on fire.

As I drove away, I watched in the driver's-side mirror as flames engulfed the truck. I lost sight of it as I went around the bend in the road. Everything went silent. Then a boom from the fire hitting the gas tank a few seconds later.

Nothing could ever make me go back to that property again. The land there had died with that bison. *How was I going to get a dead bison out of the trailer?* Like trying to move a car without wheels. I'd need help. But first, I had to get the fuck away from here. The closest neighbours were a long way out, and most people kept to themselves anyway. But a flurry of gunshots followed by an explosion might change that.

Numb. Like nothing had happened and the world just kept going on. I was surprised that I didn't feel angrier, scared, something, but there was nothing. An empty head. If I hadn't acted, or things had gone another way, it would be my body burning up right now. He probably would have lit the truck and livestock trailer on fire with all the buffalo still in it. My father had taught me that once you pull a trigger, you can never take that bullet back, so you'd better make damn sure you know what you're aiming at and where that bullet can go. I would never take that bullet back. I'd make that shot again and again.

On the outskirts of the city, I found a truck stop and an A&W. I parked the truck as far away as I could get from the glaring neon sign that lit up the parking lot. I still had a few hours to go until I could drop the buffalo off in the park. There was dried saliva on my cheek where the dead man had licked it. I could feel myself covered in the blood and shit that had exploded out of his intestine. But when I looked at myself in the truck cab mirror,

I didn't see anything. The taste and smell lingered on me, though, and I knew if I didn't clean up, it would never leave. I thought about eating something; it had been hours, probably, since the banana and bannock with chokecherry jam I'd taken from my parents' place when I left this morning. A lifetime ago.

Inside the truck stop, a table of four sloppy white men wearing crusty, wrinkled sweatpants and stained t-shirts stared at me as I walked through the door. Their patchy beards holding mayo and other condiments, and the table covered in the remains of burgers, leftover fries, chicken bones, used ketchup packets, and pop cups. I avoided their leers. They were straining, trying to catch my eye. One of the guys leaned way over so I had to turn sideways to avoid touching him as I went by. I wanted to drag his tongue out of his mouth and tie it around a urinal puck. But I kept going, eyes fixed on the prize of a women's washroom that probably wasn't used that often. I wished I still had the rifle. So if one of them thought about following me in, I could turn around and put him through the sink. All I wanted was cold, crisp water on my face. To wash away the past few hours.

The prize of the women's washroom didn't play out. A clogged toilet that, instead of plunging, people had shit on top of until shit filled the bowl. I kicked the lid closed with my boot so I wouldn't have to look at it. Toilet paper was strewn everywhere, and it looked like people had begun pissing in a corner. Someone had used white-out or paint to cover all the graffiti but didn't do anything after, so it just sat there in a different shade to the rest of the nicotine-yellow paint. Thankfully there was a paper towel dispenser in there and not an air dryer. I grabbed a handful of towels and wiped down the counter around the sink. Hot water started coming out of the tap, and I cupped my hands under it and then splashed the water all over my face. I grabbed more paper towels, wet them, and then scrubbed my cheek where the dead man had slobbered on me. I used the paper towel to clean where I thought his blood had stained my jeans. I really couldn't tell with the dark denim, but I scrubbed anyway. I scrubbed everything. If I could have filled the sink up with water and then got in it like a child at bath time, I would have. My entire body ached to get clean, to soak, lay back, and sleep. Back at Auntie May's, the first thing I'd do would be to take a long bath in a real tub loaded up with lavender scent from the endless vials she kept next to it.

"Two Teen Burgers, onion rings, and a large black coffee, please," I ordered. The Filipina lady working the till smiled and put my order in.

"Wow, hungry lady for someone so skinny," the trucker in line behind me said. "You better watch it, girly, or you're going to get a big belly." He started laughing. I ignored him and walked over to the side to wait for my order. I pulled out my phone and pretended to text someone.

"Five-piece Chubby Chicken meal and a Mama Burger," the trucker ordered. "You know I like my mamas," he added, then winked at the lady working the till. Then he turned to me. "Why don't you sit that pretty little butt down and join me for supper?"

"Sure!" I said. He looked startled. "Then, I'll crawl under the table and suck your tiny little dick if I can find it." His face dropped. My food came out. I grabbed the bag. "Go fuck yourself," I said as I walked by him.

"*Yeeeeoooooowww*," one of the truckers sitting at the table called out as I stepped through the doors and walked back to the truck.

I checked on the buffalo. They seemed okay despite the dead one lying on the floor of the trailer. Maybe? What went through a bison's skull, even? I used to think I knew a lot about bison. I used to think I knew a lot of things. The last few hours had torn that notion apart. Inside the truck, I unwrapped one of the burgers, pushed the lettuce back into place, and took a big bite. I didn't taste anything. I took another big bite. My stomach clenched, and I set the burger back inside the brown paper bag. Grease from the onion rings was already sliming up the bottom of it. I grabbed one of them and ate it. It was just the fried dough, no onion inside of it. I started laughing. My granny was a lady who'd loved onions. She would eat them like apples, or cut them up and put them on white bread with bologna for a sandwich, or when she didn't have any meat, just have a raw onion sandwich straight up. And she'd really loved onion rings. That was the treat we always brought her after she moved out of Pembina Creek and into a seniors' building in the city. What I wouldn't give to drive over to her little apartment, drop her off these onion rings, and drink tea with her into the late hours of the night. She passed away years ago. At least, it felt like years ago. I didn't understand time anymore. She'd got sick, and then her memory had faded. I reached up and grabbed the little tanned-hide medicine bag that my father kept hanging from the rear-view mirror in the cab of the truck. Granny had made it for him. For his safety. She'd beaded a six-petal flower in blues, reds, and white on the brown hide. I moved my fingertips over the beads, learning the curves of each individual one.

Granny had tried to teach me how to bead. When I was a little kid, I would place the beads on the needle for her. That was my job, and I loved every minute of it. She would feed me home-made oatmeal cookies and cups of Labrador tea while I placed five yellow beads on the needle and then five more. I tried to anticipate the colours she would use, and eventually she started letting me pick the colours out. That was a big deal. I'd like to think that she passed down teachings or history lessons to me, but all I could remember was gossip. That lady had loved to gossip. She knew everything that was happening throughout Pembina Creek and some of the neighbouring reserves. She even knew what was going on with the family that had moved to the city. It didn't matter if she didn't have all the facts or had to make some of it up herself. She loved to tell a good story. There was no need for television or soap operas when her extensive Métis kinship network provided everything needed for entertainment. I couldn't remember much about her own story, but I did know that her sister had chewed through husbands like a puppy with a stick.

I forced myself to finish one of the burgers. My head felt stronger and clearer. I had to figure out what to do with the dead bison. The worst thing would be to let all that meat and the hide spoil. I would never forgive myself if that happened. I could unload the live ones in the park and then drive back to my parents' place and get my dad to help. But then he would wonder why there was a dead bison inside the trailer. Especially since I'd told him I needed the trailer to do a bit of contract work moving cows around for a friend's family farm. That might seem a bit suspicious.

Plus, I didn't want to get my parents involved. They had enough of their own troubles dealing with the shit of being prairie poor. The last thing either of them needed was to be an accessory to bison theft. And murder. I scrolled through the contacts on my phone. No one really stuck out. A few people from back in my activist days, maybe, though I didn't know what kind of help they could offer, since most people had no idea how to drive a truck. Most had never hunted a grouse or even a deer, let alone a bison.

I turned the radio on. CBC News was in the middle of its hourly broadcast. More buffalo trouble on the prairies:

*"An area golf course was shut down today after a herd of bison escaped from a ranch outside of Camrose sometime between last night and early this morning. They blocked traffic on Highway 833 before moving onto the Camrose golf course. City staff assisted by the local rancher are still working on rounding up the buffalo. People are asked to avoid the area until authorities tell them it's safe. Meanwhile, back in Edmonton, protestors continue to block the entrance into Dawson Park. The protest movement is now calling itself sohkapiskisow paskwawimostos, which translates from the Cree to 'Bison Strong.' Local ally Erin Green has made shirts and bumper stickers with the hashtag #bisonstrong. We have Erin with us in the studio here today . . . So, Erin, can you tell us a little bit about what you're hoping to accomplish with your shirts and bumper stickers?"*

*"Well, first off, I'd like to acknowledge that I'm on Treaty 6 territory and the ancestral homeland of the Métis peoples."*

*"Yes. We'd also like to acknowledge that. Thank you, Erin."*

*"So you know, when I first saw the bison, I thought, 'Oh my god, they*

*must belong in the River Valley.' This is, like, their home. And we took it from them. So, like, we should do everything that we can to help them stay here, you know?"*

*"Erin, can you tell us a little bit about where the proceeds from the Bison Strong sales are going?"*

*"From every shirt or sticker that's sold, I'll donate ten per cent back to the activist group. It's my way of moving forward with reconciliation and letting the bison know that they have a home here."*

*"Amazing work, Erin. And I'm sure the protestors thank you for your generosity."*

*"No problem! Thank you for having me."*

*"There you have it. You can get your stickers and shirts from bisonstrong.ca. I know I'm getting one."*

I switched the station to Windspeaker radio. They were playing Merle Haggard. It must have been the old country hour. I was surprised that Tyler hadn't weaselled his way onto the radio, and that he wasn't a part of that sticker and shirt thing. The name of the group sounded just like something he would have thought up. He would have told everyone that an Elder gave him the name in ceremony. But I know he would have just pulled the Cree dictionary app up on his phone and typed in the words "strong" and "bison."

*Fuck*, I thought. *That's who I should call.* I didn't have his phone number in my contact list anymore. I tried to remember it. 780-967-something.

I downloaded Instagram. I hadn't checked my account in months, maybe even a year. I knew he would be on it, though, looking for that instant gratification. He was always posting away and sliding into Instababes' direct messages. Another system to give him the constant attention he needed. I typed in my user-name, *maskotew*—"prairie" in Cree. My password was the same for everything, ILAG8890—*I Love Adam Gladue* and then our birth years. A relic left over from my first email account and first boyfriend back in Pembina Creek. We broke up in Grade 11. But I kept the password.

I clicked open my messages. My inbox was full of invites to events, men trying to chat me up, white people asking for advice on reconciliation. All the shit that made me delete the app in the first place. I searched for Tyler's account, *TeeCardz*. His profile picture was him holding a megaphone and standing on top of a barricade. That was from a few years back, when the railways were blockaded in solidarity with the Wet'suwet'en. He was still skinny in the photo. I clicked the message button. We didn't have any saved conversation history. That had long been deleted by one of us. I forgot who. I sent him a message:

*Hey, I need to talk to you. Please call me asap.*

Two hours later, he called. I was still sitting in the parking lot.

"Hey," I answered.

"What's up? You pregnant?" he asked.

"You're such a fucking asshole," I said.

"Cause it's not mine. We haven't hooked up in like a year."

"I'm not pregnant. Fuck you." I tried my best to control my voice. Everything in me wanted to reach through the airwaves and strangle his fat neck.

"Oh . . . Did you want to come over then?" he asked. "I haven't seen you in so long. It would be great to catch up."

"I need your help," I said.

"Pass." He started laughing. "Wait, does it pay?"

"Nope. But I still need your help."

"Why the fuck would I ever do that?" he said.

"Because without me, you wouldn't be able to go around sticking your dick in all those white girls who want to get back at their racist daddies."

He laughed again. "Grey, Grey, Grey." I could tell he was amping himself up for one of his patronizing lectures. I wasn't going to have any of that shit.

"Look, can you meet me at Terwillegar Park at one a.m.?"

"Fine."

———

The first time I caught Tyler with another woman was at an Indigenous educators conference in Toronto. We hadn't been dating for long at that point—a couple months, tops. The conference organizers had asked me to come out to speak about reconciliation within classrooms and how to create new systems of thinking for kindergarten to Grade 12 youth. An ambitious topic—one that I was more confident addressing back then than I would be now. The conference was paying for my flights, hotel room, food, and an honorarium for going out there. My policy was to get the organization to put the honorarium back into a local Indigenous youth group. But I'd take a free trip to Toronto any day. I asked Tyler if he wanted to come with me. We could split the cost of his flight and then just eat the conference food or order enough on their tab to cover our meals. He had never been to Toronto. The only place he'd ever travelled to outside the prairies was Vegas. His family went there almost every year.

We'd first met at the opening for a new Indigenous art gallery in the city. He knew who I was; I tended to speak a lot at public events, and my picture would be included on all of the organization's posts on social media, which were getting a good amount of attention thanks to the Indigenous rights and Land Back movements. But I had no idea who he was. When he introduced himself, he told me that he was studying law so he could go back and work with Indigenous people who'd been impacted by the Millennium Scoop. He stood over the group we were speaking in, a solid six inches taller than the Cree, Métis, and Nakoda men and women who were mingling in our conversational circle. He wore his hair in two long braids, and had on a tight black shirt that read *nehiyawewin* in syllabics. At one point, he ended up beside me.

"I think my favourite part about art shows is how everyone stands," he said in a low voice that wasn't meant for other people to hear. I looked up at him. I must have seemed curious or intrigued or something, because he kept going. "Look." He pointed his lips to a lady and a dude a few years older than us. "What do you think they're saying to each other right now?" I shrugged my shoulders. "*Well, I really like the juxtaposition between contrasts that the artist used here. I think that it sets the tone for how we as Canadian peoples are separate but also distinct*," he said in his best white professorial mock. "*If we analyze the abstraction of it, one can really see how the angles are parallel to what we as humans desire most.*"

"Shut up," I said, giggling under my breath. "They'll hear you."

Tyler smiled, using only the left side of his face. I wanted to hear more of his stupid jokes. I wanted to listen to his story.

"So, how do you like university?" I asked. I sounded like an auntie. What a dumb thing to say.

"That's all you academic types want to talk about: university. You need to expand a little bit there, Grey. Think of the land," he said in a teasing voice.

"Pffft. I am the land," I said.

"That could be your art show . . . *Grey: I Am the Land.* Great title. What are you going to do for your performance?" he asked.

"Whow, whow, whow, this is a performance piece now?"

"All art is performance, Grey." Then he twirled in a circle on one leg in a faux pirouette and stopped in front of me. I could feel the heat coming off his body. I wasn't sure if I wanted to make out with him or punch him in the stomach. Or maybe I could just run my hands up the inside of his shirt and feel the movement of his body.

"Easy, buddy. Save some for the Ironman," one of his friends joked from the other side of the circle. Tyler winked at me and went over to chat to the guy who had yelled at him.

Throughout the rest of the event, we kept making eye contact. But every time we did, he'd shift away suddenly and pretend to analyze some of the art. He'd hold his chin up with his hand and ponder. I'd pretend to laugh and then go back to the other conversations happening around me.

I was about to leave when he came up and asked me if I wanted to go skip rocks down at the river. I agreed. Who wouldn't want to go hang out with a good-looking Cree guy down by the most beautiful river in the world, and get to play with rocks at the same time? We headed beneath the High Level Bridge and tried to hit the concrete slabs with the most skips. The sun stayed up forever in the late spring, and we sat on the riverbank until it finally dropped its dark pink and purple hues on us. I tried to take a picture of it and Tyler laughed and told me that a picture would never do a sunset or sunrise justice. I was hooked by that. We went back to my apartment and stayed in bed fucking, smoking, and eating for a month straight. We only left to pick up takeout sandwiches and coffees or to get more wine and weed. The organization I was with already worked from home most days so I would just prop my laptop up and set it so that it said I was always online. No one ever questioned it. Then I'd go back to my new goal of finding and memorizing where every scar and mark was on Tyler's body. "Mental health days," I called them. Which felt amazing after spending the last three years working around the clock.

When Tyler fell asleep, I'd cram in as much writing and analysis as I could on the current corporate tax breaks that were being handed out to, you know, stimulate trickle-down economics. I didn't want to fall too far behind in my work, but I was sure my boss noticed that my productivity had dropped. Still, she was a rad Dene lady who would be more pissed that I hadn't told her what I was really up to than at the fact that I wasn't keeping up my normal levels of frantically cranking out opinion pieces, blog posts, and handling media requests. Tyler was between semesters, so he wasn't doing anything. I'll just get a job at the River Cree when I run out of cash, he told me. I didn't give a shit if he worked or not. All I wanted was his tongue, mouth, and hands on every inch of my body.

After that month, we got back to the reality of our lives. Tyler would drive in and out of Enoch Cree Nation on the west side of the city, where he lived with his uncle. It was only a twenty-minute drive from there to my apartment by the university, but he often just stayed over. A benefit, as our marathon sex sessions physically and mentally sustained me through a hard push at work to write a proposal around the community benefits of defunding police departments. It was hard work for something that had about the same chance of happening as the return of "Crown land" to Indigenous peoples. It's difficult to put your best work forward when you know that it's not going to go anywhere. Trying to manoeuvre within a colonial system wasn't going to work. But I did it anyway. My effort to create a better future. Whether or not that could ever happen without full-scale resistance.

I was sitting in our downtown hotel room in Toronto, trying to work out the final touches for my presentation. The view overlooked the square with the big TORONTO letters, accentuated by a medicine wheel on the left side and the classic maple leaf on the right. In my fantasies about white men in corporate worlds, they were always smoking big cigars and drinking with their brown shoes and legs man-splayed about the furniture. I could just imagine the politicians who had approved that sign sitting on the other side of the square in City Hall doing that exact thing. Reconciliation accomplished. We put up your stupid symbol. Job well done, boys.

Tyler had gone to the hotel gym to work out. I couldn't get anything done with him around. For the past month he'd taken to reading over my shoulder, inserting his thoughts and opinions into whatever I was working on that day. A particular favourite move of his was to play "devil's advocate" and ask me what the pro-pipeline/capitalist people in Indigenous communities thought of what I was doing. Devil's advocate was a privileged position to take, I'd tell him, and he'd just shrug and roll his eyes at me. Nothing made me more annoyed than him trying to constantly one-up what I was doing. I'd tell him off, and he'd just turn and pace around the room. Something he had been doing since we got there. The August humidity made the downtown Toronto heat unbearable. Anytime we stepped out, both of us started sweating immediately; just breathing made it feel like our lungs were on fire. Prairie kids through and through—dryness was all we knew.

Tyler was bored, restless. The two people he knew in Toronto hadn't responded to his text messages. He claimed they were friends, but when I pressed a bit it turned out that they had just been liking each other's photos on Instagram for a few years. Tyler wanted to feel connected to a place, like he was in charge and important, like Toronto wanted him there. Even though the city didn't give a shit. It was just a city. I kept trying to get him out of the room. He didn't want to go to the art galleries or museums or the university campus because they were colonial institutions. I reminded him that so was this whole fucking city, so was Edmonton, and so was the university.

An hour or so after he had gone to the gym I had finished the presentation, basically making sure my sources were all correct and up to date. Nothing gives white educators more authority than tearing apart an Indigenous presentation or paper because it's not cited properly. I decided to go downstairs and order us a couple coffees and sandwiches. I got out of the elevator and started walking towards the coffee shop in the lobby. Big hotel. There was a bar, a couple shops, and a restaurant, all glassed in so you could see right into the establishments when you walked through. It wasn't hard to pick Tyler out on his barstool seat. He was sitting beside a blonde woman in tight black leggings and a long green turtleneck stretched all the way over her butt. Uncomfortably close for strangers. Leaning into each other's every word over their pints of beer. Tyler's gym bag sat at the bottom of his bar stool. A similar bag sat at the bottom of hers.

I watched for a minute, and then turned away and ran back to the elevator. I pressed the button to go back to the twenty-third floor. I felt like I should be more upset. Like this wasn't just an inevitable development in our fading relationship; like we had something special worth fighting for. I tried to embody a jealous high-school kid mindset, but I didn't even have the energy for that. Though I one hundred per cent would win in a fight with the blonde, just like I used to at bush parties back in high school. I wanted to slap Tyler and hear the bartender and all the patrons laugh and *oooooh* in the background. Or I wanted to want to, but my mind and body were beyond it. An absence of feeling was something that I knew I had to work on; maybe I'd left it all in the research paper or in front of the audience. Maybe that was why he was searching for something else, because

I couldn't begin to bring any real sort of emotion to our relationship outside of the desire to have good sex. What I really wanted was to go and do my presentation and get the fuck back to Edmonton.

I got off the elevator. Then I changed my mind. I was going to high-school this shit. I got back on and pressed the button for the lobby. Back downstairs, I could still see them over at the bar. Tyler was in the middle of telling some story, and she was hanging on his every word. I walked up and sat down on the empty barstool next to him. He turned and his eyes went wide with the fear of being busted for a moment before returning to the calculated, warm, and welcoming ones I knew. Those were the same eyes I'd noticed when I caught him with an essay that he "wrote" for one of his university classes. It was just one of my Indigenous think tank opinion pieces changed up a bit. New title and the word *Métis* switched to *First Nations* without a cultural context. He'd explained that one by saying he wasn't going to validate a western institution by sharing real family history and knowledge. But apparently mine was fair game to share widely and pass off as his own. At the bar, Tyler shifted his stool back so that he was in the middle, and we could all see each other.

"Grey!" he said. "We were just talking about you."

"Oh yeah?" Fuck his gaslighting bullshit.

"This is Claire. Claire's going to be teaching on a rez up in northern Ontario next year."

"Congrats," I said. Claire looked confused. Was I a lover, a co-worker, a friend? I could tell she was trying to place me. Tyler gave nothing. I gave nothing.

"You know, I was just talking to Tyler about how, like, I just want to make sure that I'm becoming one with the community. I want to make sure that I can, like, bring in the Elders' teachings, really have them heard in the classroom," Claire said.

"Elder and knowledge-keeper teachings are very important, aren't they, Grey?" Tyler said. It wasn't a question. It was meant to tell me that this was his moment. That he owned it.

"Very important," I said.

"You need to remember to respect protocols and cultures. But us Indigenous peoples have such a wealth of knowledge." Tyler kept going. He took a big swig of his beer, motioned with his eyes towards the glass, and then looked at me. I shook my head. He ordered another.

"Oh, I know," Claire said. "I took this course, Indigenous Education. It was, like, mandatory for all teachers. We did a blanket exercise, and I learned so much. I know how impactful, like, intergenerational trauma is now." She looked at me, still trying to place who I was. I knew from having that exact gaze on me many times that she was trying to figure out how authentically Indigenous I was. And if I was someone that she needed to worry about. Did I stand in the way of her side dalliance with a Cree man before returning to the suburbs and an eventual accountant husband? "I know how important, like, matriarchy is in Indigenous communities," she continued.

"I think you'll do just fine. The kids will love you," Tyler said. "Grey's actually giving a talk here tomorrow morning. You should go to it."

"Oh yeah? What about?" Claire asked.

"Destroying the western education system," I said. Tyler let out a fake laugh. Claire looked worried and then followed his lead.

"Good one. No, it's really on how educators just need to change their mindsets around how they approach teaching kids Indigenous topics," Tyler said. He continued his fake laugh.

"No," I said. "It's about fucking smashing schools with a sledgehammer." Tyler shot me a look that said I should help him try to fuck this blonde lady. His form of reconciliation.

"That's not what it was about earlier," he said. "Well, I should probably get back to helping Grey with the presentation. Sounds like we have a lot of work left to do still." He stood up and slammed back what was left of the beer he just ordered. He leaned down on one knee to grab his gym bag. I watched his hand graze Claire's black legging as he stood back up and waved to the bartender to catch his attention. "Charge this to room 2302, please, and put her drinks on it, too," Tyler said to the bartender, then turned back to Claire. "Great to meet you! I wish you all the best in your new job, and congratulations again on it. You'll make a great difference in our communities."

"You can't fucking buy someone else a drink on the tab!" I said when we got back to the hotel room.

"Why not? It's not like we have to pay for it. I should buy everyone drinks on it, really."

"Because then they would never invite me back. They might not even pay for it. What if they charge me for it? I don't want to pay for your beers."

"What do you care? You hate capitalism, remember?"

"And who the fuck was she?"

"Just a teacher I met. Relax. You're the one who told me that I should be going out and meeting people." I didn't remember saying anything like that. I did remember saying that he should go have a drink with his friends so he would get out of the hotel room and quit mansplaining shit to me.

"You shouldn't tell those people that they're going to make a great difference in our communities. Who's the 'our'? She's not part of my community. Pretty soon she'll be wearing beaded earrings, brown contacts, and dyeing her hair black with a new love for a long-lost great-great-great Métis uncle."

"Relax already," Tyler said.

I sat in the hard hotel room chair, then turned and looked out over the square with the medicine wheel. I was sick of him trying to needle his way out of everything and at the same time make me the bad person. He could never do anything wrong. Me, on the other hand . . . I was the reason that our relationship was fading. Well, if he wanted me to turn out the light, I'd fucking turn out the light alright.

"And really, I'm just promoting your talk. It's a good thing, getting the word out there about it. More educators will learn, and then we'll create a better future for the next generations."

We ordered expensive room service later that night. Halfway through our twenty-buck chicken wings and forty-dollar pizza, Tyler's phone pinged. He grabbed it a little too quickly and got hot sauce all over the screen. He wiped it on his jeans and then looked at it without even attempting to hide the little grin on his face.

"Hey, what about that. My friend got back to me. I'm going to meet him for a beer later tonight," he said.

"What time?"

"Like nine-ish. Do you want to come?" He didn't sound like he wanted me to come. "It might be a bit boring. We'll just be yapping about our hockey-boy days."

"No, I should get a good sleep before the presentation tomorrow."

"You sure? Just one drink?"

"It's okay." I wasn't an idiot. But I also didn't want him around the room anymore.

It would be easy to look back in retrospect and see all the ways he was manipulating me. I could build myself up in my head and say that I saw it coming or that I had a sense of autonomy within it. Still, I really did want to believe that he was just going to see a friend. That he was just encouraging a new teacher, who was nervous about moving to a reserve for her first teaching gig. That he wasn't trying to overshadow and take control of me and the work I was doing. I wanted to believe that we were in this together. That we really were working to create a better future. And even if I said or acted differently, I honestly did like being in the spotlight and hearing my voice ring out across a room. Not many Indigenous women ever got that opportunity. I always imagined their collective voices joining in with mine.

In the months after the trip, Tyler became more of a fixture on Edmonton's activist scene. He started accompanying me to rallies, marches, and other protest events. He'd join me when I went to speak to classes at the local universities and colleges. He'd be right there when I was doing workshops with youth groups. It didn't take long before my friends were his friends. I couldn't tell where he ended, and I began. I had spoken so often about not letting the Canadian state's patriarchal imposition on Indigenous leadership infiltrate how we operated, and now here I was with this guy confidently taking over all the work we had been doing as a community.

At first, it was nice to have the support, and I encouraged his presence. Tyler had shown up right when Ezzy left. The timing couldn't have been any better if it had all been planned. Ezzy was supposed to have been at that art gallery opening the night I met Tyler, but he had been ditching out on almost everything. That happened regularly in my world. People got infatuated with the idea of systemic change, but when they saw the work needed, they didn't actually want to bash their heads into a wall for the rest of their lives to make a tiny little dent in it. Especially things that were scheduled outside of office hours.

I never asked Ezzy what was going on. Maybe I should have, but it was way too late. At the time, I didn't think twice about it. Ezzy was just another participant, and Tyler came in like a chinook wind. Strong and welcome at first, as it melted off the winter's snow, but eventually really annoying when all you wanted was quiet from the incessant howling.

Tyler started getting asked to attend events and speak about Indigenous history in the Edmonton area. He jumped on every opportunity—"building his brand," he called it. A descendant of Treaty 6 signatories who was going to hold the government accountable for their failure to follow up on their obligations.

It turned out that he wasn't actually in law school like he had mentioned that first night—he planned to get there eventually, he said, but had really just finished his first year of the transition program for Indigenous students at the University of Alberta. Then he dropped out before starting his second year so he could concentrate more on our movement. That was how he always framed it: *our movement.* And people loved him. He was charming, he spoke well, and he specialized in making white liberal settlers not feel guilty about their role in colonization. They loved hearing from him about how they could be better allies, and he made everyone feel like his best friend. Which is probably why I stuck around even after that Toronto trip. I did my talk and got invited to join a couple others who spoke on a panel to end the conference, then got roasted by an old white professor emeritus. "I see that the government is doing lots to give back to reconciliation," he said, "but what are Indigenous people doing?" I lost it, and then I lost the crowd—until Tyler got on stage uninvited and said that Indigenous peoples were committed to sharing the land, culture, and values with non-Indigenous people, and to walk side by side with them. I wanted to strangle him. I wasn't committed to sharing anything. But something about his ability to draw people in . . . to make them feel like they were his best friend, even if he had just met them a moment ago, kept me coming back. Usually it was just because I wanted to kick the shit out of him, but then at some point I'd get over that.

We fought and fucked, and then eventually had enough. We ended it in the back seat of my Honda CR-V in the parking lot behind the River Cree Casino and Resort, where he was working as a bartender. While riding him that last time I pushed my hips down as hard as I could, taking his cock deep inside me. I wanted to smother him, to swallow him whole inside me, to ride him so hard his fucking dick would break off. Then I'd toss it out into the snowbank with all the other discarded condoms and cigarette butts where it could rot with the snow mould. It wasn't sex anymore. I wanted to grind him into a pile of bones.

I drove the truck down to the park where I was going to drop off the bison, then waited in the darkness. The city felt empty late at night. Twenty minutes after one in the morning, I saw the headlights of the Toyota 4Runner coming down the road. Tyler parked beside me and got out. There was no characteristic grin on his face this time.

"Jesus Christ, Grey. Fuck are you doing?" he said.

I shrugged and waved to the trailer.

"You're the one who dropped the bison off in Dawson?" he said. "I should have known." He shook his head.

"We need to get them unloaded. But there's a problem."

"What? Where the fuck did you get buffalo at?"

"One's dead."

"How?"

"Do you think your cousin could help with it? I don't want it to go to waste." I worried he was going to ask about the dead guy, but of course he wouldn't know about that at all. The thought kept coming into my head, though. That somehow he knew. That somehow everyone knew I had killed a man.

"Yeah, sure, whatever," he said. "Shit, this is serious, Grey."

"You don't even know."

Tyler lit a cigarette. He offered me the pack. I shook my head.

"Okay, get in the 4Runner," I told him. "I'm going to swing the gates open and then get back in the truck. The bison should come running out, but if they don't, just honk a couple times until they do."

"What if they don't move?" He exhaled up into the air, a mix of breath and smoke that hung under the city's permanent glow.

"They will. They don't want to stay in that fucking trailer," I said. "Then I'll drive to the end of the road, close the trailer doors, and follow you out to your cousin's. Cool?"

"Why doesn't your new boyfriend help you do this?" Tyler asked. "Whatever. Fine. We'll go to my uncle's then. We can put it in the garage there." He got back in his 4Runner and rolled the window down. "Grey, be careful." He buckled up his seatbelt and rolled the window back up.

I pulled a hammer out of the truck's box and walked to the back of the trailer. Inside, the bison were in motion. They anticipated something. One of them bellowed out. I undid the first latch and then the second. I swung the doors open and ran back to the cab of the truck, clanging the trailer with the hammer as I went by. The clanging reverberated and the bison tore out at full speed. The hooves stomping everywhere, mixing with their movement against the metal of the trailer, brought back memories from terrible undergraduate concerts. One of the calves hit the ground and tumbled over before righting itself and running off after its mother. They disappeared into the park's darkness, letting out buffs and snorts and braying their way into the night, and then just as fast as it had all happened, the city went quiet.

Tyler tore off in his 4Runner, going at least twenty over. I lost sight of him immediately. I stuck to the speed limit as I pulled out onto the freeway to Enoch. I didn't want to draw any attention. The trailer banged around back and forth now that there wasn't a load holding it down. Every bump felt like a mountain, or a police spike belt, as we clanked and clanked our way out to the reserve. Tyler lived near the casino with his uncle. You had to go down the main road to get there, which was always a beat-up mess. Neither the city, the county, nor the reserve wanted to take responsibility for it, so it turned caved-in and potholed, even though it was the primary route in and out of the area. The trailer really screamed as we went along, and each bump sent me flying into the roof of the cab. I had forgotten to put my seatbelt on, and when I tried to reach back for it, it wouldn't pull out. Every outside noise sounded like a siren. I kept waiting for a roadblock from the RCMP or city police, and every passing headlight had me jumping until we pulled into Tyler's uncle's driveway, where we were greeted by two German shepherd mutts that ran out to intimidate the vehicle. They barked until Tyler yelled at them to get lost, then went back to where they had been sleeping under the deck, on a bed made from a small square hay bale.

He opened the garage door. It was more of a shack than anything. Old, unheated, detached. Tyler had moved his uncle's tables to the side to make room for the bison. I circled around the yard with the truck and backed the rig up to the garage's open door.

"How are we going to move it?" I asked as I stepped out of the truck. Tyler pulled his red Chicago Bulls toque off and shook out his hair. No braids today.

"When my uncle gets a moose, he uses the quad to tow it out of the back of his truck and in here," he said.

"How?"

Tyler pointed his lips to the back door of the garage. He walked over and opened the door to the shed. There was a quad parked and waiting. Tyler hopped on it, started it up, and dragged a long brown rope back through the door, through the garage, and into the trailer. I almost gagged as I went inside. The bison had shit and pissed everywhere. Combined with the dead bison's blood, the whole trailer reeked like an old feedlot. I helped Tyler wrap the rope around the bison's legs. Then he walked back to the quad and drove it forward, pulling the bison onto the garage's cement floor.

"That should do it," he said as he hopped off the quad. He shut it off, and the roar of the motor died out. The animal had left a red blood smear on the land. I reached down and touched the blood with my fingertips, then put them into my mouth to lick it off. It tasted of earth and iron and soil and dirt and bone and steel and gunpowder and memory. Tyler watched me without saying a word, a solemn look on his face. I guess even he understood that some things didn't need a commentary. "My cousin will swing by first thing tomorrow morning. He'll know what to do with it."

I shook my head. I wanted to run off into the trees and keep going until I hit the North Saskatchewan River and throw myself into it, but instead I knelt next to the bison and let the dark-red blood stain the knees of my jeans. If I hadn't gone out to that farm today, this animal would have been running around in the pasture right about now, butting heads with the other young bulls and sleeping under starlit northern skies. This bison had died because of selfishness.

"It's just a bison, Grey," Tyler said. "It's okay."

"No, it's not," I said.

He walked over to me and put his hand on my back. I could feel the heat through the fabric of my hoodie. "Come on," he said. "I'll make you a cup of tea."

I woke up with a start. The pitch-black room closed in on me. The walls felt like they were pulsing in the darkness. I didn't know where I was. Why was it so dark? I closed my eyes and I saw the dead guy staring back up at me. I heard his final breath again and again. I lay perfectly still, scared to breathe. I didn't want to sound like him. I wanted to sound alive. I could feel my clothes on me. I reached down and checked. My jeans and hoodie were still on. I was wrapped up in a kohkum quilt. As my eyes adjusted, I recognized the Edmonton Oilers flag hanging behind a television mounted on the wall. Then it all clicked. I was in Tyler's bed. I got up and straightened out my clothes. Nothing seemed out of the ordinary. The house was quiet. I looked at my phone. Seven in the morning. It wouldn't be dark out for long. I started tiptoeing my way towards the front door. I recognized Tyler's soft snores coming from the living room. I didn't want to wake him up. The less we talked, the better. I didn't have time to bullshit. I had to get the livestock trailer and truck back up to my parents' before people started recognizing it and looking for it.

Or maybe they would never look for it. Maybe I had gone unnoticed. I didn't know. I just needed to clean it out and be rid of it. I started putting my boots on. The snores stopped.

"Grey," I heard Tyler call out. The tableside lamp turned on. He stood up, wearing only his boxers. The dim light brought out his best features and hid the worst ones. From this angle, he looked like he did twenty pounds ago, back when we first started seeing each other. I felt a twinge of lust run through me. I pressed it down. It could be so easy to fall back into bed right now and just forget about the truck, trailer, bison, Ezzy, that dead man, all of it. We could hide out here forever.

"I have to go," I said.

"My cousin Ryan will be by in an hour or so. You want to wait around for him?"

"Nope. I need to get this trailer back to my parents."

"Let me make you a coffee for the road," he said.

"I really can't. I have to go now." I left the house and walked as fast as I could towards the truck. I would not run. Running was weak. But I was weak. The dead man was weak. That's why he was dead. Ezzy was weak. Tyler was definitely weak. The land was strong. It supported all of our weak-asses.

# THREE

# EZZY

"Can you count down backwards from ten, sir?" the nurse asked. She put a mask with some sort of knockout juice over my face.

"What, you mean like just normal counting?"

And then everything went dark.

I woke up in a panic in an empty room, surrounded by empty hospital cots. I felt cold, the kind of cold that comes from fear, and my head didn't seem to work normally. Reminded me of those fogs I would get when I didn't eat much. I lay back dazed and looked down at my leg. It was wrapped up in a cast. I started touching the cold plastic and fiddling with the buckles.

"Pretty neat, eh?" A big white guy with long blond hair walked towards me. He looked identical to the pictures of Jesus that had been all over the social workers' offices back in my little-kid days. "Beats the old plaster casts. You can actually take this one on and off for bathing and eventually sleeping and such."

"Must not be in hell if I have a cast on," I said. "Probably wouldn't need one down there."

"Do you know where you are?" he asked.

"Edmonton? No, wait. Sherwood Park," I replied. "Just so used to saying Edmonton."

"You *are* in Edmonton. Do you not remember when we transferred you to the Royal Alex Hospital?" he asked. I had no recollection of that. "Sherwood Park doesn't have the capacity to do the surgery that you needed. What's your name?"

"Ezzy," I replied. He gave me a concerned look. "Uhhh, Isidore, Isidore Desjarlais." He checked something off on a clipboard. "Call me Ezzy, though."

"Okay, Ezzy, we're going to be moving you over to the post-surgery ward. A doctor will see you there in a bit and talk to you about your surgery."

"Fuck yeah, buddy," I said. *Why did I say that?* Everything seemed strangely funny. I giggled at the nurse's big dumb hair. Looked like something out of one of those eighties or nineties workout videos. "You know, when I was a kid, I used to love penguins. My grandpa gave me a stuffed one I called Me-Me. Maybe I'll turn into a penguin now."

"Maybe you will," the nurse said. "Oh man, I love this job," he said to some other nurse. "Okay, Ezzy, we're going to wheel you over to the ward now. Hold on."

"Giddy up," I said. I giggled again. Imagine a giant-ass penguin pushing a hospital gurney with another penguin on it. They'd just slip around in penguin hospital crashing into each other.

There'd probably be a great spot to go swimming and catch fish, and then, come visiting time, cousins from the mall aquarium would come over and slip around with them. *Penguin hospital is the best it gets*, I thought.

Nurse Jesus passed me off to a crew of other nurses who all looked like every teacher or social worker I'd ever had. A blur of short blonde hair spiked in the back and parted over the front, brown bobs. Guaranteed they loved wearing jewels when they got off shift. I was placed onto a hospital bed and they closed the curtains around me. "Watch that one with the drugs," Nurse Jesus said from beyond the curtain.

I drifted in and out of sleep. My dreams filled with characters I both knew and didn't. I dreamt of sitting around with a family. People I had never met before. We were all laughing as some of the dads and uncles told joke after joke. I didn't know what the jokes were exactly, but I knew we were having the best time. A lady came out of the fog with a plate full of hot dogs and a plate full of ripple chips and dip. The dream switched and I was running around the park with a kid named Jesse that I lived with in a foster home once. We were playing grounders, but instead of kids on the sand underneath the playground, there were these giant worms, *Tremors*-style, that would swallow us whole if we touched the ground. Jesse kept tempting fate by swinging back and forth across the monkey bars while the worms snapped up at him from the sand below. He kept telling me to follow him. I looked down at my body and was ten years old again. A chubby little curly-haired kid without a mangled leg. I swung out after him and felt my grip slipping. A worm sprang up and grabbed my leg and pulled me down. My hands kept slipping. Jesse was yelling something at me. I tried desperately to grab back onto the bar, but I couldn't. My hands slipped, and the worm pulled me down into the sand. In the background, I could hear Jesse crying. Then I woke up.

Someone in the curtained gurney next to me started bawling. "It fucking hurts," they kept saying over and over again. I wasn't quite sure if it was a teenager or an older lady. My mind couldn't place their voice. The nurses ignored the cries and kept working. I wanted to go over and comfort whoever was next to me. But I couldn't figure out how to move. I was tied into a bunch of wires and tubes and machines, and anyway I didn't even know if my leg would work.

"Hey, I need to pee," I yelled out. A nurse came over to see me.

"Sir, please use the buzzer. Then you don't have to yell," she said.

"Sorry, I didn't know."

"We told you about it when you came in. It's okay. Here, I'll help you." She assisted me in sitting up. "Do you know how to use crutches?" she asked.

"Yeah."

"Okay, you're going to need to use these ones here to get over to the washroom. I can move the stand here for you." She gestured towards the thing that all my tubes and wires were plugged into.

"You should help that person." I gestured with my head towards the closed curtain where the sobs were coming from. The nurse gave me a look that told me to shut up.

"I'm going to wait out here. Call out if you need my assistance," she said.

I got myself into the washroom. I pulled back the nightgown and tried to pee but nothing came out. I kept pushing and pushing. I'd had to pee when I was lying down in the bed. I didn't get why I couldn't go now. I stood there for what felt like forever. My head started clouding over. I began to get dizzy. My hospital gown fell back down, and I leaned into the crutches. Pain shot through my leg and inched through my body.

"Isidore, are you okay?" the nurse called through the door.

"Yeah, I'm good." I turned around to leave the bathroom. Then I felt piss running down my leg. The warm stickiness shook the confusion out of my head. "Fuck," I said. I tried to manoeuvre back to the toilet as quickly as I could. The crutch tip went into the small puddle of pee and slipped, and as I fell pee was still coming out and soaking my hospital gown and getting all over the floor. My leg banged and the impact eclipsed all other pains that shook my body. I screamed until a nurse came in.

"Ah, shit," she said. She helped me clean myself up and then changed me into a fresh hospital nightie. Someone else came and started cleaning the floor. The nurse helped me crutch-hobble back to my bed. The curtained stall beside me had gone quiet.

They pumped me full of some drug. It killed the pain, and I fell back asleep. I dreamt my grandfather had wings, and in this dream, he pirouetted higher and higher in the air above where I sat on green grass fresh with morning dew. A pair of owls flanked him, and the three of them circled up until they became little black dots in the crisp blue sky. Then they would dive down at me and stop an inch from my face. I could see their blood-stained talons. They kept doing this over and over. I lay back on the grass. I could watch them do this forever. Then there was a noise. The sound of someone blowing long and hard into a trumpet. Like something from *Lord of the Rings* when the orcs or other villains came for the castle, or those RPGs we played in the homes. A warning. When it faded, two thousand crows shot up from the trees all around the clearing where I lay on my back. They swarmed together, blocking out the sun's rays. I could feel the heat and warmth leaving my body. The murder of crows chased after my grandfather and the two owls. From all sides, their screeching caws hammered into my brain. I tried to cover my ears. The crows circled up and up into the sky after my grandfather and the owls.

"GO," I cried out. "GO." The crows gained on them. The faster crows dive-bombed at the owls. My grandfather flew ahead of everyone. A swarm of crows surrounded one of the owls, and I watched as it fell out of the sky, a screaming ball of feathers and talons. The owl reached out as it descended and grabbed on to one of the crows and used its razor-sharp beak to tear out the crow's throat, and cast it aside. More crows started swarming the owl, and it disappeared in a black fury of wings. When the crows disbanded, the owl was gone. My grandfather was outpacing the murder. The other owl was falling behind.

"GO," I cried out again. Then all the crows stopped moving. They turned around in the air, and four thousand avian eyes locked on to me as I lay helpless on the grass. For the first time, they seemed to notice me. I watched as all the crows blinked in unison and then charged down out of the air towards me, talons and beaks extended. They wanted me to feel pain. I cried out again. The black dots that were my grandfather and the other owl flew out of my vision. The crows were everywhere. All I could see was black flapping wings. Then I woke up.

"You're going to need to stay off of your leg for a couple months," the doctor said. "You broke the tibia, fibula, and ankle. But you're fortunate that it was just bones and not ligaments and tendons. Those take a long time to heal. The surgery went well. As you can see here"—the doctor held up an x-ray picture—"we put a rod in the middle of the leg and a plate here and here." She pointed to the prominent metal on the photo. "And there are two screws. One here and one here."

"Shit, that looks rough," I said. "How long do I have to keep that crap in there?"

"Well, unless it really starts irritating you later, then probably forever. There's no need to remove it otherwise." She clipped the x-ray picture back onto the chart, signalling that the conversation was over. "Do you have any questions?" she asked.

"I'm good," I said.

"Okay, the nurses will arrange for your follow-up sessions. Take care, Isidore."

"Do you have anyone you can call to pick you up?" a nurse asked.

"Great question!" I laughed.

When I got discharged the next day, Auntie May came to get me from the hospital. The air cast cost a hundred bucks or so, and she paid for that.

"You're going to pay me back, you know," she said.

"I know," I said, though we both knew that was never going to happen.

Auntie May had already grabbed a pair of crutches that were kicking around the storage locker at her office. She brought them with her and gave them to me. I hobbled out of the hospital and into her car. We drove to the nearest pharmacy to fill my prescription for oxycodone and Tylenol 4s. Every bump in the road sent pain stabbing through my leg. May went inside and came out with the drugs. I reached for the brown paper bag, but she held it back.

"I'm going to give these out to you," she said. "You don't get to touch them."

"Please give me something right now. This is killing me." Even the shaking from the comedown hurt my leg. Any movement broke me. I felt like I would never feel anything but pain again. All I wanted was to lie down and let the world pass me by. Auntie May gave me two of the oxycodone. I put them on the back of my tongue and swallowed them down dry. We drove back to her house.

The radio DJs were talking about making a "Sexy Bison of Edmonton" calendar. I wondered how Grey had made out. I had been thinking about her and felt like an idiot for not being able to help or communicate, not that we would have even if I did have a phone. Grey kept it tight. It must have been days since she'd dropped me off. Time had become a blur. Grey and the bison had become a blur. I had needed the sexy bison calendar reminder to jolt me back awake and into the reality of what was going down.

"You heard from Grey at all?" I asked Auntie May.

"Not since she left the other day," Auntie May said. "What the hell happened, Ezzy? Are you going to tell me the real reason why you're calling me up with a broken leg?"

"I told you! I got hit by a truck," I said, which wasn't that big of a lie. A bison was a prairie truck in my eyes.

"Bullshit. Don't lie to your auntie."

I reclined my seat to try to get more comfortable.

"I'm serious," I said.

"You know I can tell when someone's lying to me, right? I deal with little shits like you all day every day, but at least they're teenagers and not grown-ass men."

I closed my eyes. Maybe she'd think I was sleeping.

"I also know that move." She laughed. "I was worried when I saw the hospital number come up on my phone. I expected something bad to have happened to one of the kids on my caseload. But nope, it's my nephew with a broken leg."

I opened my eyes back up.

"I'm sorry, Auntie," I said. "I'm sorry about everything."

"Don't be, Ezzy."

Auntie May smiled at me and I felt small. Here I was, a grown-ass man relying on the charity of family to keep me going. I was more of a burden to Grey and Auntie May than help. Working with Grey gave me a sense of purpose. I only ever felt like I belonged somewhere when I was with her doing something. If she told me to jump off a bridge, I'd do it. Big lemming guy right here. I didn't know how to express my concern about Grey to Auntie May. I thought about asking her if she'd heard about the bison or anything going on, but I figured it was better if she just brought it up naturally. I didn't want to drag her into anything that would jeopardize her. Auntie May was the only stable person in my life. If there was one thing I knew, it was that stability could get rocked down with one little thing. I didn't want to be that thing. Being a burden was one thing. Ruining someone's life was another.

We pulled up in front of the house. Auntie May helped me out of the car and onto the crutches. I slowly hobbled up towards the door. The old wood stairs in front of her bungalow seemed as intimidating as a mountain. *One step at a time*, I thought to myself. I wished I had paid more attention when the nurse gave me a talk about how to manage stairs effectively on crutches. *How hard could it be? They're just fucking stairs.* They were not just fucking stairs, turns out. They were a series of rope ladders rotting away over molten lava. Auntie May began laughing behind me.

"You remind me of a kohkum right now."

"I'm trying! It's fucking hard."

"Oh, this is going to be fun," she said between all the giggles. "Here, old man, let me help you out." She came up beside me, and I leaned on her and the railing as I hopped up each step. We got inside the house. All I wanted was to lie down and rest. I looked over at the stairs leading down into the basement where I usually stayed. Even worse than the ones leading into the house. They shot straight down the way they always did in old homes. And the only bathroom was upstairs on the main level.

Auntie May saw the look on my face, and her laugh started up again.

"Relax, I made up the couch for you," she said.

She had placed a couple folded fake Pendleton blankets on it. There were three pillows. One to elevate my leg on and a couple for my head. To me that couch looked like the fanciest king-sized bed in the penthouse suite at the Fairmont Hotel downtown. The royalty suite. I was a goddamn Métis king. I lay down on the couch.

"More drugs, please," I called out to Auntie May. She was in the kitchen, defrosting a frozen yogurt container full of moose stew.

"Nope. Not for a few more hours."

I looked around from my couch. I didn't know what the hell I was going to do for a couple months. The old television sat across from me. It seemed massive compared to every TV out there now. Thing still had a butt on it. I was sure May had got it from some thrift store years ago. I had never seen it turned on before. I doubted she had cable or anything. On the shelves underneath the TV, there were a bunch of old Disney DVDs and box sets of *Grey's Anatomy*, *The O.C.*, *Dawson's Creek*, and *North of 60*. Nothing great, but they would have to do. My throne of boredom, of more waiting around. But I had been waiting my entire life. A couple more months wouldn't do me in just yet. Hey, maybe I'd even read a book.

Sleep came and went. At least on the upstairs couch I could judge if it was day or not by the sun. If I'd been downstairs, I'm sure I would have lost track of that too. Still, with the drugs, the pain, and the fleeting sleep, I couldn't really grasp on to what day it was. Weeks or days could have gone by and I wouldn't have known the difference, and it didn't really matter. Time was for people with jobs and places to be. The only time I cared about was when I'd get my next fix.

"Grey stopped by," Auntie May said. She'd brought me a bowl of stew, a cup of tea, and some oxys.

"You're just telling me now? Why didn't you wake me up?" What was May's problem? Here I was, and all I wanted was to see Grey—didn't she get that? What the hell else did I have going on right now other than wanting to see my only friend in the world?

What would Grey think of me all laid out, though? Just straight pathetic.

"You passed out. Sleeping like a wee little baby," she said. "Oh, you were such a cute fat baby."

"You don't know what I was like as a baby," I said. "You were too fucked up." Her face dropped, the smile replaced by sorrow. "None of you gave a shit."

"I do remember," she said. She walked out of the living room and into the kitchen. "More than you would ever know."

"Auntie, I'm sorry, I didn't mean it," I said. I could hear her sniffling in the kitchen. I hammered back the oxys and took a swig of the Red Rose tea to wash it down. Why the fuck had I said that? Here was the one lady who was taking care of me and I couldn't just be nice. I stirred the stew. The chunks of moose mixed with lopped-off carrots and hunks of potato in a brown sauce couldn't have looked less appetizing. Could have been a bowl of vomit for all I knew. Normally I'd have gone to town on that bowl, but I couldn't bring myself to take a spoonful. Auntie May kept sniffling in the kitchen. "Fuck, quit crying already," I yelled. I pushed the puke bowl away.

I'd spent most of my life resenting my mom, dad, grandpa, auntie—all of them who didn't want me. My first memories were of anger, pure rage, just a red mind that didn't understand why I didn't have a family. I hadn't understood why my dad had run off long before I was born. Now I knew that he probably hadn't even known I was alive or that he had a kid. But try to explain that to a toddler who falls asleep every night to the sounds of the older kids being beaten in the foster home. All I dreamt about was a father figure who would protect me from the people I was forced to live with. I didn't understand where my mom was until a social worker told me with a straight face and no emotion that she drank so much she froze to death in a prairie snowbank one night long ago.

There were always connections for what the social workers liked to call the "kinship visits." Random cousins, my grandfather, Auntie May. But they also liked to try to limit those and keep us as far apart as possible. They knew that when kids ran away, they ran back to their families, or at least tried to seek them out. It was the same reason the government shipped kids off to faraway residential schools. If they were close, they could get back to their families. It made sense for the government to try to put a mountain range in the way, or a lake, or a forest, or towns filled with settlers who loved nothing more than finding NDN kids alone in the woods. We at least just had city blocks or highways to contend with. But there were still the same predators out there. On those court-mandated family visits, my grandpa and Auntie May would come and meet me in a park, usually with a playground where the social worker who drove me would sit on a bench and monitor our family interactions, taking notes the entire time. Before we got there, the social worker would tell me to make sure to be careful around my family. That they were unpredictable, that they didn't have their shit together, and that's why I had to live away from them. That made my rage kick up again. I didn't understand why my grandpa or Auntie May couldn't get their shit together to bring me home to live with one of them. And on our visits I would lash out at them or try to run away, and the social worker would just say that was to be expected. That we'd better get back to the foster home where I was safe so I could try and hide from the drunk man who forced me to call him daddy.

I was a fucking kid. It wasn't like I could figure out the legislation and the government's policies that prevented families from staying together. How does a kid comprehend those things? And it wasn't like anyone in my family on those supervised visits was in a state to explain it to me. How does a kid forgive his family when the government is actively trying to keep them apart? It's hard to remember my exact emotions or what I thought like when I was young. But I do know that I spent every minute of my time in those foster homes dreaming of the family that would come and pick me up and take me away to someplace better. I just never imagined that it would be my actual family that did it. I assumed it would be some white suburban mom and dad who would come swooping in, and I'd grow up playing recreational hockey and going to weekend barbecues. The kind of thing that I saw on TV, and what other kids who came in and out of the homes talked about. Middle-class lifestyles. Probably didn't even eat real baloney sandwiches.

I've never been able to recall or figure out the depths of my family trauma and the history and legacies that go along with that, whether for good or for bad. I didn't have the privilege that created a disassociation from it that allowed me to analyze it. That's the kind of thing Grey would have said anyways. I didn't know what analyzing really meant or why I would have to do it. I'm still trying to figure some of that shit out. Probably will be my entire life.

When I turned eighteen and aged out of the child welfare system, I did exactly what the social workers all expected me to do and went to find Auntie May and my grandfather. We'd always been in contact, but it wasn't until then that I truly felt like we could start building an actual relationship away from the prying eyes of child welfare and social worker judgement. For our families, someone coming back wasn't unexpected. It had been happening for years and just seemed an inevitability. Everyone went through one of the assimilation systems. It was just a matter of time until we found our way home.

"Grey said she'll be back later. She was going to check on a few things in the city," Auntie May said. She came back into the room with a pot of tea, refilled my cup, and then sat down on a chair across from me. Her eyes were puffy and red from crying. "Don't you ever say that I didn't care."

"I didn't say that."

"Yeah, you did, even if those weren't your exact words." She looked at me. No hiding the anger and pain behind her eyes. "And just so you know, we loved you with all our hearts. Don't you ever insult the memory of my sister and father by saying that we didn't."

I closed my eyes. I wondered how many more months would I have to lie here.

"You were your mother's whole world. All she ever wanted was a child like you to love and hold and be close to. She wanted to give you the life that she . . . well . . . all of us, could never have."

"Then why didn't that ever happen?" My leg twitched. Pain. "Why did I never get a chance to truly meet her?" I had no recollection of my mother. Auntie May had a few photos lying around, but they may as well have been of a stranger.

"I'm going to tell you a story. Maybe it'll sink into that thick skull of yours that sometimes things happen that aren't anyone's fault. You don't have to blame me, or your mom, or your dad, or anyone. You've never asked about your mother, always trying to be too tough of a kid. But I'm going to tell you so that you can have some story to grasp on to. So you know what really happened. She'd want that for you," Auntie May said. I picked up my teacup. The smell of the black tea, the familiar routine of sipping it, brought me some comfort.

"Your mother went to a party, just like any other twenty-four-year-old would do. She drank too much, and she died of exposure. That was it. If it was the summer, she probably would still be alive." Auntie May exhaled loudly. "I know the social workers and foster families and group homes told you she was just another dumb, drunk Métis woman. But she was not that. Not at all. She wanted to give you a different future. She worked for a cleaning agency during the day and took courses at night to get her high school. She wanted to work in one of the office towers downtown doing books or accounting or something. When we were little girls, we'd stare out at the cranes as they were building all those towers. They were like nothing we had ever seen before. We'd sit on the front steps of our foster home and watch every day as new storeys were added onto them. Your mom thought it would be so cool to be up in the clouds. That we disagreed on. I've always liked my feet on the ground, thank you very much. I was worried that one day she would actually go into one of those towers and it would tip over." Auntie May took a sip of tea. "It's funny the things we're scared of when we're kids."

"Did you ever meet my dad?" I asked. I needed my auntie's voice to soothe me. To tell me the stories I never had a chance to hear when I was a kid. When I'd needed them the most.

"Yeah. He was just a young guy. I couldn't even tell you his name now. Well, we were all young. I don't think he even knew that your mom was pregnant or that you were born. Darrell maybe? Derek? She wanted you all to herself. I remember asking her if she was going to tell him, and she said what for?"

"You ever see him again?"

"No, he was from southern Saskatchewan. Headed for a hard life, you know. I'd be shocked if he was still alive." I stared up at the ceiling. I tried to picture in my head what they would look like now, but nothing came to me. I had never been good at visualizing.

"You want to know something?" Auntie May asked. I nodded. She refilled my teacup again, and I took a sip. "I wasn't an addict before your mom died. Sure, I liked to go out and have a good time, but it wasn't anything serious. Just having fun with your mom and all our friends. But after she died, something snapped in my head. The booze wasn't just for having a good time anymore. It was to forget that she was gone. And when I drank, I started to remember all the horrible shit we had to go through when we were in those foster homes. Your mom and I were beautiful children, and those creepy fucks loved that about us. I had forgotten about it or repressed it, but when she died, it all came bubbling back to the surface. I think because we had always been together and able to deal with it as sisters, family, that it didn't seem that bad. But then she was gone. And I didn't have my older sister around to protect me anymore from all the demons that raced around in my body. Fuck I need a cigarette." She got up and went out onto the porch. I watched her through the window as she stood in her shawl, shivering against the cold fall wind.

I remembered the last foster home I'd stayed in. The people who ran it were strictly in it for the money that the government would give them. Me and the other two foster kids ate knock-off mac and cheese almost every meal while the family and their own two children ate these incredible steak or chicken dinners. My head always felt like I was in a fog. I couldn't concentrate at school, and it made me so angry that I'd lash out when the teachers made fun of me for not being able to learn math or writing. The other kids made fun of me for being a foster kid. I don't know how anybody figured that shit out, but they always knew. Every new school I went to, every program, I carried the weight of that label. *Foster kid.* That was enough to set me up as the one who got picked on in the hierarchies of elementary school and junior high until I'd finally had enough and dropped out. I must have been twelve or thirteen at that point. My first year of junior high. No one really cared. The school was glad to get rid of me. I'd have half-assed attempts from social workers to get me to go back. But they didn't care either. There were no Auntie May types in my life who lived and died for the kids they worked with. I just had a series of old burnout social workers who hated that they were supposed to take me to powwows, camps, round dances, all that shit. They spent more time talking about how long it would be until they could collect their pensions than they ever did asking me how I was doing.

I remembered the last foster home I'd stayed in so well because they had a dog. A big fat yellow Labrador retriever named Kevin that loved everyone and everything. The dog would come into the basement and lie at my feet while I played video games with the other foster kids. I'd always miss my starting boosts in Mario Kart 64 because I'd be too busy giving the dog pets. In the morning, I could hear the dog waking up from its bed in the kitchen. Its nails would tick-tack as it raced to come down the stairs. I'd lie in my bed, giggling, as I waited for Kevin to come bounding through the door that didn't latch properly and jump up on my bed and lick my face. Then I hit puberty and the foster parents got scared of me. I wasn't this chubby-cheeked, cute, curly-haired kid anymore. I got big. Fast. I've been the same size since I was twelve. Nothing scares foster parents more than that. So they got rid of me. It broke my heart that I had to leave that dog. But the social worker came and got me, and she knew that I could never go to another foster home. It was too late for me. It was group homes from there on out.

Last I heard, pretty much everyone I'd ever met in a group home was either in jail or dead. Not many people got out of the cycle. They were just training environments for a life of being institutionalized. The social workers and their assistants were basically just glorified guards. We were expected to join in on the routines that we were given. Kids were constantly smuggling in contraband cigarettes, drugs, booze, and weapons. Everyone was angry. There was no love in places like that. Auntie May told me that they were legally obligated to try to connect us to family, culture, history, and heritage. That was written into their social work legislation—those exact words, or something just like them. But no one ever tried to do anything like that for us, besides little token gestures here and there. Once a year, they'd throw us all on a bus and drive us out to an Aboriginal Day celebration and call it reconciliation. No one I knew had any clue who they were or where they came from.

The best thing that happened in group homes was the introduction of booze into my life. Right from the first sip of vodka, I knew that this was something I could get into in a big way. I fucking loved it. Booze gave me the confidence to start talking. When I drank, the people I was with became my friends. In the summers, we'd hide out in parks off the main drags and in alleys with stolen cases of beer and cheap bottles of wine and whatever hard alcohol we could get our hands on. We'd build makeshift beer bongs, and my party trick was to dump a mickey of vodka in one and slam it back. In the winters, we'd hit up the back hallways of the malls. Other kids came and went. There was never a consistent group of friends. We were all so used to when someone just wasn't there anymore that we stopped noticing. Another kid in a similar situation would replace them soon enough. Sometimes kids got shipped to other parts of the city. Some went to juvie, some got picked up by the fucking losers who took advantage of our situations. What could we do? We had no control. The only thing I could kind of control was the amount of fucked-up I could get.

Auntie May came back inside the house. She checked her drug schedule on the fridge door and gave me two oxys. I washed them down with the lukewarm tea. Instant relief swept through my body, and I curled up under the blanket.

"You know, I tried to get custody of you after your mom died. But the government wouldn't let me. They wouldn't even give me a chance. When I went to court for it, they pulled out the documentation that detailed how I grew up in foster care. They said that I wasn't a qualified parent because of that. I wanted to scream at them, 'You fucking raised me, and now you're saying that's the reason I can't take care of my nephew.' Hypocrites. They basically just admitted that their system doesn't work. But it didn't matter. They made their decision, and that was that.

"Not having you or your mother around in my life anymore sent me spiralling. Then I thought, if I can't have you, then I'll have my own kids. Something to replace the memory of you and your mother. Something to hold on to in the long hours of the night when I couldn't hold either of you. I thought about it all the time. The only time I didn't was when I was too fucked up to think about anything. Every day I walked around, wishing that I had a couple of little babies to hold on to. I wanted to sing songs to them because I couldn't sing songs for you.

"Then I got pregnant. I stopped getting fucked up as soon as

I learned. I wanted my baby to be strong. Just like his auntie, just like you were when you were born. When I went into labour, I was so excited to meet my new family. And I had twins, if you could believe it. My family doubled just like that. I didn't even know I was going to have twins until they came. But I never even got to hold them. The hospital nurses had said I was fucked up with booze and drugs, but that was a lie. I was dead sober. They called the social workers. And the same as with you, they pulled my file, my police record, and didn't even give me a chance. I never even got to hold them." She burst out sobbing. I didn't say anything. She had a good cry for a couple of minutes, then sniffed back the tears and snot and started laughing. "So if you say some bullshit like that again I'll break the other leg. You hear me?"

I had never heard this before. I never knew Auntie May had kids. We had never spoken about something like that before and it had never occurred to me that would have been a thing. It was like that with a lot of families and people I knew. Nobody mentioned the ones who'd left when they were young. Too much pain there.

All night I drifted in and out of restless sleep. I'd wake up in a cold sweat, bracing my lower leg with every movement, and reach out for the pills that Auntie May had left on the little table beside the couch. Anything to kill this feeling. She'd only put two oxys out. I took both the first time I woke up and regretted it immediately when I woke up the next time and didn't have anything. I thought about getting up and tearing through the kitchen cupboards and bathroom to look for where she'd hidden the bottle. But the thought of trying to stand and the pain that would come with it kept me couchbound. At one point, Grey came into the house. Not in her physical form, though. She was a magpie showing off her iridescent purple and green feathers as she walked by me. At least I think she did. She may have just been silently hopping into the kitchen, looking for crumbs from Auntie May's cooking. I wanted the magpie to come over and wrap me in her wings and carry me out of the house to the top of the tallest downtown tower where we could watch the sunrise together. I dreamt of my grandfather calling out to two black bears on a mountainside. The snowcap the bears walked on was slipping away, and my grandfather kept calling to them to come down. Everything tended to blend together in the darkness. I couldn't tell my hallucinations from the remnants of dreams. I woke up with the chills again. Grey brought me over a cup of coffee from the kitchen.

"I dreamt you were here. But you were a magpie," I said. She started laughing. I couldn't tell if she was real or not. There was a subtle fade between reality and the drug-induced dream world I had been existing in.

"I'd never be a magpie, you know. I'm more of a raven," she said.

"Tall, dark, mysterious, yeah, I can see that." I took a sip of the coffee. It helped calm me down. "Where's Auntie?" I asked.

"She's at work," Grey said.

"What time is it?"

"Eleven or so. You conked out."

"I haven't been sleeping well. It's the fucking pain. Keeps waking me up."

"The drugs don't help either. Those things numb and then increase," Grey said. "Here." She passed me two more oxys.

"Where'd you get those from?"

"Auntie May gave them to me. Don't you even think about trying to find them."

I struggled to sit upright on the couch, then stood up on my good leg and grabbed the crutches that were leaning on the side table. I hobbled off to the washroom. Grey looked different. Not physically or anything. Maybe she was just tired.

"What happened with the bison?" I asked when I got back to the couch. I resolved to sit upright. I was sick of lying down all the time.

"Long story," Grey said.

"I got nothing but time."

She pulled up a news article on her phone. She passed it over to me to read.

*New Bison Herd Shows Up in Terwillegar Park*. I smiled and looked up to catch her eyes. She ignored me and stared out the window.

*Another bison herd showed up in Terwillegar Park. Early riser dog walkers noticed eleven bison eating grass in the main field and reported it to the authorities. Pete McGup, the Manager of Parks and Recreation, urged caution when going to the park. "Bison are dangerous, wild animals. Please avoid the areas they are in, and if you do find yourself around one, please give it space and respect." The city is urging citizens to avoid the park until further notice.*

"How many did we have in the truck again?" I asked.

"Twelve," Grey said.

"Did one of them get lost or something?"

"Something like that." Grey stared out the window. I kept trying to make eye contact, but she just ignored me.

"What's wrong?"

"I have something to do. I'll be back later?"

"What are you doing? Can I come with you? I need to get out of here." But she had fled out the door before I could finish asking, and from the couch I watched her hop in her CR-V. The tires kicked up gravel from the street as she hammered the gas and sped off. *Fuck was that about?*

I propped myself up with the crutches and moved over to the window and stared down the road, half expecting her to turn around. Was it because I'd broken my leg and she'd had to deal with everything by herself? She had lots of experience unloading bison and cows—I don't think she'd even really needed me there the first time. Maybe just for some comic relief. I crutched my way into the kitchen. Auntie May had my pill schedule written down on the fridge. One to two every six to eight hours or so. She had even noted the time she'd given Grey the other ones to give to me. But it wasn't like Auntie counted from the bottle or anything. She didn't have any idea how many were in there. When they ran out, she could just go and get my prescription refilled. It's not like any doctor gave a shit if I was sticking to the schedule written on the stupid bottle. It was all just money to them.

In the distance, I heard sirens wailing away. I thought of Grey speeding off and briefly worried she'd gotten in a crash. Then I reminded myself that sirens were a constant in Auntie May's neighbourhood. Grey could take care of herself. I could also take care of myself. I didn't need anyone to regulate my pill schedule. I knew my body and when I needed them. They didn't know anything.

I began ripping through the kitchen cupboards looking for the pill bottle. I opened the fridge, freezer, even checked the cutlery drawer. When I got to the bathroom, there were other pill bottles of Auntie May's in the medicine cabinet and the T4s that the doctor had prescribed me to ease off the oxys. I took two and stashed a few more in my sweatpants pocket in case I couldn't find the hard pills. I put the bottle back and headed to May's bedroom. There was nothing on the top of her dresser except for a couple bundles of sage, an abalone shell, and a pack of cigarettes wrapped in ribbon.

I avoided the mirror hanging above the dresser and went to the bedside table. I opened the drawer and saw a blue vibrator and slammed it back shut. *Fuck me*, I thought. I started laughing. Grey would love this story. I shook my head and let out a half howl. I didn't need any more pills. I looked up and saw my reflection in the mirror. It was bad. I had big bluish-black circles under my eyes and it looked like I hadn't eaten in weeks. My cheeks, usually a bit chubby, had swallowed in on themselves, exposing a bit of jawbone. A scraggly and terrible goatee had appeared on my chin and made me look like a bass player in a nineties rock band, just like that guy from Limp Bizkit. I realized I hadn't looked at myself since before I broke my leg. My eyes didn't have anything left in them. I looked away from the mirror after a half second. I had seen too much. And Grey wouldn't love this story. She would hate to hear about me scrounging around in my auntie's house trying to find pills, broken leg or no broken leg. I hobbled back to the couch.

I turned the radio on to Windspeaker. *"Hey, this is Dave Cardinal. I'm your host of* Conversational Cree *brought to you by Windspeaker radio. Today we'll learn how to count to ten."* Dave Cardinal. I wondered if he was related to Tyler. There was that old saying—you could throw a rock down 118th Avenue and it would hit a Cardinal. *"Peyak. One. As in peyak nitotem. My one friend."* Another voice chimed in on the program: *"One friend, pffffttt, you don't even have that. Peyak atim—one dog, maybe."* They laughed at each other. I started laughing with them.

*"I thought you were my friend?"* Dave said to his co-host. *"At least you said you were when cows and plows came in."* They both burst out laughing even harder. I could get into this. It took them an hour to count to ten because Dave would give an example, and then his co-host bugged him about it. I made a mental note that the program came on the radio at eleven in the morning. I'd make sure to turn it on again the next day.

When Auntie May got home from work that night, I waited for her to confront me about the pill bottle, but she didn't even notice I'd gone into her bedroom. I felt pretty shitty about looking for the oxys; I just wanted the pain to go away so I could get back to whatever the hell it was I was supposed to do. I really couldn't figure it out. The chances of anyone hiring an ex-convict to do anything meaningful were slim. And I couldn't see myself grunting away in concrete or scaffolding or something like that. It wasn't worth the money. I'd rather just go and camp out in the River Valley if it came down to it. I had done enough of that with the group homes as a teenager. I didn't mind the idea of sleeping in a makeshift tarp-town tent. Winters would get long, but it would beat someone yelling at me because I didn't swing a hammer hard enough.

"I was thinking about our conversation yesterday," Auntie May said. She sat down in the old pink lazy boy recliner by the couch. "Oh god, you stink. We need to get you showered up."

"I smell like saskatoon berry pie," I said.

"No, you don't," she replied. Then she went serious. "I know where my kids ended up. The ones that were taken away from me all those years ago." She paused and took a couple deep breaths. "They ended up in a suburb way down on the southside of the city. So far south, they may as well be in Calgary." She laughed. "They're old now. Twenty-two. The same age I was when I had them. They both graduated from university this year."

"How do you know?" I asked.

"I googled them," Auntie May said.

I laughed. "No, ha. How did you find them, I mean?"

"*Oh.* My friend who used to work with me. She pulled my old file when she transferred over to the ministry and was able to find their assigned file numbers from that, and she grabbed them. Her bosses definitely would have fired and probably charged her if they'd found out."

"Whatever. Fuck 'em," I said.

"Exactly. Anyways, that was a few years back now. I went and crept the house they were living in. Big house. I had never been to a neighbourhood like that before. It didn't have alleys. There was nowhere to park your car because of driveways. It was right on a lake that you could go swimming in and everything. Super-fancy place."

"Hey, we used to go swimming in Rundle Park lake all the time. That was fancy," I said.

"That's not fancy. You get the itch swimming in there. Greasy storm pond. This lake has like a turbo thing that kicks up the water, so you don't get the itch," she said.

"Okay, I get it," I laughed. "Rich place. Did you talk to them?"

"No."

"Why not?" I asked. "You're always talking about how the kids you work with need to connect back with their families and communities."

"It's different. I didn't want to take away from what they have now." Auntie May lit a cigarette inside. Something she never did. "I didn't want them to have to learn all about this." She waved her hand around the room. The smoke trailed behind her movements.

"You should meet them," I said.

"Maybe someday. Not now. I have a big sucky baby on my couch already. I don't need any more." She laughed and then stood up and walked out onto the porch to finish her cigarette.

# FOUR

I couldn't stand looking at Ezzy. His body writhing in pain through sweaty, disturbed sleeps. He was banged-up on the couch. I didn't know if he would ever walk normally again. There was always that chance. And I had fucking killed someone and let a bison die. Some government people would just load the bison onto a truck and bring them back. The bull had died for nothing.

That guy, though?

I thought I'd feel something about killing him, but I didn't. He'd lost his humanity when he shot the bison. The rapey shit was just clichéd. But killing the bison had brought him down to the same level he'd put me. Fucking loser. I was glad he was dead. People like that didn't deserve to be on the same territory as the bison. They never had and they never would. Growing up and helping with the farm work, you got numb to certain elements of the butchering and slaughtering process. That's how I felt. Though I didn't think I'd ever be numb to the bison, and I didn't think anyone in any generation of our family would have either.

I started driving. I wasn't sure where I was going to go. I didn't have any friends I felt comfortable enough calling up. I didn't want to go into the River Valley and see the herds. I doubted the cops or anyone looking into it could pin or place anything on me directly, so I thought about going down and joining the protestors. Probably safer anyways. But I also knew a lot of the people down there. I didn't want to chat with them or talk about bison anymore, read about bison, see bison. All I wanted was for them to join the River Valley and then forget any of this had ever happened. I went out on the Anthony Henday, the giant ring road that circled the city, and started doing laps. It took a full hour and a bit to go all the way around. When I was in high school, the small-town boys would drive laps around the three streets in Pembina Creek. I remembered wondering what they could possibly find entertaining about it. But as I started into my third lap around the ring road, I figured they'd been doing what I was doing now. Looking for something, anything really, to bring me back to reality, to a past I'd never had, or propel me into a future I wasn't sure about. Or maybe they'd just been cruising for babes.

I turned off towards Enoch and drove to Tyler's uncle's place. When I arrived, I saw that Tyler's 4Runner was gone, but his cousin's old Dodge truck still sat in the driveway, the door to the garage wide open. I could see his cousin working away on the shot bison when I pulled in. He looked up and smiled when he saw my CR-V, and set his knife down and washed his hands in an old 4L ice cream pail he had loaded up with warm soapy water.

"What's going on, Grey?" the cousin asked when I stepped out of the vehicle. I wrapped my arms around myself to shelter against the cold wind whipping across the yard. I started walking towards him. "Tyler's not here right now if you're looking for him. I think he went down to join in with those protestors in the River Valley."

"Yeah, I figured as much," I said. "How are you?"

"I'm good. Thanks for the bison, by the way. My wife is going to take the hide over to the school and do some teachings with the kids on how to tan it."

"That's good," I said.

"Holay though, they are big." He pulled off his black Oilers hat and wiped the sweat off his brow. "I'm used to doing up moose. But this . . . is a lot."

He had the cuts from two quarters all processed. Big chunks of meat that he could further cut down into steaks or ground up into burger or jerky.

"Need any help?" I asked.

"I've got it," he said. I looked at the bison. It was just meat. Red flesh. Not the living, snorting, stomping animal that it had been. I started walking back towards my vehicle, staring down at the gravel crunching underneath my feet, when the cousin called back out. "Actually, why don't you help me wrap up everything. I'm going to drop some of it off at the Elders centre later today. We can get that ready to go."

"Okay," I said. I looked up at Tyler's cousin and he gave me a look that said everything was under control. I hadn't butchered an animal since high school. Back then, I used to go hunting with my dad, and we'd cut up the deer or moose in the garage. I'd never had to butcher up any of the animals from the farm, only the ones from hunting. I think my dad knew that I had an attachment to the farm animals; he or his friends and cousins that worked for him would harvest them. Since we had a barn set up for butchering meat, people from the community would always drop by to use our equipment to process the animals they hunted. I remember being a little girl and standing outside as my dad tied a chain around the legs of a giant bull moose and raised it into the air with the tractor. The two old boys that had hunted it couldn't walk that well anymore, and they definitely couldn't bend down to work on it. So, my dad hung it up in the air for them to field-dress and skin out. He ended up doing most of the work for them, though it wasn't for a lack of trying on their part. They both had large families at home to feed. And moose still filled the freezer during lean times.

Back in my undergrad days, I went on a few dates with a white guy who thought of himself as a hunter. He spent good money on camouflage and different scents that were supposed to mask his or make deer attracted to him, and the sheer number of different pieces of gear that he had just to go out and hunt a deer made me cringe. The tarps, and sleds, and cameras, and different lures, calls, decoys, ammo, and the thousands of dollars put into specialty camouflage was ridiculous. Everyone I knew who hunted wore their regular work clothes—usually blue jeans and a flannel shirt—and carried some ropes, water, and their knives.

That was it. Besides the gun. That's how the aunties went out, that's how my dad and his buddies went out, that's how I went out, and we all seemed to do okay. For all this guy's talk and gear, he never did get his trophy buck. And he spent most of his time driving around in a truck, which made me wonder why he was wearing camo. His dream in life was to hunt a moose, and he was quite resentful that I had done so since I was a kid on the settlement. When I told him that my dad went every fall during the rut to get a bull, he told me it was bullshit that we could hunt whenever we wanted, but he had to wait to get drawn for a tag. I called it with him after that. Probably should never have got involved in the first place.

I walked over to the folding wood table Tyler's cousin had put the meat cuts on. The cuts ready to get cleaned and wrapped up in brown butcher paper waited in a blue plastic tub. I washed my hands in the soapy water he had set out and then picked up one of the knives lying on the table.

"Just sharpened that one last night. Should be good," he said. I took out one of the football-sized roasts that he had taken off the leg and began trimming away the silver skin and fat. That was usually what held the wild game flavour that people didn't like. "Feel the weight on that, eh? It could feed fifteen people."

"Crazy," I said. "I'm going to make it a bit more manageable." I sliced the roast into three different sections and wrapped each one up in brown butcher paper. I found a Sharpie over on the tool bench and wrote bison roast on each package with the year. "You can see how one of these animals would have fed a community for a long time," I said.

"Yeah. Just gorgeous, gorgeous creatures," he said. He had a front quarter propped up on the table and took his time working around the dark, bloodied flesh where one of the bullets had entered. I thought about the dead man. Did his body have the same blood clots hemorrhaging around the hole that the bullet had made? A shrunken cavity that exposed bone, flesh, and blood? I tried to concentrate on prepping and packaging up the bison meat. Once I had each package ready, I labelled it and threw it into a blue Coleman. When the Coleman was full, I dragged it over to the big freezer they had in the garage and loaded it up.

"I'm going to have a smoke. Do you want one?" Tyler's cousin asked me. We had been working away in silence for nearly two hours. He walked over to the old ice cream pail and washed his knives and hands. I did the same. The water that was once warm was now freezing, red sludge. "I'll get some clean water," he said. He brought the pail over to a corner of the yard and emptied it. The huge German shepherd mutts came running over from where they'd been lying on a flattened spot of grass in the sun, and licked and bit at the grass where he dumped the water.

"They're excited," he said. "They know they'll be getting some bones later today." He laughed, then lit a cigarette and passed me the pack. I hadn't smoked in a long time, but right then felt like a good time for one.

"How're your kids?" I asked.

"Big . . . Holay." He laughed again. "You should see Jeremy. He reminds me of my chapan somedays, and others he reminds me of a little rabbit just bouncing around. And Melanie is graduating this year. She's going to university. The band already said they'd fund her. Which is great, no way I could pay for it. Back in the day, nobody got funding unless you had some weird connection to the Indian agent, or the band manager."

"That's good," I replied.

"Can you imagine? My daughter going to university. Kohkum and Mushum would be so proud." His eyes started tearing up. "That sun, so bright," he said, and wiped the tears away with his sleeve.

"Sure, the sun," I said. We both laughed. I hoped that the university system had changed in the few years since I'd graduated, so that it wouldn't be smacking them in the face with colonialism all the time. But I knew that it hadn't. Still, it was a good way to meet other Indigenous people from all over who wanted to change the inequities in it. That's what I had gotten out of my undergraduate—an escape into a different world.

"Want to see something?" he asked. I nodded. We walked back over to the garage. He pulled out another Coleman from under one of the folding tables. Inside it was the most enormous heart I had ever seen.

"That's the size of my head!" I said.

"Bigger. The size of my head!" he said. "One of the Elders wants it. I'll bring it over to him later tonight."

We stubbed out our cigarettes and he went back into the house to get clean hot water. When he left, I opened up the cooler again. I had seen moose hearts before and cow hearts, but this bison heart was on a different level. One look at it and I could see how intense the animals were, how they were able to carry themselves over the prairie for such long distances, outrunning and fighting anything in their path. I thought about lifting it up, or trying to, at least. I wanted to weigh it. Then I heard Tyler's cousin humming as he came back to the garage with the water. I closed the cooler and got back to work.

We stopped when the sun went down. The inside of the garage shack wasn't insulated, so the fall chill had created the perfect meat locker temperature inside of it. If it was any colder out the meat would really start to freeze. Any warmer and it wouldn't sit well. I helped lift the two quarters that we hadn't got to up on ropes tied to the rafters. The whole shack creaked, and I thought it was going to tumble in under the weight. Tyler's cousin seemed confident in the structure, though, so I went with it. I helped him load up a couple of coolers' worth of meat that he would drop off at the Elders centre on his way through the townsite. I thought about hanging out until Tyler got home, but then decided that I didn't want to be around when he got back. Though if he wasn't here already, he must have gone straight to his job at the River Cree.

"I'm going to be back at it again tomorrow if you feel like coming by," Tyler's cousin said.

"We'll see," I replied. He got in his truck and drove off. The two dogs followed his truck to the end of the driveway and then turned around and went back to where they had been lying around all day.

I got into my vehicle. Bison blood had caked under my fingernails. My hands smelled like the earth and prairie grasses that the bison had eaten, with a warm iron scent layered overtop of it. I could use a shower. If it had been a few months ago, in the summer heat, I would have driven down to the river to go for a swim. The first ice flows were starting to build up now, though. Instead, I turned back out to the Anthony Henday ring road and did a couple more laps. It was well into the night when I drove back to Auntie May's house.

Auntie May was already in bed. Ezzy twitched away on the couch in his painkiller-induced sleep. I walked over to him and leaned down and kissed his forehead. His skin felt cold and clammy, and I tasted the sweat and salt of someone who hadn't bathed in days. I went and got in the shower and then went to bed.

Sleep evaded me. Animal metaphors had been rolling through my head for the last few days, and I imagined a lone caribou running from a pack of wolves until they pinned it up against an exposed section of pipeline. The last of a herd animal that had once roamed all throughout the mountains and foothills forests, now gone. I wanted to live as a caribou, but I was becoming more of the wolf: taking down bison and men. Sirens wailed throughout the neighbourhood, and urban coyotes answered back with their own howls. I didn't know what I was going to do anymore. Before, my plan had been to get another group of bison and then drop them off in a different park, maybe even shift my attention to some of the towns or other cities around Edmonton. But I kept thinking the city might start watching the parks more closely now since I'd dropped off the second herd. It was time to take it easy for a bit. If there was one thing my years of organizing had taught me, it was to know when to back off and when to attack. I told myself that I would tell Ezzy about the dead man and the bison in the morning.

—

Auntie May had made saskatoon berry yogurt bowls for breakfast and left them out on the counter. I picked up a note she had written that told me when to give Ezzy the painkillers and where they were. Auntie May had made sure to leave it up on the top of the fridge, just in case Ezzy came wandering into the kitchen. She had hidden the bottle of pills inside an empty coffee can on the shelf. The letter said to make sure he didn't see the hiding spot. If he did see it, then I was to just hold on to the pills until she could find a different place to put them. In her note, she mentioned that she was headed to court and would be there all day. I set the note down on the kitchen table.

I peeked into the living room. Ezzy was lying on the couch, a homemade blanket tucked around him except for his feet, which hung out the bottom. I remembered that he could never sleep with his feet inside a blanket, or socks, or enclosed in anything. *Ready to run*, he told me once. His eyes were open, and he was staring at the ceiling. I filled up two cups of coffee from the lukewarm pot that sat in the maker and threw them in the microwave, and watched him as the clock ticked down. He avoided my eyes. He still hadn't turned to the kitchen to acknowledge me yet.

"Morning, Ezzy." I sat down in the chair beside his couch and placed a cup of black coffee on the side table.

"Morning," he said.

"What's going on?" I asked. "How are you feeling?" He shrugged and kept staring at the ceiling. "Do you need me to get you anything?"

"I need some meds. My leg is killing me," he replied.

"You'll get your pills in a couple hours."

"What are you of all people doing subscribing to this stupid western notion of time?" he said. I saw his eyes turn up at the corners when he spoke.

"You're going to have to wean yourself off, you know," I said.

"Who the fuck are you to tell me that? If it wasn't for your stupid plan, I wouldn't be laid on this couch," he said. I sunk back into the chair. The coffee tasted burnt yet cold. "Fucking everyone's a preacher now, eh."

"I'm sorry," I said.

"This is worse than jail, you know. Worse than the group homes. This is the absolute fucking worst."

"I know," I said.

"No, you don't, Grey," he said. "You don't know shit. You're just a steaming pile of it, not the real thing, you know. When have you ever thought about me?"

"It doesn't—I don't think . . ."

"Are you sure? Cause it really seems like that's the case. Just another fucking pawn," he muttered. He tried to sit up, and I saw him wince in pain. Then he just resigned himself to lying down. "I just want this all to go away."

"What can I do?" I said.

"Get me those pills."

"I can't do that. You know I can't do that."

"Then make something happen."

I didn't say anything. Tyler's cousin would have started butchering the second half of that bison by now. I could just leave and drive out there and help him. Or I could drive back to Pembina Creek and stay with my parents for a while, or I could go to Vancouver and never come back to this fucking city. We sat there for a long time. Ezzy never once looked over at me. He kept his stare pinned to the ceiling until he closed his eyes.

"I have to tell you something," I said.

"What?" he asked.

"A man came to my uncle's old place when I was parked there waiting for darkness."

Ezzy looked over at me for the first time that day. "Was he driving a blue truck?" he asked.

"Yeah." I responded. *What the hell? How did he know that?*

"Fuck me," he said. "I got in a fight with that guy at a gas station a couple days after we moved the first herd of bison."

"You what?" I asked.

"He picked me up at the driveway going into your uncle's place. Then he tried to hustle me for cash. So I beat him up a bit. Nothing serious, though."

"Are you fucking kidding me?"

"Huh? What?"

"He's fucking dead. That's what happened. He showed up in the yard and tried to rape me. Then you know what he did? He killed one of the bison. He shot one in the trailer. And then he tried to kill me."

Ezzy sat there, staring at me. He didn't say anything.

"So I fucking shot him. And now he's dead. He's fucking dead. The bison is dead. He's dead. Everyone is fucking dead." I could feel tears welling up. "All because you couldn't control your fucking anger."

"Grey . . . I—"

"No, enough. My uncle's trailer is gone, along with the bison, and I'm a murderer." I shook my head. "Did anyone see you fight this guy?"

"Someone at the gas station might have. I don't know. I didn't think about it."

"Did you know what happened with my uncle's trailer?" I asked.

"I wasn't sure. I mean. I don't know."

"It sounds to me like you did know. You knew that someone was out there, angry enough to burn down a fucking trailer, and you didn't think to tell me?"

"I didn't realize . . . I just didn't think it would go any further than that."

"Well, it fucking did." I got up and left the house. My hands fumbled for the keys in my pocket. I shook so hard I dropped them on the gravel. I reached down, picked them up, unlocked the car, took a deep breath, and began heading towards Enoch. Then I changed my mind and went towards the river. I couldn't believe Ezzy hadn't told me about the man. He'd known who burned down the trailer. I would never have gone back there if I had known. How could he have been so stupid? He of all people should have known that things don't just end. That people always come back for revenge. You can't just beat up a fucking guy at a gas station and expect it to be over. I would have even driven out and rammed that vehicle off the road if I had known that someone was coming after us. After him. Whatever. I slammed my fists into the steering wheel. The horn honked, and the people in the car next to me turned to watch as I kept punching away, each blow accompanied by a beep. They drove away when the light turned and left me hammering away on the horn by myself, stalled at the intersection.

I parked at the same spot overlooking the River Valley that Ezzy and I had stopped at after I found him at the halfway house. That felt like such a long time ago now. I wondered why I'd bothered contacting him. He would have been content to play cards and drink coffee forever, or until he was deemed a successful candidate for re-entry into society and moved out on his own. From this vantage point, I could see the protestors set up farther down in the River Valley. There were significantly fewer of them now. The main crowds had dwindled after the first few days. Now the organizers would put a call out for people to come down if something was happening. To witness the authorities, how easily they could just move those bison out. But for city councillors who had built their election platforms on the joke of reconciliation, it wasn't that simple. They'd have to make it seem like it was an Indigenous idea or else it wouldn't work, especially here. My friends in university liked to call it an NDN city. When I toured around a few years back, I'd noticed prairie cities like Saskatoon, Regina, Winnipeg, they were NDN cities too. But if you went to Toronto or Montreal or Vancouver or Calgary, it wasn't the same. Those cities were content with artwork and trivializing the populations whose land they'd imposed on. In NDN cities, we were starting to have an active voice in city politics, and in this NDN city in particular, they really wanted to appear progressive. Because of that, our stupid bison idea might just work out.

That's probably why I'd gotten Ezzy involved. He wouldn't question, or get in the way, or try to take it over. He'd just do what

I asked and not think twice. But then he'd also do other stupid shit and not tell me about it, apparently. If he'd just told me about the dead man before he died, I would have found somewhere else to hide out and not have gone back to the trailer. Possibly. I don't know. I probably would have just avoided it. I think that was why I'd just never brought up the prospect of Ezzy meeting Tyler. Ezzy would have beaten the shit out of him if he'd made one of his little quips. He might not have had a western education, but he wasn't dumb. He could tell if someone was making fun of him or not. And if Tyler got beat up, it would start a whole thing; Tyler wouldn't just let something like that go away without his idea of justice being served, which probably would have meant the cops getting involved, and I preferred to avoid that. As much as people like Tyler liked to talk about abolishing the police, they were still usually their first call.

I used to come to this spot and study when I was at the university. At the time, I could see where a big osprey had made its nest overlooking the River Valley. It would soar in circles overhead of the North Saskatchewan banks, looking for fish in the clear fall waters. I could watch a bird like that all day long. I saw an eagle here once, too. At least I thought I did. It was a long way off, but it was big. I was pretty sure I saw the white markings on its tail even though it was way up in the sky. I'd had so many ideas back then. I still thought this world had a chance when it came to reversing climate change. I had believed the Land Back work we did made a difference. Now, I saw it as just another token gesture, something for corporate boards to eventually pick up on for their equity and diversity and inclusion policies. Now it was about survival. How one lived.

For the first time since I'd come to the city at seventeen, I thought about going back home to Pembina Creek permanently. My parents would be okay with me moving back in. I could wait it out and see if anyone had an old cabin or, worst case, a house in town that I could rent off them. People usually abandoned those places when they were forced into the city by age or for work. I could take up the kind of rural existence that I'd avoided for most of my life. The one that urban yuppies and NDNS idealized without realizing the work that went into living it.

I drove to Terwillegar Park. Tyler had moved other people over there for the protests, and they had a different vibe than the Dawson protest. I didn't see his 4Runner in the parking lot. He must have gone back to Dawson. At Dawson Park, people had rallied around the bison. In Terwillegar, the city couldn't control the flow of people, so they'd just decided to shut it all down and put up big blockades on the roads in and out for the time being. Same kind of move they would do when coyote populations got out of control and started biting everyone or attacking dogs. It was a park in a suburban area, for affluent people who wanted to stay close to the downtown core but still own their McMansions with massive yards and have enough space for their king-sized beds. People were pissed about the bison. They needed a space to walk their dogs and do fitness classes. When that was taken away from them, even if it was just temporary, they came out with the kind of ferocity that we'd tried to rile up in climate change protests back in the day. This was natural, though. Hard to force it.

One side was full of university-age students who'd set up barricades and signs that proclaimed BISON RECLAMATION and

LAND BACK. On the other side, a group of thirty or so were standing across from the protestors and screaming at them, mainly older white people in their fifties and sixties. I parked my car off to the side and rolled down the window so I could hear and see better.

"Fucking go back to your avocado toast, you entitled little shits," one of the counter-protestors yelled.

"You get that from *Reader's Digest*?" a protestor countered.

"You're the reason this world is so fucked up," another counter-protestor yelled.

Two hundred yards away, at the end of the clearing, I could see the bison moving back and forth through the trees and munching on grass. Oblivious to everything around them, content to just hang out where the food was.

"Get a real job, you fucking bums," an old white guy wearing a brown fedora with a feather in it yelled at the protestors. Very recognizable. I remembered him attending climate change protests and marching with us back in the day.

"Professor David?" one of the protestors yelled back. I watched as the man in the fedora turned red. People beside him picked up his slack and began pouring it onto the protestors. The racism, homophobia, and bigotry really ramped up. It was like any Canadian internet news article comment section, just spewing hate in every form possible. I needed to pull a CBC and turn off the comments on articles about Indigenous peoples.

I drove the twenty minutes over to Dawson Park. Protestors had set up semi-permanently with separate wall tents for food, health services, cultural support, and rest areas for everyone down there supporting the bison. The community here could rally pretty hard. A couple cops and bylaw officers watched from across the road. There were no counter-protesters here, which kind of surprised me because of the wealthy houses in the neighbourhood. I didn't recognize anyone, though I hadn't recognized anyone at Terwillegar, either. Everyone that I had known from years ago was long gone to warmer climates, to attend graduate schools or work jobs with pensions and benefits. I hoped the protestors kept it up. If the bison could establish themselves in the River Valley, that would be wild. The ones in Terwillegar might go back to the farmer, but I couldn't see why the Elk Island ones couldn't stay.

When I talked to biologists out there, they always said that they had to get rid of bison because the two herds were at maximum carrying capacity for the size of the land they were on. When I asked where the bison went, they kind of just shrugged. Some went to establish other herds, most went to the slaughterhouse. An old Leonard Cohen song that my dad used to listen to came into my head. *First we take the River Valley, then we take Berlin.* Seeing the setup made me want to get out of my vehicle and join in. I hadn't felt that for such a long time. It took everything I had to stay at a safe distance and just watch the goings-on, but what I saw there encouraged me. It looked like they were working seamlessly together. I knew from experience that there would always be some drama happening behind the scenes. Even that had a place, though. People always got incredibly emotional when they invested their energy into a cause and the stakes were high. I myself was guilty of starting drama many times. But if I joined back in, I wouldn't have to think about Ezzy, or the bison, or the dead man.

It was easy to lose your responsibilities for a cause. People did it all the time, throwing away all that life put in the way and justifying it because they were helping out for the greater good. I knew that everyone burned out. I'd seen it happen so often. The balance of life and protest was a hard thing to achieve. I hadn't been able to do it, and part of me felt like that was okay because it could make me forget.

I didn't see Tyler or his 4Runner at Dawson, either.

Ezzy. I didn't know if I'd be able to forgive him. I wanted to punch him, or break his other leg. Anything to get back at him. What would have happened if the two of us had been in that trailer when the dead man lit it on fire? Shoot me any day over getting burned alive. What a terrible way to go. Though I guess it doesn't really matter. Death is just death. My phone buzzed. It was a text from Tyler:

*Hey! How are you? My cousin and I are going to drop the meat off in the community. Want to come over after? Like 2ish?*

*Sure,*

*Okay sweet. I'll see you then* ☺

Emoticon happy face? *Since when did Tyler use emoticons?*

"Where is your uncle, anyways?" I sat down with a cup of tea on the same couch that Tyler had slept on a couple nights back.

"He's in Saskatchewan. An Elders gathering at the university or something," Tyler said. He sat down in an armchair across from me. His uncle had a massive flat-screen TV that dominated one wall. Beside it, an eagle statue sat on top of a cat climbing tree. On the wall hung school pictures of Tyler and all his cousins throughout the years. I'd looked through them all in detail back when we dated. I found the spot on the wall where Tyler's Grade 12 graduation photo hung.

"Awh, look at little preppy boy T," I said. In the photo, Tyler had a short ski-jump haircut. "I'm surprised you didn't have frosted tips."

"Frosted tips haven't been cool since the nineties, Grey."

"They're still cool up in Pembina Creek," I said. "I was thinking of getting them done, actually." I instinctively reached into my pocket to grab my phone. It wasn't there. I must have left it out in my SUV.

"That would be a good look for you. Switch it up a bit."

I leaned back into the couch and took a sip of tea. The warmth felt good. Outside I heard the German shepherd mutts start barking. I turned to look out the front window. They were chasing off into the woods after something.

"Probably a coyote," Tyler said.

"You gave all the meat away?" I asked.

"Yup. It's all gone except for what we left for my uncle here."

We sat there and watched the dogs rip up and down the tree line.

"Are you going to tell me where the bison came from?"

"I don't think so. No."

"People were asking why we had so much meat."

"Just tell them it was a donation from a local farmer," I said. "Someone who wants to start their own reconciliation journey."

Tyler snorted. "A forced reconciliation journey?"

"A bit forced. But not any different than anyone else's."

"So who shot that bison then?" he asked. I didn't say anything. Just sipped away at my tea. "Grey. I need to know what's happening. What if one of the RCMP hears about it? Don't you think they'll ask us questions? Especially if I'm already down at those bison protests, and now I'm giving away meat?"

"You didn't have to do that part. You could have just let your cousin do it," I said. But I knew that Tyler wanted the community to see him as a provider.

"It was a lot of work. I heard you came by and helped yesterday?"

"Yeah, for a bit."

"Why? Did you want to see me or something?" Tyler asked. He grinned and shifted his weight closer to me on the couch.

"Not particularly. I just wanted to see someone else less, I guess."

"Pay me back for helping you out the other night or something?" he said. It was framed like a question. But it was more of a request.

"Since when are you such a capitalist? You should really give back to the community, you know," I replied. "Not everything has to be a transaction." He kept staring at me. "Consider your payment the fact that I'm giving you an opportunity to meet new women."

"It's not like that anymore," he said.

"I don't believe you."

"It's true."

"I've heard that one before," I said. "What, did you think I was coming out to fuck you?"

"So why are you here?" Tyler asked. He was serious.

"I don't know."

"Me neither."

"You're such a prick," I said. I wanted to throw my teacup at him, but I didn't, only out of respect for his uncle's house. I stood up to leave.

"Grey. Wait," he said as I was at the door, putting my boots on.

"You know, if you were just a little bit nicer, then I might have fucked you. But since you're such an asshole . . ."

"Who shot the bison?" he asked.

"I did. It was out of control. I thought it was going to hurt the other ones," I lied. "You happy now?"

"These things happen, Grey. It's okay," he said. I was sick of his new calm attitude. Same bullshit underneath.

I got to my vehicle. Tyler didn't follow me to the door this time. Only the two dogs came back to see who was in the yard. I checked my phone. I had ten missed calls and a couple texts from Auntie May.

*Where are you? Answer please*

*GREY PLZ PICK UP*

*Ezzy is in the hospital. He OD'd. We're at Royal Alex.*

I drove as fast as I could. If Ezzy died, that was two men and a bison that I'd killed because of my carelessness. All within the last few days. Fucking poor Ezzy. The world never gave that guy a chance. If he could just stay alive, maybe we could start over. I could help him find a new path. We could get him thinking more about a future, maybe go to school, something, I don't know.

All the feelings that I had been trying to avoid came raining down on me. I pushed the pedal down. I could speed everything away. That lost pup in a garbage dump. I couldn't call or text

Auntie May and I decided to just wait until I got to the hospital to find out if Ezzy made it. If he was dead, then fuck if I knew what I would do. Auntie May had done so much good for the community and herself for so long. But this was the kind of thing that sent someone back over the edge again.

*Grey PLZ CALL*

I parked without paying and ran to the emergency room entrance. Auntie May was standing outside the doors smoking. Her face had turned pale. She was shaking. Years of hard living had come back on her. She stared at me as I ran up but didn't say a word. She held out her pack of cigarettes. I took one. We smoked in silence and stared out at the traffic coming out of downtown. In the distance, the office towers loomed with people probably looking down on us. A large digital billboard on the one building flashed an advertisement with three beautiful blonde women drinking cocktails at a downtown club. *See and Be Seen.*

Auntie May lit a second cigarette with the butt of her first. A couple kids in sweatpants and Hustle Gang hoodies wandered by and asked if they could bum smokes. May gave them a smoke each, and they ran off towards the mall.

"What happened?" I asked. Auntie May kept staring off in the direction that the kids had run.

"I came home, and he was unconscious on the floor. Barely breathing. He'd turned blue, his face, everything." She took a drag and the exhaled smoke combined with the cold air to create a vast cloud that rose towards the hospital's rafters. She shook her head. "The fucking idiot, he found the note I left. It was right beside him. I should have just texted you all of that."

I tried not to cry. I couldn't say anything. I should have put the note away. I didn't even think twice about it, I had left the house so fast. There it was, just sitting on the kitchen table, ready for him to figure out where the medication was that could make the pain and thoughts disappear.

We couldn't make eye contact. We stood there with the city hum buzzing all around until we finished our cigarettes. Then Auntie May started giggling. I looked at her, puzzled.

"I might have broken his nose when I jammed the spray up there." Her giggles intensified. "All that training at work . . . never thought I'd have to do it with my nephew."

"He didn't have the prettiest nose to begin with," I said. Now she burst out laughing, but then her laughs switched back to sobs. I gave her a hug. We held each other close. She felt cold. I wanted to warm her up so badly. "I don't know how much longer he had. If I hadn't come home, then he would be dead." I held her tighter. My own tears soaked the back of her coat.

"I'm so sorry," I said. My words muffled by snot and tears and my face buried in May's black coat. "I'm so sorry."

"It's not your fault," Auntie May said.

"It is. I should have hidden the note. I forgot. It's all my fault." And then I really started crying and blubbering. "It's all my fault."

"Grey, look at me." We broke apart from our hug. Auntie May's hands grasped my shoulders. Now I was the one who avoided her eyes. "Look at me, Grey!" she repeated. I raised my eyes. I wiped away tears with my hand. "Where were you?" she asked. A group of nurses in their scrubs walked by without looking directly at us.

"We had a fight. I couldn't be there anymore. I had to go."

"Go where?"

"To see the bison. I had to do something. I'm so sorry."

"It's okay. It's not your fault." And even though she said it, I still had the feeling deep down that she didn't believe it.

"Can we go in and see him?" I asked.

"He's sleeping right now. He's stable, though. Thank god we only live five minutes away from here."

"Thank god you got home when you did," I said. "I don't know what I'd do if we lost him."

"Me either."

We lit another round of cigarettes and smoked them right as the sun set, its pink and orange hues reflecting off the glass from the towers downtown.

"You should probably go home," Auntie May said. I nodded. We both knew that home meant somewhere other than the city. A place to recharge and get away from the chaos I had caused. We gave each other a hug and held on tight. I wanted her to tell me everything was okay. I didn't want the hug to end. We broke apart, and I started walking towards my vehicle. "Take care of yourself, Grey," Auntie May called out.

Moving back in with your parents in your late twenties was as depressing as it sounds. I had been on my own in the city since I was seventeen. Don't get me wrong, I loved my mom and dad, and the full-on thoughtful care that they provided, but three weeks of my mom barging into my room and asking if I was hungry started annoying me. And there was no internet out on the Pembina Creek Métis Settlement, so I had to drive into the townsite of Pembina Creek itself and park at the McDonald's to use their Wi-Fi if I wanted to check anything. I typically went there after supper. An excellent excuse to go for a drive and get out of the house, at least.

Besides those excursions into town, my days fell into a routine that resembled the summers of my high school years. I'd wake up in the morning, fill my to-go mug from the pot of cheap Nabob coffee my dad would leave on the burner when he left for work, then wander around the farmyard, checking in on the different animals. The chickens were still chicken-ing. The horses weren't the ones from when I'd lived there and they didn't give a shit about me, not like the ones in high school that would follow me everywhere I went in the farmyard, hoping for a chance apple or carrot. After my walk, I'd cruise through the books I'd left behind, mainly old fantasy and science fiction novels. There were a couple old textbooks I'd dropped off here after I finished my undergraduate, too; I'd read passages and snippets, but wouldn't invest the time into actually starting and finishing one.

My mom kept bugging me about some of the local boys. At first, she thought I'd come back because Ezzy and I broke up. She couldn't grasp that we had been living together in the trailer in a platonic friendship, and thought that we had to have been fucking or something; two people in their twenties didn't just live together. I insisted that I just needed a break from the city, though, and both my parents definitely understood that. My dad started leaving lists of chores to do around the yard and the house to get everything ready for the coming winter. I'd putter away at those in the afternoon, then I'd go for a walk through the back forest that bordered the farmyard with one of my parents' big farm mutts. I liked seeing the St. Bernard crossed with malamute and god knows what else ripping in and out of the trees. It was impressive how agile the 200-plus-pound dog was. My dad told me that, a few years back, it got in a fight with a cougar in the night and ended up killing it and dragging its carcass back to the house. When my dad woke up in the morning for work, there was the dead cougar outside the front door. He found Tiny sleeping in his doghouse, all cut up but no serious wounds. It took a strong dog to defend itself from a cougar one-on-one.

Mine and Tiny's walks would take us through white birch and poplar groves that mixed in with the dominant pine trees. We wandered down old game trails that moose and deer had carved into the forest. I thought about the thousands of years that these same deer and moose and their descendants would have walked through these same forests. Their trails probably didn't deviate that far. I thought about my own family, and how my ancestors had walked similar trails over countless generations, even the same ones I was walking now. This was as home as you could get. The land held all our footsteps, and would continue to hold the generations' to come. Eventually Tiny and I would end up at the Pembina Creek, the body of water the settlement and town were named after. Back in junior high and high school, this had been my cousins' and friends' and my swimming hole. We'd sneak coolers and Old Style Pilsners out of our parents' places and come down here to lie around in the sun and jump off the cliffs at the creek's bend, where the water was the deepest. We always hit bottom, but it was deep enough that it didn't hurt. I didn't know if Ezzy had ever been swimming in his entire life. He once told me a story about swimming in the legislature fountains when he was a kid attending inner-city youth camps. They couldn't afford to take the kids to the pools, so they would just bring them to the fountains around town instead. I asked him if that had been weird and he just shrugged and said it was the way it was. No one thought twice about it.

We'd sit down at 6 p.m. for supper every night. My mom was a big fan of the "meat, starch, vegetable" style of cooking. Spices outside of salt and pepper weren't a thing in her kitchen, and even then, those two were used pretty sparingly with the hunks of steak, carrots, and potatoes. That was supper. I craved spice, but then, I hadn't exactly been eating well, or eating at all, really, the last few weeks before coming here. Being back in my mom's overbearing food world, I could feel myself start to put weight back on. In the northern bush, you don't find too many truly skinny people. Everyone carries weight in some form. When I looked in the mirror, I noticed that my body was filling out more. I could grab my stomach, something I had never been able to do in my adult life. It felt good. Colour had started to come back into my face from all the time outside with the animals. I could have sworn my hair had taken on a different shine to it, too. Stress will take down a person.

I knew I had to move on. There was no way I could bring the dead bison or the man I had killed back, or Ezzy from his OD. Still, at night, when I lay awake in my childhood bed staring at the glow-in-the-dark stars I had plastered on the roof a long time ago, I couldn't get rid of the image of Ezzy dying on the floor from a drug overdose, or of the dead man's flesh exploding in a red mist when I pulled the trigger. I tried to tell myself that I couldn't have done anything different, but at the end of the day, it all came back down to my stupid plan. *I hope those stupid bison are happy*, I thought, then I laughed at how ridiculous it was to humanize an animal. I didn't know if it was worth it or not. There was no way to add it all up. There was no equalization. It just was what it was and I had to live with that.

One night, a few weeks into my home stint, we were having supper. "You remember Ian, yeah?" my mom asked. I looked up at her from the shake-and-bake chicken I had just been shovelling into my mouth. She liked to bring up random guys who were still single and about town. It was an almost nightly occurrence.

"Oh yeah! The guy who wore way too much Axe body spray back in high school," I replied. "Stinky Ian." My mom frowned at me. At the other end of the table, my dad ignored all of this and stared out the window at where Tiny was rolling around in the fresh snow.

"I ran into him at the grocery store the other day. He's a very nice boy. Did you know that he got a salary job at the mill? Those are very good jobs, you know. Right, Dave?"

"Very good jobs," my dad replied. He turned his attention from the dog to the second baked potato on his plate. He loaded it up with sour cream and bacon bits.

"Sweet, maybe I'll head over to his trailer after supper then," I said. "See if he wants to start making you some grandbabies."

My dad looked like he had started choking on the mouthful of baked potato.

"Grey. All I'm saying is that he's a nice boy and you should maybe go out on a date with him. He told me he'd be interested in that," my mom said. She was frowning at me. "Chicken?"

The wild part is that I actually considered going out with Stinky Ian. I would have done anything to get out of those late-night funks where I just lay there in a stew of my own guilt and what-ifs. But then the thought of trying to describe climate change activism and eliminating the global capitalist economy while distributing wealth to marginalized communities to him gave me a bigger headache than cheap body spray. I wasn't sure if I was ready to lay all of that down, forget about it, and roll into a nice lower-middle-class rural existence on the settlement.

On the nights when I couldn't sleep, I took to aimlessly scrolling through Instagram and Twitter. Not that I ever posted anything, or even liked or commented. But the algorithm hooked me in, and I kept wanting to see more. More memes about how shitty Canadian politics were. More updates about babies and houses from high school and university friends. More graduation and first-job posts from my activist friends who had long ago taken off for grad school. Those were the posts that got to me. If I had left after my undergraduate, I would be wrapping up a Ph.D. and most likely looking for a tenured position somewhere by now. Friends from my protest days kept getting jobs across the country. I started googling their names. I'd read through their master's theses and academic journal articles. I looked into the conference presentations they gave and the undergraduate courses they taught. A lot had changed since my undergraduate days. There were now Indigenous professors and thought leaders all throughout post-secondaries. When I was in school, it was still white men teaching about Indigenous history and governance structures. I went deep into it. After a couple nights, my doom-scrolling on social media shifted to different graduate program websites.

One night I was coming back from my daily walk with Tiny. We crossed over the hill and into the farmyard. At the crest, I looked down and froze in fear. My uncle's Dodge pickup was parked in the yard. I hadn't talked to him in months. Long before the trailer burned down. He had to have driven here from Grande Prairie, a good four hours away. I could only assume there was one reason that he'd come, and it wasn't just to drop in and chat with my parents. I thought about turning around and running back into the woods. I could probably get to town in a couple hours. But I'd have to hitchhike back to the city if I did that. Bus service had stopped coming through Pembina Creek years ago, and hitchhiking around here was a death sentence for Métis women.

I collected myself at the top of the hill. Tiny sat down and tried to fit his butt on my boot. I leaned over and wrapped him up in a big hug. He didn't like that. He shook me off and went towards the house and the new vehicle in the driveway. I followed him back to whatever fate my uncle had brought with him.

Inside the house, my dad, mom, and uncle were all sitting around the kitchen table. My dad and uncle each had an Old Style in front of them. My mom had put on a pot of tea. They all looked at once when I came inside the house.

"Hey uncle, how's it going?" I asked

"Grey, come and sit down," my mom called. She poured me a cup of tea. I grabbed a piece of bannock from the plate on the table and loaded it up with saskatoon berry jam. I pretended to inspect the dish that my mom had put the jam in.

"I really like the pheasants on this dish," I said. "And the cute little dogs chasing them."

"Grey, what happened to my trailer?" my uncle asked. I leaned back in my chair.

"It's gone," I said.

"And you never thought to fucking tell me? What the fuck happened?" He crushed in the sides of his Pilsner can as he lifted it to his lips. He wiped the foam from his dark moustache. My dad lit a cigarette. Something my mom had forbidden inside the house years ago. She ignored it this time.

"I didn't want to bother you," I said.

"I get a phone call from the fucking police. And they tell me that my trailer's gone and that there's a burnt-out truck with a body in it."

"Grey, what happened?" my mom asked. "You can tell us."

"Honestly, I don't know. I wasn't staying there. I drove into the yard one day and saw the trailer and the truck." I started crying. "When I saw the body inside the truck, I panicked and left."

"Why didn't you call the police?" she asked. My dad, uncle, and I all stared at her. My dad crinkled his eyes up, then went back to smoking and looking out the window. She took a sip of tea and leaned back in her chair, holding the cup in her hands.

"Why didn't you call me, then?" my uncle said.

"I didn't think about it. I didn't want to get involved in whatever happened."

"Fuck, Grey. They're going to be investigating it, you know," my uncle said.

"Let them. I didn't have anything to do with it."

"You can tell us if you did, sweetie," my mom said.

"I didn't. Fuck, how many times do I have to say that?"

"It's okay. We know you didn't," my mom said. She got up and came around the table and hugged me. I was still crying. My uncle didn't look convinced. He finished his beer, and my dad got him another one from the fridge.

"I still don't get why you didn't call me. I would have preferred to have heard about it from you rather than the cops," my uncle said.

"What exactly did they say?" I asked.

"Someone was out deer hunting. They followed the road back into the place and found the burnt-up trailer and truck. Then they called the cops."

"Maybe that person was crashing in there? I hadn't been there for a while," I said. If I told myself that enough times, maybe it would start becoming the truth. I sniffed back a snot bubble.

"Who knows," my dad said. His first and only bit of input into the conversation.

"Wait. Where was your friend Ezzy when all this happened?" my mom asked.

"We were staying at his auntie's place in the city. He was looking for work," I said. A lie. "It was easier for me to come and go from her place with that contract work I had for those farmers."

"If a cop asks, could she back that up?" my uncle asked. I

regretted mentioning Auntie May instantly. I didn't want to get her involved in this at all.

"I'm sure she could. Don't bother her though," I said. "She's got enough on her plate right now."

"What about your, uh, friend Ezzy?" my mom asked.

"He's in the hospital right now. At least I think he is."

"Why?"

"He overdosed on painkillers."

"Oh, sweetie." My mom continued her hug. I leaned back into her arms.

"If the cops ask, why don't I just tell them that I've been here the entire time?" I asked.

"I might not get the insurance payout then. I think there's some bullshit about having someone check in on a place every couple of days, or else your insurance isn't valid," my uncle said. The idea that my uncle had insurance on the place, that he had even read the policy, seemed wildly out of place. The guy only had paperwork for vehicles sporadically, let alone a random trailer out in the woods. I had been sure it was just an old squatting spot, road-allowance style.

"I don't know what to do," I said.

"We don't do anything. Let the cops do their investigation. If something comes up, we just tell them as little as possible. They'll try and throw all of us in jail if they can," my uncle said. "Fucking bastards."

"I don't think they would do that," my mom said.

"Really? Still just living with your head in horse manure, eh?" my uncle asked her.

"*Enough*," my dad said. "He's right. We don't tell them anything. Grey was at Ezzy's aunt's. Some weirdo torched it all. End of story."

"I better be able to get my insurance money," my uncle said. My mom stood up and went into the living room.

"What insurance money? That trailer was worth five bucks tops," my dad said.

"I might have already mentioned that my niece was staying out at the trailer," my uncle continued. "When they asked me, they didn't start out with the trailer burned down. They asked if I knew who was out at the trailer. I said, yeah, my niece is. And then they mentioned that it was burned down, and a body was found."

"So they know about me being there?" I asked. My head felt heavy. I wanted to rest it on the cold table.

"I guess they do," my uncle said. "Sorry. Shit, I didn't know. I was worried it was you that had died."

I lowered my head until my forehead rested against the table edge. I wanted to drive it straight though, just to feel something, but I couldn't. I couldn't feel anything.

The RCMP came by my parents' property the next day. I was sitting upstairs in my bedroom, looking at grad school forms and requirements, when two cars pulled into the driveway with their lights off. I had decided that I'd better fill out an application quickly. They weren't due until mid-January, a couple months away from now, but if I didn't get them done, I thought I might be stuck in Pembina Creek forever. Or in Drumheller or Bowden for murder. I didn't know how investigations worked. Would they be able to identify the body if it was burned up? Could they tell that it had been shot beforehand? Would they find fingerprints on the gun? Or did fingerprints burn away too? In my head, university kept me out of prison. The applications occupied me. I waited for the avalanche. I tried to concentrate on something so the questions would stop for a while. For the first time, I wondered if the man I had killed had a family or friends. If he did, had they reported him missing? Had anyone noticed that he was gone? I remembered the way his tongue felt when he licked my cheek. How badly he smelled when he pressed himself close to me. I'd shoot him again if I had the chance.

There were two Mounties, a lady in the first car and a man in the second. Thank god my parents were both off at work when they came by. They were still hurting from the conversation with my uncle. I saved my applications and watched from the window as the Mounties walked up to the house. I started downstairs to meet them. Part of me wanted to just hide away in the bedroom. They wouldn't know any better. They couldn't come inside without a warrant. At least, I thought they couldn't. That was how it worked on television shows, I was pretty sure. For someone who had put so much effort into the work of defunding the police and abolishing prisons, I really didn't know much about the daily procedures of either.

They knocked on the door. I opened it up and stepped out onto the porch.

"Grey Ginther?" the lady asked. The man stood behind her, trying to do his best to be intimidating, but his fat features just made him look comical, like a little sausage trying to squeeze out of his khaki cop casing.

"What can I do for you?" I asked.

"I'm Detective Janzen. This is my partner, Detective Harrison. We're with RCMP K Division," she said. "We want to ask you a few questions. Would you be willing to come to the station in Pembina Creek with us?"

"Am I being charged with anything?" I asked. I tried to remember the little info packets that the activist group used to make for front-line protestors. They'd had a short tip sheet on what to do if police officers approached you. For the number of them that I'd handed out over the years, I would have thought I'd have it memorized by now. But I still knew the basics of not giving them anything extra. Just simple answers.

"No."

"Then I'm fine right here."

"Can we come in then?" she asked. The other cop maintained his attempt at an intimidating posture. He tried to look angry, but his cheeks swallowed up his eyes.

"Nope, here is fine," I said.

"Okay then. How did you know Brian Krushinski?"

"Who?"

"He turned up dead at your uncle's trailer. The one that your uncle told us you were living in."

I didn't say anything. I wasn't going to respond.

"Was the trailer vacant?"

"Yes," I said. Fuck my uncle's stupid insurance money.

"So you don't know anything about why the trailer was burned down, and Brian's body was found in a burnt truck?"

"I don't."

"Are you sure?"

"Positive," I said. The lady RCMP officer looked at the big boy. She turned to me.

"Grey. Where were you staying if you weren't staying at the trailer?"

"Here or at my friend's auntie's place in the city."

"Is this friend named Isidore Desjarlais?"

"Who?"

"Isidore Desjarlais. Is that the friend with the auntie whose house you were staying at? And his aunt, that's Marsha Desjarlais?" I had never heard Auntie May's full name before. If this was a different situation, I'd have laughed. Marsha! No wonder she went by May.

"Yes."

"Would they be able to confirm that you were staying with them?"

"They would."

"Are you sure about that?"

"One hundo."

"Pardon me?"

"One hundred per cent," I replied. "Look, I'm very busy."

"You don't care that a man died out at your uncle's trailer? The one that you've been staying at?"

"I haven't been staying there. I already told you that. And I don't know anything about it. So yes, you're right. I don't care. I don't know who that person is."

"Grey, when someone dies, we need to secure justice for them," the sausage cop said, his first words coming out squeaky. I saw why he'd tried to present as imposing and silent. His voice betrayed him. His look did too. He was flabby and placid. The lady cop, though, she was ripped.

"That's a new one," I replied.

"Your friend Isidore. He has a lengthy criminal record, doesn't he?" the lady cop asked. I did my best to kill her with my eyes.

"That's none of my business," I said.

"It wasn't that long ago that he was released from prison. Do you think he wants to go back? Or do you think that he'd avoid it? What would he do to avoid going back to jail, Grey? We've already talked to him, and he had some interesting things to say."

"Look. I'm busy. If I'm not being charged, I'm going to go back inside," I replied.

"Thanks for your time, Ms. Ginther. We'll be in touch." They walked back to their cars. I tried my best to look stoic, like I didn't give a shit, and waved at them as they drove off. As soon as they got out of sight, I ran back into the house, up to my room, and jumped in bed and hid under the covers. I'd kill myself before I went to jail. I couldn't imagine anything worse than being unable to go outside and hear birds sing or feel the warm sun on your back. Jail was always a possibility, especially when organizing protest movements, but if I got charged with murder, that was a lot of time compared to public nuisance or whatever bullshit charges they threw at protestors. I needed to get a hold of Ezzy and Auntie May.

I sent Auntie May a text: *Hey can you call me when you get a chance? I need to talk to you.*

*Sure thing*, she replied. *Give me a couple hours though okay?*

I turned on my computer and typed out the rest of my graduate school applications with a fury. Maybe if I was able to get them all submitted, then everything else would go away. My drug had always been to work so hard that you didn't feel feelings or think about what was going on around you. I would throw myself head-first into Word documents and social media posts and organizing briefs, or writing speeches to be delivered at protests that I helped coordinate. I turned that energy into getting into school. I let them consume me. McGill, University of British Columbia, Toronto Metropolitan, University of Toronto, Dalhousie. A few former-professors-turned-friends agreed to send reference letters for me; they just asked for my proposal so they could write them based on that. Two of them sent emails expressing genuine surprise that I hadn't decided to go to graduate school earlier. One of them asked me why I wasn't applying to the University of Alberta campus in Edmonton. I ignored the question.

# EZZY

I could hear the last flocks honking south. It wasn't that long ago that the circling cranes that started the migration had spiralled overhead. The last of the big northern geese made their way across the rehab centre. After they left, it would just be the cedar waxwings, addicts in their own way for all the good berries lying around. The staff member out there, Joe, had told me all about the cedar waxwings, including what they were called. I only ever knew them as those little ones who moved from berry tree to berry tree in drunken flocks. They liked when the berries fermented and turned red. I just liked the noise they made and how it would break the silence of the snow on the land around the place. The staff shovelled out pathways through the grounds, and one of the staff found these little spikes to go on the end of my crutches so I wouldn't slip when I walked outside on them.

I liked the days at the centre. Good food, good people, good conversation, good exercise, good routine. I didn't have much of an appetite still, which was too bad because the cook knew what was going on. She was from Trinidad and would crank out rice and peas and jerk chicken on Friday nights. I had never eaten anything like that. She told me it was all in the scotch bonnet and the allspice berries, and however she combined them blew my limited palate out of the water. The people running the place talked about how we all need routine in life, even if it's something as simple as making the bed in the morning. I thought they might pull some AA shit and make us swear our lives away to Jesus Christ, but that never came up. I struggled to remember if my days on the outside ever had anything resembling a routine, or even a self-imposed one at that. I'd definitely had one in jail, but not a fun one. Wake up at six, someone counts heads. Get breakfast, go to work, go back to the cell, have lunch, get counted another time, go back to work or exercise, go back to the cell, have supper, get counted again, go to a help program or something, go back to the cell, get counted, go to sleep. The group homes tried to establish something similar. Grey and I had never really got in a routine at the trailer. I'd just wanted to drink Luckys and play cards and pass the days.

People liked talking about the bison at the centre, and there were regular updates on what was taking place. In our circle conversations, someone always mentioned how happy they were to see bison in the River Valley. They hoped the city would let them stay. Maybe even if it was just Dawson Park and they could make that an area specifically for them. But other people worried it would turn into some wild-animal zoo. I thought we should set it up so that the bison could be in the park forever. I wasn't sure how to do that, though. I guessed people would get used to them, but all it would take was one incident and the city would shut it down fast. Grey always talked about how bison represented the past before colonialism and settler movement onto the prairies. That their very existence pissed off the government internally, even if they didn't know it. That the government would prefer Indigenous peoples assimilate into settler society, rather than demonstrating there are other ways to live peacefully and successfully. In their minds, bison and Indigenous peoples shouldn't live on the prairies anymore. That was the whole point. They shouldn't be there, all modern and existing, and they definitely shouldn't be thriving independently within a settler society. But I didn't know how to make a space for the bison to flourish forever in the vast herds. We'd definitely need Saskatchewan, or at least central Alberta. How could we shut down farming operations and revert the land back to a natural state? Fuck if I knew.

I didn't tell anyone my thoughts, though. We all just wanted to survive. Us and the bison. It was fun hearing about something I'd helped create, and sometimes in the circles, I wanted to talk about what had happened but I worried I would sound delusional, and I didn't want people to see me that way. I knew the circles were mostly safe places where addicts could say anything. But shit still left the circles, and people had to be careful when they talked. And forget about the staff, who would have to report something illegal if I mentioned it.

Joe was one staff Elder I bonded with. We called Joe an Elder, even though he would never call himself one. He was probably in his seventies or eighties or something, but could have been in his sixties. He told us about his own journey to recovery, and how connection with and knowing his Cree community back in northern Saskatchewan and his roots from had helped him move through life. When I met him, we'd started bullshitting about our families, and it turned out he knew Auntie May from their social-work diploma days. From that, we figured out he also knew my grandfather. They'd spent a bit of time together on the outskirts of downtown. After our circle wrapped, if someone else didn't grab him for a chat, I would crutch my way over and sit with him. Early on, he began teaching me how to bead Métis-style.

"You know about the flower petals, eh?" Joe asked.

"Don't know anything about flower petals."

"They say a four-petal flower is for something sacred. You know, your tobacco pouch, medicine bag, something like that. Goes back to the four directions and the teachings around that. A five-petal flower is to represent the strength and leadership of the women in our community. And a six-petal flower, you know that one?"

"I don't."

"That's to look like a peacock of the prairies." He started laughing. I joined in. It felt good to laugh about something like beadwork.

"My stitches look terrible," I said. I held up the flower I had been beading on a piece of felt for practice. "They're all uneven and spaced out weird."

"What flower looks perfect in the world? Each one has its own quirks and personality, you know."

I looked at the flower he had been creating. All the beads lined up tight to each other. I couldn't see the hide or thread underneath the beads at all. Mine had so many spaces and white threads coming out each and every way. My needle had almost bent to the point of snapping.

"How many needles you break?" I asked.

"I go through a needle every five or six days, or so I guess."

"Wild."

"I've been doing this for years, remember? You've only done it for a week," Joe said. I was trying to tack down five orange beads, but I had too much thread, and it kept getting tangled up. "Your grandfather was more of a music man than a beader. He didn't have the patience to sit down and do this."

"Honestly, I don't know if I would normally, either. But . . ." I nodded at my leg. "This fucking thing." From across the room, one of the staff gave me a stern look. "Yeah, yeah, nice language, sorry," I said to them. They went back to staring at the show on the television.

"He had an old guitar he'd drag out to where we were all staying in the River Valley," Joe said. "I'm pretty sure it only had four or five strings on it. And he had taught himself how to play these old country songs from listening to the radio. We'd sit there and listen to him strumming and singing. Those were always good nights."

"When he used to come to pick me up for visits, he'd always have a song for me," I said.

"He loved nothing more than to change the lyrics to popular songs to suit himself. He'd always be replacing things like 'Arkansas' with 'Alberta' or 'me' with 'Métis.' Little things like that. But it made it fun."

"I used to be so mad at him," I said. "I didn't get why he couldn't take me back to live with him. Why I had to go live in all of those stupid places."

"Do you still feel that way?"

"A little. I don't know," I said. I cut the thread I was fiddling with and stretched out two arms' lengths of a new thread. "I'm really good at threading the needle, though." I started laughing. "That's what you said was the hardest part, right?"

"It's hard to think about sometimes. But we need to forgive those who came before us just as much as we need to forgive ourselves."

"I think I'm angrier now that I never got to learn anything from him. I never really got to talk with him, as an adult, you know. I never got to hear those stories."

"Your aunt would know some of those stories," Joe said. "They spent quite a bit of time together before he passed."

"Yeah. We never really talk about it. Well, a little bit about my mom. But never really about my grandfather or family or anything."

"A lot of people go through life without the connections and support that you have. Your auntie and grandfather loved you. They had their own battles to deal with. But nothing takes away that love. It's out there. It exists even if it's something we can't see or touch. Just having that energy and connection on the wind is what matters. It'll find you eventually."

Joe stood up from the table. He passed me the flower he had been working on. Five petals. Turquoise beads lined the outside and red beads filled in the petals. The centre was a deep yellow with one little orange bead tucked in for good measure. "What do you think?"

"Mmm, it's okay, I guess." I winked at him.

"Just okay? Holay. Guess my sweetheart won't want it then."

"What's with the orange bead?" I asked.

"Spirit bead, my boy," he said.

---

Auntie May came out to visit a couple times, but I hadn't seen Grey yet. In all the years that I had known Grey and been around her, I had never heard her once express a violent thought. Even when white supremacists came to the rallies to stir shit up, she would still advocate for non-violent measures to counteract them. I didn't have the patience for that. I'd beat them if it was up to me. But then, as many therapists have said, that was why conflict followed me around. Grey didn't think like that. She used to host training sessions for protestors on how to deal with conflict when it came up. Looking back, I wished I had attended one of those. Maybe things would have ended up differently then. Or maybe they would still be the same. Joe kept telling me about things happening for a reason. But I couldn't see why everything that brought me here needed to happen. He told me that I would know in time.

I thought about Grey a lot at the centre. I wanted her to know I was alright. When Auntie May visited I asked if they talked, but she never answered me, just said that Grey had gone back to Pembina Creek. I didn't have a cell phone, and my only email address was from junior high school, and I couldn't remember the password. I wouldn't have even known how to begin a letter anyways. What did they always teach in the job prep workshops? Start your cover letter with *To whom it may concern*. But who actually talked like that? I'd never once heard the word *whom* said in my life. I wasn't even sure what I would say to her anyways. *What's up? Leg's healing. Sorry about taking all those drugs and the redneck. Hope you're well.*

———

Detox was hard, and the transition to a lighter pain medication was even worse. I kept waking up with the shakes and sweats. My head was clear, though, for the first time in a long time. If there was pain, I'd just have to deal with it. Joe gave me lots of different plants for teas and poultices, and they helped a little. He told me that in the summer, when my leg was all better, he'd take me out and show me where they grew and how to harvest them. Nothing felt like the chemicals of oxys, though. That shit was potent.

Auntie May had signed me up for the ninety-day treatment plan. I couldn't argue. In the ninety-day program, one of the requirements was that in-patients worked towards a goal. Most of the people chose schoolwork or their safety tickets like H2S Alive, Confined Space, First Aid. I didn't want to do the safety tickets. Reading about social studies from a textbook seemed so far removed from what Joe said when he talked about the land

and how interconnected everything was. He encouraged me to do some work towards a GED, and Auntie May loved that idea when she visited, so I rolled with it. I still didn't see what good a GED would do for me, though. I told Auntie May it would turn me into a clog. A word I'd stolen from one of Grey's speeches. But Auntie May told me that if I wanted to stay with her when I got out, I'd need to either get a job or do a lot of volunteering over at the friendship centre, so GED it was. If I had to do it to keep people from bugging me, I was good for it. Might not pass, but I could try. The staff said I could get one in three months if I applied myself. That just triggered memories of all the social workers and counsellors who would tell me the same thing. Could just picture that guidance counsellor back in Grade 10 telling me that if I just did my homework, I could achieve greatness. I'd like to have seen him try to do something like that in the group home I was in at the time. We all knew that it didn't matter if we did our homework or not. Applying yourself wasn't the problem. Survival on the daily was. Still is.

The best part of the whole thing, though, was bugging Joe for stories about my grandfather.

"So you're saying that there used to be a reserve right in Edmonton?" I asked one day. We were back at the informal beading table in the recreation room. A couple other patients had joined us.

"Yeah, Papaschase 136. Southside, right a bit north of where Millwoods is now," Joe said. He was helping someone thread their needle. "Big chunk of land."

"Why isn't it there anymore?"

"Long story. But basically, the government realized the land was worth something, and they took away everyone's status who lived there, even though they had just signed Treaty 6. Turned it into plots of land to sell off."

"Where'd the people go?" I asked.

"Some went to Lesser Slave Lake, some to Enoch, Maskwacis, some to the bush north of St. Paul, Saddle Lake. Some stuck around Edmonton. It was pretty widespread."

"And my grandfather was a part of this?" I asked.

"No, it would have been his grandmother. It all happened in the 1880s."

"Do you know where my family went?" I asked.

"Your grandfather came to the city from north of St. Paul, so I'd assume that area. Every once in a while, when he scraped together enough cash, he'd leave and go back and visit his granny, who still lived up there. That was, of course, a long, long, long time ago now, when we were all still young men. Even if he had some cash, he'd still hitchhike up so he could give it all to his wife, your granny." Joe started laughing.

"What?"

"I don't think your grandfather ever had a dollar to his name. He'd spend it or give it away as soon as he got one. He wasn't big on money."

"Who is?"

"Need it to survive now. That's just the way it is," Joe said. "Back in the day, we'd trade in furs and bison meat. But those days are long done. Hey, what do you think of the bison in the River Valley?"

"I don't know much about it," I said, which felt truer every single day.

"Well, they said they're probably going to let the Dawson Park herd stay. But the Terwillegar herd is getting returned to the farmer."

"Farmer?" I asked.

"Yeah, they might even be gone already. I read that in the papers on the weekend. Turns out the bison came from a farm. It's a whole big thing in the media now. Apparently, they found a stolen vehicle on the farmer's property. So now they're trying to figure out how the bison were moved into the River Valley."

"You think it was the same people who moved the Dawson Park herd in?" I asked.

"Of course it is. Even the dumbest Mountie could figure that out."

"Wild."

"All I know is, if we let them, the bison will take the prairie back."

"Would that be a bad thing?" I asked.

"For some people, yes. For other people, no."

Joe would ask me how my schooling was going. All my courses at the centre were okay except for Aboriginal Studies. They gave us module-style booklets we had to work through. The person who'd written the modules kept referring to everything as if it were finished. Like there had been a war and now it was all over. I didn't understand what the school wanted from me. Everything seemed like it was designed to make me think too much about my own life and circumstances. I already did enough of that. Now I was expected to share it with someone that I didn't even know. Write out some trauma shit and send it away to an unknown email address. I'd pass on that.

There was a tutor who walked around the room we did the schooling in. They didn't teach the subject, just helped us upload stuff onto the internet or work through some problems. Whenever I asked them a question about the Aboriginal Studies content, they said they weren't qualified to speak on it. When I got the assignment back, I didn't do well. I had written that proper Aboriginal Studies would be hanging out with Joe and not filling out these questionnaires. The invisible face that responded over the internet told me that I had to focus on what was asked of me. The tutor told me the same thing. Just answer the questions that they provide. Don't make your own.

Days passed by. I continued to wait to hear from Grey, but nothing ever came. Auntie May told me she knew I was in there. That she was giving me some space. The more time that went on, the reflection hours we went through in our circle made me want to apologize. My anger had made me responsible for the situations that got us here. I needed to own up to that in order to be able to move on. But move on to what? That was always my question.

I asked Joe that.

"You'll find your place eventually."

"What if I don't?"

"It took me a long, long, long time to find myself here, working with my family and community in a good way," he said. "What do you care about?"

The first thing that came to my mind was Grey. I pictured her sitting across from me at the card table in her uncle's trailer.

I thought about the way her hand looked as she raised the teacup to her lips. How grey had started to pepper her dark black hair. Fitting. I wanted to go back to the world just being her and me in a trailer with a deck of cards, a cooler of Luckys, and the howls of the coyotes around us.

"I don't know if I care about anything," I replied.

"You do," he said. "You do."

The cops showed up the day after we'd wrapped up our schooling sessions for the month. We had all just moved over from the schoolroom to the crafting room. I could feel the energy drop when they came through the door in their full uniforms. Two big meatheads, all muscles, guts, and trying to look cool with tattoos. All the little conversations and jokes ceased instantly. Most people kept their heads down, staring intently at the beading and sewing they were working on. A few of us glared at the cops. I wanted them to feel as uncomfortable as they were making me. Every single person in rehab with me probably had something happen at one point that they could get chucked away for. The cops started walking towards me.

"Isidore Desjarlais?"

I went to stand up and felt Joe's hand on my thigh, pushing me back down. He stood instead.

"You're not supposed to be in here," he said. He blocked the cops. They couldn't walk around him.

"Sir, please move out of the way."

"You know the rules as well as I do. You need to go through the office. Make an appointment with the director." The cops moved in and towered over Joe. They stood, arms crossed, staring down at him, but Joe didn't budge. He met their attempt at humiliation and threw it back at them. "And get out of here."

The cops continued to stick their chests and guts out, the old maximize-space technique. It might have worked better if their bellies hadn't been hanging over their belts, but they still had guns. Guns and tasers, and both those things could fuck you up something fierce. I thought about just standing up and going with them. We were only delaying the inevitable. I wondered what it was they had figured out. Most likely something to do with the burned-down trailer. Joe kept standing, though, until they finally turned and left.

Everyone in the room continued to stare at me. The easy chatter never returned. Joe slumped down in his seat at the table.

"Assholes. They would never try and pull that crap at a white, rich rehab facility. But at the native one, it's all shits and giggles."

"Maybe they didn't know," one of the staff said.

"They knew exactly what they were doing." Joe turned to me. "We may as well get ready to head down to the intake room."

"We?" I asked.

"I'm coming with you. Not going to let them try and pull any more bullshit."

"I'll be fine." He gave me a look that said *I don't believe you.* I poured myself a cup of coffee and sat back down. I tried to start beading again, but it wasn't going to happen. My hands trembled. I didn't want to go back to jail. I tried to sip the coffee but splashed it on the table. I started wiping it up with a napkin. Then an aide came in and requested that I go and meet with the director and the police. When I walked into the intake room, everyone was standing around the table even though there were chairs pulled out.

"Isidore Desjarlais, you're under arrest for car theft and violation of your probation conditions."

"Wait," Joe said. "That's not enough to pull him out of here. Usually, they let someone run out their time here first."

"Joe, the authorities have deemed Ezzy a flight risk," the director said. He hiked up the back of his falling-down black dress pants. One of the cops came up behind me and put handcuffs on. When no one was looking, he gave them an extra squeeze to cut off the circulation to my hands.

"How am I supposed to crutch around with handcuffs on?" I asked.

"Flight risk? The guy can barely walk," Joe said.

"Isidore is also being investigated for other potentially linked crimes," one of the officers said.

"Bullshit," Joe said. "You can't just pull someone out of here when they're doing well in the program. That's not how this works."

The director shrugged his shoulders. The one cop asked the aide to find a wheelchair for me.

"There's nothing I can do. Policy is policy," the director said. The aide came back with a wheelchair.

"Sit," the one cop barked at me. I sneered at him and sat down in the chair. They started wheeling me out of the building.

"Ezzy," Joe called out after me, "you don't have to tell them anything. Wait until you get a lawyer."

We got to the parked cop car.

"Move," the one cop grunted. I stood up on one leg and tried to put a bit of weight on the air cast on my other leg. The pain shot up my body. The other cop opened the back door. I hopped over and into the car. They closed the door, locking me back into my old world.

Turns out, they'd run fingerprints collected from the stolen Jeep through their database and those matched the ones on file for me. There was another set of prints in the car, too—had to be Grey's, but they didn't have a match for those. They grilled me for days about it. It was pretty apparent that I had stolen the car. They could charge me for that, no problem. Now they were conflicted because everything pointed towards the fact that I was involved with the stolen bison. For obvious reasons, the stolen car had turned up in the pasture where the bison were moved from. But then they didn't think that I had the capacity for something like that. Not everyone could just move bison around. Especially a busted-up and drug-addicted criminal. Why had I left the car out in the field? Who had I been with? How did I move the bison? Why was I moving bison into the city? I just stared during their questions. What was the worst they could do? Lock me up harder?

They did try to threaten me with a longer sentence, and when that didn't work, they changed their tactics and offered a lower sentence if I gave up the person I was with. The cops also told me there was no way I would make bail. With my priors and the severity of stealing a car, the judge would put me away for sure. Now, if I was going to chat about who I was with, then they could maybe make something work, or at least let me go back to rehab first. But I knew that if I ended up doing that, they would just turn around and charge me with the theft of all the bison. I was sure they could lay down some crazy charges with something like that.

I would love to hear how it was read out. *You are being charged with the illegal seizure and transportation of a bison herd from a pasture to a park. How do you plead?* Guilty as fuck, your honour.

They kept trying to figure out why I would move a herd of bison. They scrambled to connect this last bit. I was surprised that they didn't mention my hospital records. I was sure they had access to those. Maybe they didn't. When they finally realized that their interrogation was going nowhere and I wasn't going to snitch on anyone, they changed tactics again.

"Your friend Grey. She's quite the troublemaker, eh?" one of the cops asked.

"Grey who?"

"Grey Ginther. She's a known activist in the city here," the other cop said.

"And we have reason to believe that she's involved in some heavy stuff. Arson for sure. Potentially murder too."

"Is this the kind of person you're friends with, Isidore?" the cop chimed in again.

"I've hung out with worse," I said.

"You were living with her out at the trailer, weren't you?"

"I've been staying at my auntie's for a while now."

"How long's a while?"

"Long enough to know that this is fucking stupid."

"Now you're a smart guy too, eh? Was Grey involved with the bison at all? Or just burning down the trailer?"

"Look. I don't know what the fuck you're talking about."

"Isidore, we found your fingerprints on a stolen vehicle at the farm where twelve bison were taken. Those bison showed up in

Terwillegar Park. Then, not long after that, we found the trailer where you and Grey Ginther had been staying burned down next to a truck with a body inside. And you mean to tell us that you don't know anything about any of that?"

"Yup."

"Do you think we're dumb or something?"

"Yup."

"Look. We know you're having a rough go. If you're cooperative, we can figure out how to look at your sentence differently. You might be able to go to a minimum-security prison. We might even let you go back to rehab before that. But you need to give us something. If this does go to a bail hearing, then the judge will throw the book at you. I promise you that."

"I'll take my chances," I said.

I really didn't like that they'd brought Grey into this. Obviously they had found the trailer. If only that fucking redneck hadn't shown up, things might have been a lot different right now. Grey and I would be back out there, still playing cards, and I'd be sipping away on a Lucky while she went over to the park to watch the sunsets and the bison herds in the last light. Instead of me being held waiting for bail. And Grey, shit. I hoped she was doing okay. Maybe that's why I hadn't heard from her yet. Because of these cops coming in hot. Part of me hoped that Grey would just pin everything on me. The man, the trailer, the bison. Whatever it took to keep her out of trouble.

After the interrogation ended, I waited for my bail hearing. Back to the waiting game. The ceremonies and stories with Joe and the other patients had made everything seem so new and light.

I didn't even mind the schooling compared to the dull boredom of sitting around in a prison cell. No wonder they'd used prison operations to destroy us on the plains. Hard to build a resistance when all the young men and women were constantly getting removed from community and the old teachings and histories. The creation of a system that isolated us from our own lands and languages was necessary if they were truly gonna settle here and tame a country that didn't want to be tamed. But no one was meant to stay caged up—birds, bison, Métis . . . no one. I figured that however this played out, when I got released I would go back to rehab and keep learning from Joe. Plus, they had painkillers everywhere in prison. Probably more accessible than they were back on the outside. I'd have to watch out.

At the bail hearing, the cops and their lawyer told the judge I was a flight risk. They presented their case and insinuated a connection to additional crimes, but they hadn't figured those out yet. The judge looked at me. He took off his glasses, polished them, and put them back on.

"Isidore, are you physically able to walk?" the judge asked.

"No, Your Honour. Not without crutches, at least."

"And have you ever left Edmonton?"

"Not really. I mean, I went to the mountains with a youth-group thing back in the day."

"Where were you when you were arrested?"

"In rehab, Your Honour."

"And you're being charged with theft of a motor vehicle? The motor vehicle, which was valued at less than five thousand dollars?"

"I don't know how much the vehicle costs, Your Honour. But yes, those are the charges."

"Could you drive a vehicle right now?"

"No, Your Honour. Not well, at least."

"You've had a few offences in the past."

"I have, sir."

"I don't see anything violent on here. Isidore, are you a violent man?"

"I try not to be, Your Honour," I said.

"If I grant you bail, what are you going to do?" the judge asked.

"Go back to rehab, Your Honour."

Auntie May posted bail for me. She gave me a lecture on how I'd need to attend my court dates or she'd be screwed. Bail was a lot of money to deposit on nothing. Especially when you didn't have any money to begin with. I told her she didn't have to worry. I'd just sit it out until trial. She wasn't having it. She wanted me to get through rehab, at least. I think she was just as worried about the availability of oxy in remand as I was. Even just thinking about those painkillers made me want to get back on them.

We stopped at a McDonald's on our way to the rehab centre. I thought back to when I was a little kid, and I'd go on a drive to a new foster family or a group home and how the social worker would stop in at a McDonald's. Like a Happy Meal with a cheap-ass plastic toy could make everything right. I'd sit in the back of the social worker's car, eating my Chicken McNuggets and fries and dreaming that this would be the place that would work out. Where I would be treated like one of the family, eat the same meals, make friends, have adults that actually gave a shit about me, and live the life all the kids I went to school with seemed to have. With every nugget-dip into the sweet and sour sauce, I'd fantasize about how it would play out. Eventually, the realization that it would never happen kicked in—right around the time the nuggets turned cold and stale. But in Auntie May's car, eating those same Chicken McNuggets and fries as an adult, I had a similar feeling. Would this be the place that finally worked out for me? Prison was inevitable, but I had a few months until trial to figure my shit out.

"You know, sometimes they can reduce a sentence if you can show how you're getting your life back on track." She always got a Big Mac and a Diet Coke, no fries. She reached over and grabbed a couple of mine.

"Hey! Get your own,"

"I just want a taste," she replied. Then she quickly grabbed a handful and pushed them all into her mouth at once.

"Real mature," I said.

"Joe told me that you were doing quite well."

"Yeah. He's a good guy."

"You spend time with him. He'll tune you up."

"I'm already tuned. Like the finest fiddle you ever did see."

"Here, let me have another fry." She cleaned the last of them out of the cardboard container. "I'm going to go do something."

"What? You asking Joe out?" I said.

"Gross, no. He's like as old as my dad," Auntie May replied.

"Age is just a number," I said.

"Not that." She took a sip of her Diet Coke, then lit a cigarette. "I'm going to reach out to my kids." Her eyes teared up. She wiped them away with her sleeve. "But I'm scared."

"I think it's a good idea. Why'd you change your mind?" I asked.

"Oh, I don't know. Everything's so fickle. What if one day I'm gone? Or they're gone? I'd never forgive myself for not really knowing."

I wondered if she would have decided to do this if not for me and my shit. If it was the predicament of losing me that had moved her to push forward in her own life.

"Auntie. I can tell you this from experience. There's nothing that I wouldn't give or do to be able to meet my mom." I paused. "Absolutely nothing in the world that I want more than that."

---

When I was a kid, I dreamt so hard of being adopted. Late at night, when I couldn't sleep, which was pretty much every single night, I would sit there and think about my future family. I based them on television families from daytime sitcoms, as that's all I had to go off. None of us knew what a real family was like. There would be the working dad, coming home from an office job with his suit and tie undone to show that he was now relaxed. He'd come barging into the house, so excited to see me after a day away at work, and he'd pick me up and swing me around, and we'd go to a park or play baseball or basketball or shoot pucks at a net in the driveway. The kind of thing that TV dads did with their kids. My mom would be cooking all day. Just big, beautiful meals of turkey sandwiches, tomato soup, salads, everything and anything that wasn't a can of Alphagetti or Chef Boyardee ravioli. I'd never see that fake tomato sauce again in my life. In the summers we'd go to our cabin, and in the winters, Disneyland or Mexico. My imagined family would all be white, European—probably Ukrainian or something like that. I wouldn't have to be a Métis kid anymore. I could just be a Canadian and the family would love me for it. I'd forget all about the beatings in the group and foster homes. I'd forget all about the creeper social workers and the people who got a little too close to us kids. This family would love me for who I was, and they'd never let me go.

I spent days that turned into weeks that turned into months that turned into years sitting there waiting for this to happen. I wasn't the only kid who did that. There were lots of us. The older kids would make fun of us. We were wimps, pussies, little bitches to them, but we knew that in their hearts they also held on to a small sliver of hope that they would find a family. Even if they told us that we were wasting our time, in the backs of their minds they always believed that someone would come get them, too, if they just waited long enough. We dreamt of families and knew that they weren't far away. Families that wouldn't just take us in because of the government money that went to the parents—families that wanted us for who we were. That would adopt us and take us away from everything in our pasts. Every time someone new pulled into the parking lot of a group home or someone pulled up outside a foster home, my heart jumped. This could finally be it. Enough freedom and love to finally be a kid. That's what I was told, to wait, and if I waited long enough and I was good enough while waiting, someone would eventually call me family. I'd wait forever for that.

SIX

# GREY

My parents and I were playing radio bingo when we learned about the third herd. My mom had five cards laid out in front of her. She absently tapped away on them with one hand as the announcer called out the numbers on the station. In her other hand, she had her phone open and was scrolling through Facebook. Whenever she saw something interesting, she'd begin talking to my dad about it. Usually, it was family or community gossip that got her going—that or weird conspiracy theories other people shared. My dad had two cards in front of him. He told me he liked to concentrate on the numbers, and with just two cards, he felt he was more connected to luck. When my mom started chatting about whatever she was reading, they would both get distracted and start missing numbers. It wasn't the most solid bingo strategy, that's for sure. I don't think either of them ever won. But they loved it, and it kept them busy a couple nights a week through the northern winters, so I joined in with them. I had submitted all my grad school applications and was back to sitting around the house all day. It was just a matter of time.

"Hey, did you hear about this?" my mom asked. My dad raised his eyebrows but didn't look up from the cards. In the background, the caller announced B10. My dad and I both marked it. I reached over and marked it on one of my mom's cards when she missed it. "They're saying that ten bison showed up in Calgary in a park off the river."

My mom's news sources weren't the best.

"Where'd you hear that?" I asked.

"My friend Sherry—do you remember Sherry? Cousins with Doug? I think she lives down in the city now and works for some bank. No, not a bank. It's the government, but it's some sort of finance job. I wonder how her kids are doing. They must be big by now. When was the last time they were up this way? It must have been seven years ago now, holay! Her youngest baby would be all grown-up and in high school by now . . ."

"So Sherry posted it?" I asked. "What website?"

"*Edmonton Journal*," my mom said.

"You're both missing the numbers," my dad said, exasperation in his voice.

"Oh, sorry." My mom looked back at her cards. "What did I miss?" She grabbed my dad's.

"Can I see your phone?" I asked. My mom tossed it to me, her focus now elsewhere.

The article didn't say much. It just mentioned that ten bison had appeared in downtown Calgary, in Prince's Island Park. It related them back to the two bison herds that had appeared in Edmonton. It said that, at this point, authorities were trying to figure out where the bison had come from and were advising people to avoid the area until further notice. I passed the phone back to my mom, my bingo cards long gone at this point. Maybe I'd get in on the next game. I pulled out my own phone to search for more information about the new bison herd. There was a text from Tyler waiting on it.

*You down in Calgary now? Thought you were at your parents . . .*

*No, still up here. Are you down there?* I texted back.

*Nope. But media calling me up to ask about the new herd. What should I tell them?*

*Dunno? That's on you. Just don't mention me please.*

*Cops came by to ask questions about you a couple weeks back.*

*Good for them,* I texted. That didn't surprise me. I was surprised that Tyler hadn't got involved in this herd, though. I sent a follow-up text. *You say anything?*

*What do you think . . . I'm going to go down to Calgary and check this out.*

*Have fun!*

*You sure you're not in Calgary?* Tyler texted. I didn't respond.

Google didn't have much more to say about the herd than what the *Edmonton Journal* article had mentioned. I'd check again in the morning and see if something new came up. I went back to the bingo cards.

Overnight, two more herds popped up in Saskatchewan—one in Meewasin Park in Saskatoon and one in Wascana Park in Regina. They called the Meewasin Park herd an extension of the bison living in Wanuskewin, just north of where they appeared.

No one was sure where the Wascana herd had come from. But really, no one was quite certain where these bison came from at all. None of them seemed to have any apparent tags on their ears that could link them back to a particular area or farm. And all the herds were small, ten or twelve bison at most. Social media started bumping with people trying to speculate: the Saskatchewan ones seemed planned, but maybe the Calgary one was just coincidental.

It became a national media frenzy.

The number-one trending topic on regional Twitter was #bison followed by #landback. People were fired up. My feeds were filled with people supporting the bison and calling for the parks to keep them there. But a quick search brought up a different side of the conversation too—people mad about the bison coming back into parks they used on a regular basis. The comments got racist fast, but that was expected. I couldn't remember any protest or talk that didn't bring out old racist people to yell about something. I was more curious now about who was bringing these bison in. It wasn't me. It wasn't Tyler. It definitely wasn't Ezzy. Other activists, maybe. Usually something like that needed some coordination. And shit was it hard to not feel a bit of jealousy towards those who were doing the organizing. There was a certain high, a thrill that came from seeing good plans followed through. I wasn't going to be able to do that for a while. But whoever had taken it up was doing a good job.

I sent Auntie May a text to let her know that I wanted to see Ezzy and was going whether she liked it or not. She didn't say anything about whether it was a good time to visit, just gave me a heads-up that the cops had recently pulled Ezzy in and charged him with vehicle theft, and that he was out on bail and back at rehab. I didn't ask her about any of the particulars. I wasn't sure how much information cops could pull off phones, but between the texts with Tyler and Auntie May, I worried that there was enough incriminating evidence on there to put me away. I tried to google what information police could obtain from a phone. Everything just directed me to American sites, and it was hard to find any information for Canada. The cops hadn't come back to my parents' place since that one visit, but I figured they were just trying to put together a case to bring me in. I wasn't worried about Ezzy saying anything. Tyler might if he thought it would work to his advantage, or if they cornered him. But he didn't know anything except that I had stolen and released bison in the River Valley. Part of me wouldn't have been surprised if he started grandstanding and taking credit for all of it. Or maybe I was just hoping.

I pulled into the rehab-centre grounds. Overnight, snow had blanketed the trees that lined the road going up to the main building. The entire drive down, I had nervously tried to figure out what to say to Ezzy. Should I apologize for running out and leaving him on his own with the pill bottle? Should we just forget that that had ever happened? Just thinking about how it could have played out so differently started triggering visions. Ezzy unconscious on the floor, blue in the face, convulsing, Auntie May not making it there in time to give him a naloxone shot. The last breaths leaving Ezzy's body. The peaceful look on his face as he faded into death.

The visiting room was gorgeous. The building had recently undergone renovations, and the centre had turned it into a circle with arching poles that tilted as they got closer to the roof. The wall facing out towards the grounds was one giant window that let light in. There were couches with actual Pendletons wrapped on the backs of them and bison hides splayed on the ground. A little pedestal stood in the centre of the room, and laid on it was sage, sweetgrass, diamond willow fungus, and a cast iron pan. Ezzy wasn't there yet. The staff member let me know he was in a counselling session and would join me after. I sat down on one of the bison hides. Soft and warm. I could smell the smoke from the tannery lingering in the fur. I wanted to wrap myself up in it and lie down by a fire and listen to someone telling me beautiful stories. How nice it would be to spend a winter doing something like that.

I pulled out my phone and used the front camera to check my teeth. My mom had packed me a couple baloney sandwiches for the drive, and I had eaten them both before arriving. If I ever got into online dating, that would be in my profile: *must feed me bologna, mustard, and bannock sandwiches.* I picked a piece of the bannock out of my teeth and nibbled it. I got nervous. I lay down on the hide and stared at the ceiling.

"Bison rug looks good on yah," Ezzy said. I hadn't heard him come into the room. I jumped up a little too fast and a ton of blood rushed to my head. I collected myself. Ezzy looked healthy. He didn't have that same swollen look he had when he was laid up on the couch at Auntie May's. Colour had come back into his face and his eyes were no longer sunken. He had even started to put on a bit of a belly. Beside him, there was an older man who looked at me with a smile on his face. The first thing I noticed about him was his posture. Tall and composed. There was something about his face that made me think he would bust out a dad joke at any minute and then launch into a story. That would have fit very well with the room's whole theme and the snow falling outside the big glass window. Some Hallmark Christmas-movie shit.

"Hey!" I said. "Ezzy, you look so good."

"You too," Ezzy replied. "Grey, I want you to meet my friend Joe."

"Joe Gladue nitisiyihkasôn kiya mâka tânisi kitisiyihkâson?"

"Grey Ginther nitisiyihkasôn," I replied.

"Miwasin, tânitê ohci kiya kayahtê?" Joe asked. I had to try and think back to the Cree language courses I'd taken at university. It was a long time since those lessons. My dad spoke a bit of it still, but my mom had never learned the language.

"Pembina Creek ohci niya," I replied. "Kiya mâka?"

"Amiskwaciwâskahikanihk ohci niya êkota mîna mêkwâc niwîkin," he said. I got that he lived in Edmonton, but I wasn't sure about the last part. "You speak good Cree."

"It's been a long time."

"You should keep learning," he said. "This one too." He pointed his lips at Ezzy, who sat down on the couch. His leg was still in a cast, but he looked a lot more comfortable with it on. "Anyways, I just wanted to meet you. This one talks about you so much that I thought I better come shake hands with the famous Grey Ginther."

I blushed. Joe smiled at me and took my hand and shook it without applying any pressure. I felt myself melting into the warmth of his palm.

"Great meeting you," I stammered.

"You as well. We'll talk soon."

He turned and left, and the room went silent. I started to move towards the couch where Ezzy was sitting. Then I hesitated and went and stood by the smudge station in the centre of the room.

"You can light it if you want," Ezzy said.

"I'm okay," I replied.

"Grey," he said. "You know I struggle. I'm trying to learn how to deal with it." I moved towards the window and stared out at the small songbirds that were flying from tree to tree. "I'm trying, Grey. I'm really doing good in here."

"You look good," I said. I could feel myself start to tear up.

"I got a bannock baby going on," he replied. He started laughing and patted his stomach. I burst out laughing. I wiped the tears at the corner of my eyes away.

"Me too," I replied. "Me too."

"I wish things didn't turn out the way they did," he said.

"I know. We all fucked up."

"You look good, though. Healthy and shit."

"Healthy and shit? What's that mean?" I laughed. "I'm so fucking scared, Ezzy. I don't know what's happening." I sat down on the couch beside him. We both sat there in silence for a few minutes. I didn't know where to begin. Then Ezzy started talking.

"Did the cops come to see you?" he asked. I nodded. "Me too."

"Auntie May told me they pulled you in."

"Yeah, for a bit. They don't know shit."

"I don't know about that," I replied.

"Believe me. If they knew anything, they'd have us both locked up right now. They don't want us outside any more than they want those bison in the parks," Ezzy said.

"What'd they say to you?"

"They could bust me for stealing the car. That's fine. I'll eat that any day."

"Is it safe to talk in here?"

"Oh yeah. This place is legit. I mean, if we told a staff member something directly, they might have to legally report it. But that would only be for what went down back at the trailer . . ." Ezzy's voice tapered off. I could see him hesitate, not sure if he should bring up the situation or not. I looked down at the ground. "Grey, that was my fault, what happened. I created all of that with my anger issues."

"No," I said.

"Yeah, I really did. None of that should have gone down. Something Joe and I have been talking about in here. How I need to take accountability for my actions. That's what community is. Accountability."

"But you weren't the one who went through it," I replied. "You didn't have to be there. You don't have to think about it constantly. You don't have to worry about what will come of it all once the cops get their shit together. Fuck am I going to do if they figure out I shot that man?"

"I really don't know. I'm sorry," Ezzy said. He stood up and limped over to where the smudge stuff was. He lit the diamond willow fungus and started smudging himself. When he finished, he looked towards me. I didn't really feel up to it. But then I didn't want to disrespect this place or how well Ezzy was doing. I went over and smudged myself.

"I'm sorry, too. I shouldn't have left that note out," I replied.

"I was going to find them no matter what. It was just a matter of time," Ezzy said. He began laughing. "You want to hear something funny?" I smiled at him. "When I was looking for pills one time, I found a vibrator in Auntie May's drawer."

"Get out," I said. "You weirdo, going through your auntie's stuff."

"I know." He kept laughing. "So funny, though. You think that would have stopped me from searching for a while."

"Good for Auntie," I said. Then I started laughing. "You creep."

"She's thinking about going and meeting her kids, you know."

"Really? That's so awesome."

"But she's nervous about it."

"I hope it all goes okay for her," I replied.

"Me too. I can't imagine that. Like what if my father showed up out of nowhere. I don't know how I'd feel about that."

"Auntie May's solid, though. She'll do it the right way."

"I know she will. Is it bad that I might be jealous? I might not be her boy anymore," he said. I looked up at him to see if he was joking. His eyes twinkled. "I'm just bugging. I really want this for her. Plus, I need more cousins. You can't be the only one that I hang out with."

"I applied to grad school," I said.

"Really? I thought you hated the idea of that."

"It's time for a change. I need to leave here. Probably not forever, but for a while, at least."

"That's fair. Where at?"

"Out east. Or maybe Vancouver. Guess it depends if I get accepted anywhere, really."

"I'm sure you will."

"I hope so," I replied.

"That's cool. I'll come and visit you. I always wanted to go to a different city."

"Of course," I said.

"Once I'm out of here, and everything wraps up with the charges, then I'll come out for sure. Maybe I'll crash one of the undergrad courses you'll be teaching. Just start running my mouth at you about everything."

"How would that be any different than now?" I said. Ezzy chuckled.

"It wouldn't. I'd just make myself sound smarter. More intelligentable."

"I don't think that's a word."

"Yeah, it's for intelligent gentlemen. I'm learning lots of grammar in here."

"Really?"

"Getting edumacated. Maybe I'll be a prof like you one day. Buy a suit."

"Maybe . . . have you ever even worn a suit?"

"No. I should for court, though."

After visiting hours ended, I messaged Auntie May and asked if I could crash at her place. She said that was fine with her. I told her I'd pick up supper. On the drive over to her place, I stopped in at a chicken spot and grabbed us a small bucket with fries and gravy.

Auntie May wasn't home yet. I used the spare key she hid behind a loose board on the porch and went inside. The house didn't look much different than the last time I went there. She had cleaned up the area where Ezzy had slept before he went to the hospital. That part was back to normal. Everything else looked untouched. Auntie May kind of floated in and out. She never really cooked, just heated stuff up, ate, slept, and left. I turned the radio on, and after a commercial:

*"More developments in the ongoing bison story. A group out of Saskatchewan claims that they're the ones who are releasing bison across the prairies. Funded by crowdsourcing, the group is purchasing bison legally from ranches and then releasing them in the parks. The Saskatchewan government is looking into pursuing charges against the group under the Wildlife Act. The group has stated it's willing to fight the charges in court. In the meantime, local authorities have asked protestors to remove themselves from the park premises, stating that they are putting themselves and the bison at risk. We spoke with the lead organizer from the protests, Tyler Cardinal, who maintains that the protestors will be staying put until the River Valley is designated as Indigenous land and the bison have the right to stay there. Tyler, thanks for joining us today in the studio. We know it must have been hard to leave your fellow protestors to come and speak with us."*

*"Thank you for having me. It's always incredibly hard to leave the land that holds so much of my family history, memory, blood, sweat, and tears. Did you know that that area of the River Valley was once First Nations reserve land?"*

*"I did not know that. Thank you for telling us."*

*"It's good for everyone to be able to learn more about the true Indigenous histories of place—that's how we can move things forward towards a true state of reconciliation. I'd be more than happy to help educate anytime."*

*"Now, Tyler, what would an ideal outcome be for the protests?"*

*"Return all the land. To bring the bison back as they were before colonization. To return the prairies to the matriarchal governance structures of the Indigenous communities that were here beforehand. It's important to always note that it's the women and two-spirit peoples who lead these protests. We're just here to support those who are truly doing the work."*

*"Very well said. Now some people say that the bison are a threat. What do you think about that?"*

*"The bison aren't any more of a threat than the whole system of colonization is. Bison are natural here and we need to honour their kindred spirits if we're going to become whole as Indigenous peoples again. We're all in this together against a capitalist state that has turned the prairies into a massive resource-extraction enterprise. We need to move back to a true sense of collectivism if we're going to be able to progress as peoples on these territories. We need all the allies for the fight that we can get."*

*"Well said again. And you have two allies in us here. Thank you again for joining us, Tyler, and if anyone has any questions or wants to learn more, where can they do that?"*

*"You can follow me on Instagram at TeeCardz, or on Twitter. All the updates will be coming from my social media."*

*"Thank you again—or as the Cree say, hiy hiy."*

*"Hiy hiy."*

The radio moved on to hockey. I turned it off. What bullshit. He just threw as many buzzwords in as he could and tried to sell himself as a corporate trainer at the same time. I thought about messaging him to ask who these two-spirit and matriarchal leaders were . . . but then decided against it. And I thought about warning him about the legal shit the cops had brought down on us, but again, he could deal with it if it came up. He hadn't been out at the trailer, the national park, or the farm, so he was fine. And I didn't know if the cops had linked the burnt-out trailer to the bison or anything yet. They'd given vague hints, but nothing concrete. I think they were more concerned with the dead body than anything at this point. From what I could tell, the bison herd in Dawson Park had lived up to their national park domesticity and hadn't caused any issues so far. None of them had wandered off or got into downtown or the neighbourhoods yet. They seemed perfectly fine to just hang out in the River Valley. Though I bet the cops were on high alert for more people trying to bring bison into the city. I wouldn't be surprised if I saw Tyler doing something like that. Especially now that people in Saskatchewan had taken it up. A classic move; solidarity protests. I'm sure he was losing his mind that he hadn't thought of crowdsourcing for more bison so he could get that skim off the top. "Administration fees."

I put on a pot of tea and turned the oven on. I'd throw the chicken and fries in there to toast them up a bit when Auntie May got home. I knew people loved their cold leftover chicken, but I could never quite get into it. Too much congealed grease for me. I saw May had left another note on the kitchen table.

On this one, she had written the names Derek and Brittney Benn. Underneath their names was a house address for a place deep down on the southside of the city. I pulled up Instagram on my phone and searched for their names. Derek's account was private, but Brittney's was open. When I saw the first picture, it was like what I figured looking at Auntie May when she was in her early twenties would be like. They were identical—both mouth-dropping beautiful. This was definitely Auntie May's daughter. I scrolled through her feed for a bit. The pictures weren't recent. The last post was from the end of summer. But that made sense, with Instagram going the way of Facebook. Before then, most of the pictures were of her and her friends lounging in bikinis by Lake Summerside. Another photo showed her with who I assumed were her adoptive parents on a trip somewhere. The adoptive parents looked classically rich. That was the best way to describe them: nice hair, nice clothes, and no blemishes or wear and tear on their faces from years of blue-collar work. Finally, she had a picture of her and Derek standing beside a Christmas tree. I could see the resemblance between Derek and Ezzy a bit. It wasn't as pronounced as Brittney and Auntie May. But if you put the two of them side by side, you would be able to tell they were related. I scrolled a bit further down, but the pictures started getting into old high school parties. Then Auntie May walked in.

I debated if I should show Auntie May, but I figured she would just learn about them on her own time. I didn't know how these things worked. Auntie May had learned years ago how to find kids using Facebook for her work. Though I didn't know if she had ever thought of Instagram as a means for that.

"Grey! Come here," Auntie May called out as she came bursting through the front door. We wrapped each other up in a big hug. It felt so good to see her again and be in her company.

"Auntie, I missed you."

"I missed you too."

"You hungry? I have food." I put the chicken and fries on a baking tray and put them in the oven. "Give it five minutes."

"For chicken? I'd give the world," Auntie May said. She winked at me and sat down at the table. "You're looking good. Your parents must be so happy they get to spend time with you."

"They are. I think I'm too old to be living at home, though."

"It's just temporary. Enjoy these moments," Auntie May said.

"How are you? Ezzy told me that you have big news."

"Did he? That blabbermouth. Could never keep anything to himself." I motioned with my head towards the notepad on the table. Auntie May started chuckling. "Oh, you saw that? Yeah. I'm sure he told you. But I'm going to reach out to my kids."

"That's so good, May."

"I'm super nervous. This has been a long time coming. I don't want things to go wrong. And I mean, there's always the possibility they don't want to meet me."

"I'm sure it'll all work out," I said.

"Wow, you are hanging out with Elders. That sounds exactly like something one of the old ones would say." She grabbed the tray out of the oven. "I'm starving. Let's eat."

"Ezzy looks good," I said. "Way better than before."

"He's coming along. I'm glad he met Joe."

"Yeah, he introduced himself to me when I stopped in to visit Ezzy."

"He's a good guy. He was friends with my dad before he passed away. The two of them used to camp out together in the River Valley during the summer months, and the shelters during the winters."

"Now he works out there?" I asked. We dug into our food.

"He had his own rough patches to work through. A while back now, he ended up in the minimum-security. But when he was locked up, he learned a lot from a couple Elders and knowledge keepers who were also in there."

"Brutal that you have to go to prison to learn about our culture," I said.

"Tell me about it," Auntie May replied. "It's terrible." She stood up and cleared our plates into the sink. "Anyways, Joe always was a support to everyone. I guess he just transferred that support to the centre."

"He seemed very nice. Very composed," I laughed.

"He'll be good for Ezzy. Ezzy's never really had someone like that around all the time. My father came and went. But he had his own struggles. The times he spent with Ezzy were wonderful, but he wasn't able to give the support that he wanted to. The system wouldn't allow that."

"Of course it wouldn't," I said. I got up to dry the dishes.

"It's always been bad for us," Auntie May said. "Enough of that now. What's new with you? I want to hear how you've been."

"I applied to grad schools. That's pretty much it."

"Really? Where at?" she asked.

"Oh, and I've been playing lots of radio bingo but I never win!"

"Where'd you apply? Here?"

"No . . . I applied out east. And Vancouver, too," I replied. May looked hurt. "I need a change."

"I get it. I'll miss you."

"I probably won't get in."

"Oh shut up. Like that's going to happen." She wiped away tears with her sleeve. "But you'll come back for sure, eh?" She smiled.

"For sure."

Auntie May barged into the basement bedroom the next morning, and when she turned on the light to wake me I saw that tears were streaming down her face.

"Auntie! What's wrong? What happened?" I went to get out of bed, but before I could, she threw herself onto it. She kept sobbing. I tried to figure out what had happened. "Auntie? Talk to me. What's going on?" I repeated. "Did something happen with the kids?"

"It's Ezzy. He went back to jail last night."

"What? They can't arrest him. He made bail. He's fine until the court date," I said. Auntie May blew her nose on her sleeve and cleared her throat.

"I just got off the phone with Joe. Ezzy went into the social worker's office at the rehab last night and told them he had killed someone."

"What?" I could feel my blood start racing. My heart dropped. "What did he say?"

"I don't know. I'm not sure what they're charging him with. The cops came and picked him up."

"Oh no." I could feel the tears coming. May buried her face into the sheets and started crying hard, and I could hear my own muffled sobs coming.

*That fucking idiot*, I thought. What kind of shit was he trying to prove? I leaned back on the sheets and closed my eyes. Why would he do that? He wasn't anywhere near that whole thing when it went down. Did he have a plan? Or was this some bullshit sacrifice he needed to make? Was this going to bring me into it? What was he doing? The cops didn't know anything. At least that I knew of.

After that I moved into Auntie May's basement, and she and Joe pitched in on retaining a lawyer for Ezzy. We couldn't see him or talk to him while they processed him. I still had no idea if I'd eventually get pulled into it. The unknowing of it messed with me. Every day I was just there in her house, my fingers aching from the back-and-forth twitching, my feet worn from pacing. I couldn't take it. May had stopped talking about going and meeting up with her kids. Ezzy had taken over her focus again. Joe stopped by the house on his way home from the rehab centre every day. He'd bring us leftovers and would often stay and drink tea with us into the night. His presence in the room helped a lot. If it was just May and me, who knows how long we would last? I could tell Joe wasn't feeling too good about what had happened. He never said as much, but I could see that he thought he was to blame for Ezzy's decision to turn himself in. Accountability. I don't believe that Joe knew it was for something that he hadn't even done.

The story Ezzy told finally came out. He'd turned himself in for murdering the man in self-defence. Ezzy said he'd been squatting in my uncle's trailer and had gone out there because he knew it was empty from a conversation we'd had. He told the cops I didn't know anything about him being out there. That he had just taken the opportunity to move out to a free place and someone had mentioned an abandoned trailer. One day he was headed into the city to get cigarettes and beer and he got mixed up with the guy outside a gas station. In Ezzy's version, the man showed up a couple days later and tried to run him over with his truck in the yard, hence his broken leg. The man got out of his truck with his rifle and tried to shoot Ezzy but missed. Ezzy wrestled the gun away and shot him, then burned down the trailer and the truck to get rid of the evidence. When they asked him about the stolen Jeep, he said he was in the city one night and borrowed it to go home. Afterwards, he took off driving until he ran out of gas and energy, which was at that field the Jeep turned up in. He then hitchhiked his way back to the hospital.

The cops didn't give a shit about the stolen vehicle anymore. It was Edmonton—a vehicle got stolen every five minutes. Their interest had shifted completely to the dead man, and the burned-down trailer that went along with it. Murder trumped vehicle theft any day.

The cops came by to ask Auntie May some half-hearted questions, but it was obvious that to them, the case was shut, and it was time to move on to the next one. I still worried that somehow Ezzy's story would implicate me, but it never came up. Everyone seemed pretty content with how it played out except me. I debated if I should tell Auntie May and Joe about what actually went down, but decided that would just put unnecessary pressure on them. Auntie May talked to Ezzy and said he sounded okay. I wasn't sure if I was going to get to visit or speak with him. Everyone just wanted the lawyer to deal with it all. That wasn't my favourite idea. I tended not to trust people who made money off the criminal justice system.

The lawyer figured Ezzy could get the murder charge dropped to manslaughter or even assault because he'd acted in self-defence. Auntie May and I didn't want to start hoping that he might be right. But the lawyer did have a few good points that stoked our optimism. He met us at Auntie May's house and brought coffees from an Italian grocery store down the way. We sat there awkwardly making small talk about the chill of a prairie winter, letting our coffees get cold. The lawyer looked out of place in his suit surrounded by photos of old grannies and mushums, and cousins, and family. All these big, round, brown heads smiling through generations of poverty at this man that owned more than all of them combined ever would or had. Whatever. Finally, he got on with it. Ezzy's priors wouldn't hold up well when the Crown prosecutor used that against him, but thankfully none were violent. The lawyer figured they might even help in his case by showing that this was an isolated incident. Not a pattern of behaviour. Something like that.

They'd remanded Ezzy into custody, and because he was already on bail, his option for it had gone away. Not that anyone would have been able to put up that much money anyways. Nobody knew if they would charge him with arson or for the body. Maybe they'd go with both—he was going to be charged with something for sure. But the lawyer figured that since Ezzy had turned himself in, and had been doing well in rehab and school, that would help. But I had seen how the justice system treated Métis men—particularly Métis men like Ezzy—and it wasn't pretty. They still thought it was 1885 here. I didn't trust the system to work fairly. Everyone knew that it was intended to keep us locked up and away from settler colonial gazes and society. If we weren't around, then everyone could get on with their mining and railroads and oil development and forestry—anything and everything to drain this land of its lifeblood and sell it off. Wasn't that what jail was? A way to keep Indigenous people from getting in the way of a colonial dream?

But Ezzy had sacrificed himself to an activist dream. My activist dream. It was something that few people would ever think about actually doing. Myself included. Everyone was content to let dreams die when there were actual implications for their future. I'd thought that I might be different when it came down to it, but I wasn't. Maybe when you didn't have a future to begin with, the idea of sacrifice seeme a little less chaotic and final. At least, that's how I justified my decision not to go and throw myself into the bear's mouth and let the law devour me as it had Ezzy, in the hopes that his sentence would be reduced. He'd be fucking pissed off if I did that, anyways. The least I could do was try to commit myself to supporting him as best I could. I'd take and take and take from whatever grad school I ended up at, and turn it around to use against all the bullshit that came at us in this colonial existence. Every successful revolution needs soldiers just as much as it needs poets and dreamers.

# SEVEN

# EZZY

The city feels different when those big summer thunderstorm clouds move through. I walked down the back path that followed the train tracks while the train ran above ground until it disappeared into the downtown subway system. The path was long forgotten about by city planners and everyone outside of those commuters who took the train into work every day and stared out at the tent encampments that lined the green space. But even they mostly just chose to ignore it. Easier to do that than try to provide resources for those who lived here. The concrete walls behind the ramshackle and tattered tents had been spray-painted repeatedly over the years. Layers of old gang tags, slogans, callouts, and resistance graffiti. I wondered if Grey and her friends had ever written out any of the old tags. Probably not. The downtown buildings in the background reflected that purple-black light from the incoming prairie thunderstorm, and it changed the lighting throughout the alleyways and avenues. I always felt that nothing good came when the city heated up to this level. People got angry. People made bad decisions. The heat tended to fuck up fragile minds. Mine included. On nights like this, the best thing to do was to keep moving. Don't let the heat settle in and drive you down into the ground with the rest of them. Wait for the storm to come and cleanse the city.

Kids on black spray-painted bikes ripped by me. Yelling at each other about a party someone was having. They looked happy. Ready to get right into it on a hot night and see where it took them. I wanted to get into it too. But I couldn't. I wanted booze. I wanted painkillers. I wanted everything that would make me forget it all. The last fourish years in prison had kept me sober enough. There was the occasional breakdown, but I wasn't connected enough to really sustain a high and I'd kept that running ever since. Those same people in the trains assumed everyone was all fucked up who lived out here in the encampment, but that couldn't be further from the truth. Back in prison I put in enough time in the classroom to finish up my GED bullshit. Not that anyone was hiring someone coming out with my charges. There was a rumour that a basement bowling alley on the southside of the city hired anyone. But that was a long way from here, and I figured the sounds of heavy balls smashing into pins would just remind me of what it had sounded like when that bison smashed my leg. I couldn't do the loud noises anymore. Even when the train ripped by here on the early morning run I'd always wake up startled, ready to fight. Then I'd hear the snores coming from my neighbour in the old pup tent next to mine, and I'd realize that this might be as close as I ever came to belonging anywhere. I'd wrap myself up a little tighter in my old patchwork blanket and try to sleep until the sun's heat and the hot concrete wall behind the tent drove me out.

My neighbour was sprawled out on the grass outside of his ripped-up old blue Coleman tent. He had draped a big green tarp over it a few weeks back, to try to keep some of the rain out. That worked, but it made the tent unbearably hot inside on days like today.

"God I hope it rains," he said when I walked over. I laid myself out on the grass beside him.

"Me too. I'm over this heat."

"Got any water?" he asked.

"Nah."

"Shit. I hope one of those people with all the bottles wanders through here at some point."

"Me too. We could go over to that spray-park by the stadium like when we were kids."

"Maybe if they don't show up. Too hot to move right now."

"I hear ya," I said. I stretched out. A couple weeks before, the grass had been bright green. When you lay on it, it had felt like a plush luxury blanket. After the last few weeks of heat without rain, though, the grass had died. Now the brown shards that remained dug into my back and stuck to everything. I stared up at the sky and wondered when the thunderstorm was going to hit.

I hadn't told Grey I had been released. I hadn't talked to her in years anyway. I didn't plan on it at this point either. She'd kept in regular contact for a few months after I went away. Then I guess grad school got in the way or something and the calls got less frequent until they dropped off completely. I never knew what to say. Just like it had been years earlier, when I first met her and followed her and her activist friends around and the conversations were over my head. They didn't seem real to me. They didn't have that same focus on survival. When Grey did call, she had avoided talking about the bison. She never talked about what had happened at all. For the best, I thought. I made my decision and that was enough for us. No use reliving some past bullshit at this point.

I assumed that Grey would have graduated by now. But I really had no idea how long something like a master's or doctorate degree took. Not that it mattered. She'd find me if she wanted to. But I don't think she did. I represented something that I don't think she ever wanted to revisit. I'd like to think that was fine with me, but it really wasn't. I missed her company and the late-night crib games. Me and some of the other guys would play cards in prison but it was never the same. I'd wander by the cultural programming room every now and again, stop in for one of the drum-making circles, do some beadwork, but it never felt right either. Everyone could tell that it was some forced bullshit the jail had to put on, but they didn't put any thought or care into it. I never got that same feeling I got when I was sitting around bullshitting with Joe. The Elders and knowledge keepers would switch out every couple weeks, too, so you could never really build up a relationship with them in your one allotted hour a day or whatever it was. Auntie May would encourage me to keep up my attendance when she'd pop by to visit, but her visits trailed off too. She'd had a lot going on with her kids. I wondered how that all had gone for her. I hadn't spoken to her since I'd been released, and hadn't really heard any details. I figured at some point I'd wander up to her house and check it all out. But for now, I had to just chill for a bit. Prison takes something out of your heart and shatters it on the ground for everyone to stare at and, at the same time, pretend they're not looking.

Not that I wanted anyone to see me. I don't think I did, anyway. I never did tell Auntie why I really did it. Grey either, though I'm sure she thought it was to save her. The guys in prison mostly just laughed and said I played myself and that wasn't how the law worked when I told them how it went down, but if they were such legal geniuses why were they still locked up? Embarrassing, though. Hard not to think about it. Figured my audience out here might not have anything better to do than listen, but nobody really wants to hear about anyone else's problems. It's like trying to tell someone about a dream you had. Same one every time.

"You know, the only reason I even ate that murder shit was because the cops told me they were going to charge my auntie as an accomplice," I said.

"You've told me this before," my neighbour said.

"But that was bullshit, right? They could never prove that, and I mean like, she wasn't even involved anyways."

"Yeah, I've told you that before too. Fuck, get a new story already, bud. If you want to do some confessing, go wander over to Sacred Heart."

"Maybe I should . . . they would have water for sure. We could ride out the storm there?"

"If it keeps you from telling me the same shit over and over again, then yeah, let's go."

"One of those city-sponsored street-sweep gangs might come through and steal and throw out all of our shit, though. We better stay put."

"They'll toss it even if we're here . . . who cares?"

Clouds had turned the city eclipse-dark. It felt like night even in the middle of the day. The power of the prairie surrounded us in the air. Any minute now. Maybe the guys in Fort Sask were right and it really was all bullshit. I tried to turn it off. Somewhere above us the thunderbirds were drumming their wings grouse-style. I looked up. My neighbour crawled back under his tarp in anticipation of the storm ending our conversation. Heat beat the rain, I guess. I'd just keep that one between me and the thunderbirds.

I looked back up. Flashes in the gathering dark. Any minute now. Even if everything that they'd told me was bullshit, it was still real. It landed in my head that way, and it didn't matter what anyone else thought at the end of the day. A decision is a decision, and a life is a life, and the thunderbirds will still bring rain. Tomorrow will always come even if a guy's not there to see it.

# EPILOGUE
# A PRAIRIE DREAM

I dreamt of endless prairie skies. Where the herds of bison grew infinite, stretching from dawn to dusk. In the shadows of the herds, plains grizzlies, wolf packs, and Métis, Cree, and Sioux hunting parties flanked the bison. All of us trailers keeping to ourselves. The bison would provide us all with everything we'd ever need to thrive. I was riding on the front bench of our Red River cart, sitting beside Aunt May as she held the reins for the horses. In the back of the cart, my grandfather sat beside Joe, and they were telling stories to two young adults probably in their early twenties who I didn't recognize but who were hanging on to every word. The intention of listening to the Elders shone deep in their eyes and in the way they leaned their athletic bodies forward to catch every nuance of speech. I couldn't hear their exact words, but every once in a while, laughter would break out from all of them. My mother sat at the very end of the cart, an image forever captured in the picture I had of her from when she was twenty-four, taken shortly before she died. She never aged, and even though she looked to be a similar age to these young adults that I did not know, I could tell that she was vastly older in her knowledge, her wisdom, her experiences. My mother sat there beading away on a tanned bison hide that would become a gun case. Her body moved with the cart seamlessly as we ran over bump after prairie bump. Somehow, she never pricked herself with the needle even when we were bouncing high into the air as we rolled over ruts left by the bison.

I heard the fiddles playing loud, the spoons keeping time, and the travelling songs keeping the cart rhythms in check with the bison's thundering footsteps drumming their way towards the Medicine Line and eventually Turtle Mountain. I saw Grey sitting on top of one of the finest bison-runner horses, a tapestry of beaded flowers sewn into a velvet blanket that rested underneath her on the horse's back. The beads reflected the prairie grasses reaching up for the next rainfall. She stopped and I followed her gaze as she looked across the prairie. An older lady, another person that I had never met, sat on a horse beside Grey. She looked familiar, and I could tell that she was family somehow. But weren't we all? The old lady whispered something to Grey. They stopped and our whole procession stopped with them. A hundred carts halted on the sunburnt grasses that the route had worn down to the sands underneath. As we halted, the music stopped and the conversations lulled. Everyone waited for the next move. Behind us, our packs of dogs bellowed and barked into the dry heat of the summer air, and the horses whinnied and stomped restlessly. I could tell that Grey was thinking about something. She had that same look about her that she'd had when she was giving talks at the legislature grounds when we were younger. That same look she'd had when we were rounding up bison with the trucks and releasing them into the River Valley. Then, with a simple nod to the men who circled around her, we began preparing for a hunt. The men rode throughout the carts, letting us all know that this was the place where we would harvest and then process the bison. Grey and I made eye contact and she broke from her solemn look into a grin. I began laughing. I knew I would never have to wait for anything again. I knew that I belonged. That we were all together and we always would be.

Off in the distance, thunderhead clouds gathered, ready to answer the grass's call for water. I watched from my place atop the Red River cart's bench as the community moved into action. Men and women circled the carts up and the travelling horses were switched out for bison runners by the hunters. Some of the children started gathering ammunition and guns, others sharpened knives and awls and got the supplies ready for the people who would follow the hunters and process the meat. The old men and women prepared the fires to smoke and dry the meat, make pemmican, and tan hides. The community moved as one, just like the herd that stretched out before us.

The bison runners got ready, and the hunters rode out at full speed towards an extension of the herd that stood out from the main group like a dangling arm, a hanging leg. Grey was at the front of the riders, and they all moved in sync with her. We watched from the top of the hill as they got closer and closer to the young bulls that they had scoped out as the ones for this hunt. The processors rode out at a slower clip, as they would take some time to give the bison the proper respect in death. A few of the carts sat behind us, waiting; they had been emptied out and designated to carry back the hides and meat to the main encampment. As I watched all of this unfold, I felt a presence beside me. I looked over to my left and the old lady who Grey had been speaking to earlier was now sitting beside me on the cart bench, where just a moment ago Auntie May had been. She looked at me and I noticed the deep lines cracking on her face and the wrinkles around her eyes that spoke of a thousand laughs and a thousand tears.

"Welcome home," she said. "I always knew you would come back."

# ACKNOWLEDGEMENTS

To those who fight every single day with all their strength to make this world a better place for Indigenous Peoples.

To all of those from Winnipeg to Vancouver who have supported me through a very difficult/depressing summer and fall. Your love spans the prairies to the sea.

My friends who have heard me talk about this book for the past four years. There are a lot of you who have had to deal with this.

My agent, the legendary Cody Caetano, and editor, Jordan Ginsberg, for making this book what it is.

My family, who encouraged a literary existence from a young age despite not knowing anything but prairie poverty.

**CONOR KERR** is a Métis/Ukrainian writer. A member of the Métis Nation of Alberta, he is descended from the Lac Ste. Anne Metis and the Papaschase Cree Nation. His Ukrainian family are settlers in Treaty 4 and 6 territories in Saskatchewan. He is the author of the poetry collections *An Explosion of Feathers* (2021) and *Old Gods* (2023), as well as the novel *Avenue of Champions* (2021), which was shortlisted for the Amazon Canada First Novel Award, longlisted for the 2022 Giller Prize, and won the 2022 ReLIT award. In 2022 he was named one of CBC's Writers to Watch.